HEAR ME SCREAM

A Novel

R.M. JAMES

Vabella Publishing
P.O. Box 1052
Carrollton, Georgia 30112
www.vabella.com

Manufactured in the United States of America

13-digit ISBN 978-1-938230-57-8

Library of Congress Control Number 2014935138

10 9 8 7 6 5 4 3 2 1

To my son Joey, I hear you, I love you.

"The price of freedom is eternal vigilance."

Thomas Jefferson

PART ONE

ZEMI

Raven collapsed face down on the grass, her mouth wide-open. The sharp pasture stabbed at her swollen tongue. She forced her sunken eyes to blink. No tears spilled. No tears reached her dry lips. Her body weighed her down and insisted she sleep. Forever. She panicked then, heart pounding loudly in her chest. She pictured herself standing, even running. Yet the real task required some sort of effort.

The subtle sound of footsteps on brittle grass impelled her to lift her head and squint into the glaring sun.

A flash of blue hair poked through the brush. Yellow eyes gazed at her with furious intensity, the fixed stare of a feline on the prowl. The figure emerged with caution, blue locks falling along its shoulders. A girl, the healthiest young person Raven had ever seen.

"Hi, I'm Ata." Her citrus scent triggered Raven's hunger. Her stomach growled. "What's your name?"

She was not another mirage but a real person.

The girl reached into a backpack and pulled out a flask. "Here." She crouched to reach Raven's lips. "It's water, drink up."

Raven guzzled down the few ounces left and then instantly regretted consuming the stranger's offering.

"Slowly," the girl said. "Do you mind telling me your name?"

"Yes, I mind." Raven coughed, choking on her own saliva. Her throat ached. "Alone . . . I travel alone."

"Alone," the girl repeated. "It's amazing what little replenishing Sorrows need in order to recover."

"Replenishing a what?"

"Can I have your name, please?" Ata's eyes shone with goading concentration, demanding obedience.

Raven usually avoided other travelers for fear of robbery, rape, or slavery. There wasn't a single person worth trusting outside of Glasgow's suburbia. Children were the worst. Abandoned by adults, they would do anything for food and water. In Graves County, one of those starving brats had appeared out of the bushes and begged her for help. When she refused to give it, the boy's allies ambushed her. They stole her survival bag and a full jug of water. It would have lasted her another two days.

"Raven," she answered, surprised at how easily she submitted her name to a stranger.

"Hi, Raven. Where're you headed?" Ata strapped on her backpack and stood. "Maybe we can travel together?"

"No." She needed to arrive in Spencer County unseen, a problem with Ata in tow. "I'm a lone traveler."

"But I have water," Ata pointed out, "and you don't."

"Were you hiding in the farm house?" Something was off about the girl—besides her eyes and hair. "And how old are you?"

"Just turned twenty a couple of days ago. And you, Raven? How old are you?"

"I'm not sure anymore." Raven drew her knees to her chest and rolled into a sitting position. With her hands pressed on the grass, she pushed herself upright. "You look no older than sixteen." She brushed the sweat off her brow, squinted.

"And you look all better!" The girl flashed a white smile. "Do you heal quickly?"

"No," she said. "Do you?"

"Healing quickly is a sign of natural selection, you know, like the books say." When Raven didn't reply, Ata spun around several times as if giving the whirls a chance to explain her logic. "Do you read books?"

"Yes." Raven slogged her way past the grassy farmland in search of a better view over the land. She was taking chances with a stranger, and though Ata seemed harmless—

She won't hurt you, a ringing in her ears announced.

The afternoon's rare breeze failed to stir the bare trees. The decaying farmstead, a few yards away, creaked and groaned. She had ransacked the old place for valuables earlier that day before the roof collapsed. None existed. Old manure was the only indicator the stables had once sheltered horses. The cow-house, rabbit hutch, and the pig sty were also empty. Raven had loitered about the farm expecting nothing and getting nothing, not even a cart or a wheelbarrow. No ducks swam in the pond. No pond existed. No one wasted precious water on strangers.

She's not a threat.

"Can I join you?" Ata sprang from behind, close enough the scent of oranges made Raven's mouth water.

"Why do you smell like oranges?"

"I just ate one. My hands still smell like the *frrruit*." Ata pronounced fruit as if it were a new word. "Do you want an orange?"

She turned to her. "What?"

"An orange, are you hungry? I have two oranges left, two fruits."

"I don't have anything to offer you in return for your water and orange. Why are you helping me?"

The girl tipped her head up, facing the scalding sun's brightness. "I'm alone now," she said after a pause.

"You haven't been alone for long, have you?"

"No." She rummaged through her backpack and pulled out an orange. "I had to leave my home to find Zemi."

Raven snatched the fruit from Ata's hand and bit into it. A burst of citrus exploded in her mouth, igniting her unused taste buds. She devoured the orange, peel and all. "Who's Zemi?"

"I don't know." Ata said, tilting her head slightly to the left. "Zemi might be looking for me."

Raven spat the orange peel stuck in the back of her throat. "Is Zemi a family member?"

"Zemi can answer all of my questions," she said.

"What kind of questions do you want answered?"

"All of them, any of them. Zemi—"

"Well, thank you for the orange." She licked her juicy lips dry and her sticky fingers clean. "I have to get going."

"Can I come too, please?" Her desperate gaze, or maybe a foreign internal need, gave Raven no other choice but to let Ata join her, if only for the water.

And oranges, don't forget.

Borrowing water from Ata was a lot easier than stealing it from well-guarded creeks and ponds. Avaricious land owners shot at anyone who drank from their precious, muddied, disease infected, and life-sustaining liquid.

Now you're thinking.

Raven and Ata headed up a crescent hill. They hiked their way to the top where the peak revealed what to some stimulated disappointment, a longing for a lost era. For Raven, the empty highway was the quickest way to her son.

"Eureka." She didn't remember drifting from the main road in the first place. "Okay, Ata, we're going downhill, and we're going to stay on the blacktop."

"Where do you need to go?" Ata bent to scrub insects and dirt off her bare knees. "Is this going to be a long journey?"

"You need to find Zemi, and I need to find my family."

The trip ahead required another set of eyes since Raven's were more than exhausted. Her legs ached from a week of endless walking. The skin on her rough body had been peeling for days. Her stomach hurt. A persistent fever wouldn't go away. She would have lingered on any grassy bed were it not for her son. He needed his mother. She needed to find him.

"Mind over matter," Raven said. "She who thinks health gains health."

The water and the orange don't hurt, either.

"Where's your family?" Ata asked.

"Alive, I hope."

She controlled her descent and tried not to slide downhill. Her boots had already sustained an eight day journey. But smooth concrete would palliate her leg muscles.

Follow the green traffic signs to Spencer County and this time stay in Kentucky, no more wrong turns to Indiana.

Yes. She answered the buzzing noise in her ears. *I'm on track again.*

"Why wouldn't your family be alive, Raven? Do they need water?"

"They have plenty of water, a whole creek, in fact," she said. "Rebels—"

"I thought there was no such thing as rebels?"

Raven halted and glared at the girl. "Don't tell me rebels don't exist!" She grabbed Ata's arm and shook it in anger. "Rebels exist!"

Let go of her!

For as long as she could remember, the buzzing from inside her eardrums had made it almost impossible to sleep in the silence of night. To her advantage, the discomforting sound had also kept her on a steady pace forward. When had the noise become an inner voice? She waited for an answer, but was relieved when no one replied. Insanity was unacceptable. She lacked the energy for another disadvantage.

Mind over matter, she told herself, *unless my mind is the matter.*

"Do you think rebels are the reason I can't find Zemi?" Ata jerked her arm free without wincing, screeching, or even complaining about the sudden attack.

"Probably."

Raven's feet came in contact with the asphalt. Warily, she observed her surroundings. One could never be too sure. Other survivalists possibly lurked around, especially while she and Ata remained in the open. "We stay on the shoulder lane, north. If we hear any noises, we run back to the woods, over there, on the other side."

Across the road a heavily wooded area abided untouched. Hydrated trees flourished uncut. If she had noticed the woods earlier, she wouldn't have trekked through open farmlands. But there was no use in regretting the past. Besides, her companion was useful bait. Rebels were always on the prowl. If any ever approached her, she would run, leaving the brutes to have at it with Ata.

No, you will not.

Raven ignored the voice.

Ata was friendly, sure. But a girl stupid enough to share her water with a stranger while smelling like a dome of oranges and showcasing an abundant amount of shiny blue hair was asking for whatever she got.

One fact Raven never forgot on her journey north was her gender. When laws were no longer in place, women and children suffered most. Females were not as quickly killed off, not if savages could have their fun. Raven was cautious enough to dress like a boy: an old baseball cap hid her hair, and only her hands and stern face were visible to the wandering eye. Her sex was indistinguishable from a distance and nothing gave it away, not her walk, baggy garments, or her voice. Costly was the price of being a girl.

"Ata," she said.

"Yes?" Ata skipped alongside with a nursery rhyme gait.

"What happened to your fellow travelers?"

"What do you mean?"

"Why did you leave your family?" Someone like Ata was not supposed to have survived, not with all the evil lurking. "You do know someone can hurt you, don't you? I easily could have." And did.

She smiled. "Dying from thirst isn't very threatening."

"But still—"

"Raven!" Her elated pitch left an actual ringing in Raven's ear, a humming sound. "You were barely alive a little while ago. I'm positive that you, like me, are different."

"What does that mean?"

"Different." The girl grinned, sure of her nonsense. "We both need to look for Zemi."

"I need to find my family."

"Zemi will find your family." Ata was almost not worth the extra food and water—almost. "Aren't you curious to know what brought us together? I saved you from a certain death."

"No, I wasn't dying. I was thirsty. Besides, if Zemi really knew the answers to everything, he'd know where we are."

Her smile beamed with curiosity. "Do you think Zemi's a man?"

"It's always a man, Ata. If you don't even know the gender, why are you looking for him?"

"Because," she started, "because there's a lot I don't understand about the world."

"Who does?"

"I want answers."

"Answers to why the world goes round?" Raven mocked. "Who cares about that? In your search for this mythical creature, you might end up dead."

Ata's smile widened. "Mythical?" She stopped skipping. "What does that mean?"

"Who sent you to find Zemi?"

"I've always known."

Raven measured the odd girl and her bulky backpack and briefly contemplated theft. "What makes you so sure you'll find him?"

"Maybe he'll find us."

"Will he?"

Her nod was exaggerated. "I'm sure of it!"

Raven sighed. "Yeah, I'm sure he will." She lacked the strength to disagree. "Let's keep going and if we're lucky, Zemi might find us sooner."

Ata pointed ahead. "I think he already has."

The dark hooded man emerged from the trees, a lone traveler. He was disgustingly familiar, and his stink of decaying limbs stung Raven's nostrils. He limped, probably an act. His slouched and wounded appearance had to be a trick. The man would kill them both. He was no average survivalist. He was a rebel in disguise.

Run. Run now.

She sprinted with tumultuous, chaotic strides, desperate strides. Her pain lay somewhere forgotten. Raven ran for her life. The highway was no longer cracked asphalt but a runner's track. Her erratic breathing amplified with each sore stomp. She was afraid, terrified. The road dipped and then lifted sharply transforming the afternoon sun into a blinding object in her way. She ran in dizzying zigzags in case the rebel carried a weapon.

The memory of Ata's huge, amber gaze haunted Raven for a split second, a second she almost stopped to think. A violent shake of the head later, and her guilt evaporated into the muggy air.

Good luck and good riddance.

HEALER

Nico knelt to study the manmade pond. The chirping crickets and the bellowing frogs had been replaced by a silent sadness. He dipped his hand in the murky water and inspected the coat of algae clinging to his finger.

"Your pond is sick." He wiped his hand against his pants. "I hate to say it, but the surrounding trees are blocking the sun. You're going to have to sacrifice a tree or two. Or you could drain—" He could hardly instruct the farmer to let the pond die. The trees provided oxygen. "The water has to stay clean."

"Stupid pond. I knew I should've purchased property near a creek." Mr. Sears paced about, accusing the trees with an occasional glance. They were all too lush, crowding the pond. "That's well and good, Healer, but why is my son having stomach pains? Gavin's been vomiting for days. Wife says he's cramping and thirsty all the time."

"The water is polluted with whatever artificial fertilizer you use for your crops. Rain washes the excess chemicals into nearby water sources, and in your case, that's this pond. I'm guessing you haven't lived here very long and don't know the land's history, or who used it before."

"How do you know all this, kid?" The farmer's anger reddened his cheeks. Nico didn't need to look up at him to know. "Ain't you supposed to be a healer, not some pond expert? Tell me what's wrong with my damn boy!"

"I already healed your son. Your wife knows to ensure he drinks clean water." Nico paused for a moment to listen to the skittering footfalls of his father, hurrying toward them from the Sears' house. "Your boy had cholera, Mr. Sears."

"But we always boil the drinking water."

"Yeah, but I can smell your latrine."

"What does shit have to do with any of this?"

"Have other passing or maybe sick travelers used your latrine, Mr. Sears?"

"One or two in the last month, I think. They didn't strike me as sick."

"And how do you get rid of your feces?"

"Dug a hole in the ground."

"Excrement has seeped into your water from the latrine. You should find a more efficient way to dispose of your—waste."

"That's ridiculous!" Mr. Sears stomped on the ground with the ill temper of a toddler. "We always boil the water."

"Yeah, but you don't boil the bath water. All your water comes from the pond, no?"

"What's the problem with that?"

"Your son's been drinking the bath water."

Kurt, who had made it down the hill, approached Mr. Sears and patted his back. "Gavin's nine. Nine-year-olds do that sort of stuff. Why, when Nico was nine—"

"We need to get moving, Dad." Nico turned to his father. "We've spent enough time here."

"Don't go, please." Mr. Sears urged them. "Why don't you stay for a while? We have plenty of food. You know, the rebels are making their way down here, stealing land as they go. There's safety in numbers, right?"

"That sounds tempting," Kurt said. "But most of our income comes from being on the road. Others need my son's medical skills."

"I understand all that, I do." Mr. Sears spotted his daughter on the other side of the pond. He waved her over. The girl approached them with an empty water bucket in hand. "Sophie's fifteen, my lovely girl. Say hi, Sophie."

She was small, lacking the muscle of a healthy teenager. Sophie wore a stringy white dress, miserably similar to her dry, brittle hair. She was pale, with skin rougher than sand. Wounds, not properly healed, marked her legs. But it was her heart's irregular beats that bothered Nico. And so did her respiratory system's struggle to keep the girl from crumbling.

"Isn't she a beauty?" Mr. Sears asked, grinning. "If you stay, she could be your wife. If you choose to wed, that is."

"You are a beauty," Nico told the girl, not disregarding her presence as her father had. "Can I ask you something?"

"I assure you, Sophie hasn't been touched by a man." Mr. Sears felt the need to confirm. "She would make a fine wife. She can cook, sew, clean, and she's especially good at—"

"May I speak to Sophie in private, if that's not too much to ask?"

"Is that too much to ask?" The man cackled, amused. "There ain't nothing you, Healer, can ask that I won't oblige to, not after you healed my son and possibly my pond. Will you save the pond, too?"

"I already told you what's wrong with—"

"We'll speak about this later," interrupted the man. "Come, Kurt, let's give the couple some privacy."

Mr. Sears was originally wary of the two travelers believing them rebels out to steal his land. Yet it didn't take him long to offer up a worthy asset, Sophie. He had raised his daughter as a way to a better life, or a good trade. Girls were always excellent barters and sometimes, if the bid was too low, men would offer their girls for a single night. Nico found it strange that Mr. Sears hadn't bothered to keep Sophie healthy enough to tempt a man. She was malnourished, sickly, and simply unappealing.

Nico approached Sophie. "If your disease progresses, your organs are going to start failing. Are you a vegetarian?"

"What's a vegetarian?"

"Someone who doesn't eat meat."

"There's barely any meat around here, and when Father does catch a rabbit, the animal is too small to feed us all. Father needs the meat the most. He's a man."

"A selfish man." Nico reached out and stroked the girl's warm cheek. "You need protein in your diet, more so than he does."

She smiled, and the simper was pretty, in spite of her cracked lips. "What do you suggest I do? How can I become better for you?"

"You're too sick to concern yourself with marriage. Take care of yourself first. And Sophie?"

"Yes," she mouthed softly, "Healer?"

"Nico. Call me Nico."

Sophie set the empty bucket on the ground. "I used to eat eggs before the chickens died. Will I die as well?"

"Sophie." Nico took her hand, pressed it firmly. He waited for her to look him in the eyes; hers were a shallow green. "You're going to get well, but from this day forward, you have to start eating meat."

"Meat is hard to come by, Healer."

The outer wounds took seconds to rectify but normalizing her body temperature was a longer process, maybe not as long as building her immune system. Luckily, for the girl, there were no permanent damages. "All better."

"What do you mean?" she asked.

He let go of her hand. "Let's go hunting, Sophie."

Finding the warren was easy enough since the burrow's system was tunneled deep, a maze of many entrances. The dark, black hole was an indicator of the many furry creatures resting inside. Nico moved slowly, listening and settling near the creature's blind spot.

The rabbit's long ears swiveled from one side to another, detecting the slightest sound. While scanning for threats with its twitching nose and wide field vision, the creature grazed from the green pasture near its burrow. Sophie coughed. The rabbit froze in place. Nico pounced. It tried to hop away in zigzags, an escape which would have succeeded in the past. Back when Nico was a young hunter, prey running tactics had usually left him hungry. Not anymore. Once caught, the rabbit's hind legs kicked. The animal bit him in the struggle. Nico still snapped the creature's neck.

"Do you know how to make rabbit stew?" he asked Sophie.

She gaped in disbelief.

"You and your mother should prepare stew." Nico was better off not explaining how he had mastered his hunting skills. "Sophie, aren't you hungry for something other than fruits and vegetables?"

Her eyes remained glued to his grip on the bunny ears; the body dangled from side to side. "I make good stew," she finally answered.

"You go do that, then." He bagged the buck and handed Sophie the brown sack. "Run along now. I'll meet you after I've gathered a few more."

"Are you going to catch them like you did this one?" Her breathing had improved, but her immune system still struggled to regulate. "Do you catch all the animals in that fashion?"

Nico did. He was a good hunter, better than most. "I do. You should see me bringing down deer." He laughed, and she laughed as well, unaware his answer was no joke.

They left the Sears a day later. Sophie was especially unhappy, and in all fairness, Nico would have married her if only to remove her from her father. What kept him from agreeing to such a commitment was the acceptance of surrender. Natural reproduction was difficult. He could never commit to visiting the roaring city, spending days in a lab, trying to pretend he could impregnate Sophie. He had an instinctive way of meeting his mate, not that he believed she existed anymore, but if she did, if she were to beckon him.

"You're young, Nico," Kurt said. "There's no rush to tie the knot so soon, but I do doubt you'll find a prettier girl."

The sun shone bright on the narrow paved road. Nico and Kurt rode on horseback, destination unknown. Eventually, someone would need their help.

"She was sick, Dad."

"All girls look ugly and sick to you."

"She would've died if—"

"Did you heal her?"

"Yes, I did. I know what you're going to—"

"We could've bargained for more goods, doubled the price. You can't go around healing people without getting anything in return. I don't know why you think we have to spare folks hardship. Everything we have—"

"Dad." He refused to humor his father. "Would you prefer to go the bounty hunter way again?"

"Now, Nico." Kurt pulled the reins back toward him, bringing the bit backward in Sable's mouth. Sable was his mare, a gift from a man who had nothing left to exchange in return for his health. "Son, I'm not trying to make you selfish, but your mother was exactly like you, always wanting to help everyone, and now she's dead."

"Slow down, Bronte." Rarely did Nico have to pressure Bronte into stopping or decelerating. His stallion had been a faithful companion throughout the years, since his colt days, before his entire herd had died of starvation. The horse was loyal, fast and perceptive. "Easy, boy." And to his father, "I cured an innocent girl today. Mother would've been proud."

"She would've wanted you to marry the girl. She was a fertility doctor after all." Kurt wiped his forehead, sweat dripped down his face. "You show no interest in reproducing, and you hardly pretend to care about a single lady. Something can't be wrong with every girl alive. You don't give yourself time to get to know them."

"They're sick, Dad, all of them. The entire human species is sick." Nico knew for sure. "You don't see them like I do. You can't smell that . . . that stench of decay . . . that hopelessness of will. The entire species is fading, Father. Can't you taste that in the air and in their food?"

"What, by the name of pie, are you going on about?" Kurt reached inside one of his saddle bags, dug deep. He retrieved a yellow piece of paper. "I'm starting to think you're a shallow man."

His father had never quite understood him. "What do you have there, Dad?"

"A nice bounty for—"

"You said you weren't—"

"I know what I said, but this one is offering more than all the grateful farmers combined could ever afford."

"I want to see Mother's grave." Nico's need to visit Rosetta's resting place sprang from an abrupt gut ache, a cinching in his core. "I want a break, right now. I'm tired of helping, always helping. I want . . . I don't know what I want, but it sure isn't another favor for another person."

"Favors that pay aren't favors, Son."

"We have enough supplies. Let's do something different."

"Do you want to take a vacation?"

"A what?" His father often invented words. "What's a 'vacation'?"

"Time off from work," Kurt answered. "Isn't that what you want?"

"Yes, that sounds exactly like what I want. Vacation, huh?" He liked the term and was tired of battling the never-ending diseases.

Some infections affected patients more than once. Folks failed to take simple precautions. "Let's go on a vacation, see Mom."

After several aimless miles, the wind moaned and tugged at him. The fresh, fruity air eased the beating sun. Nico took a breath, happily knowing a vacation awaited him. He closed his eyes as a refreshing breeze swept in from the west. The need to follow the wind constricted his chest. The pull was new and frightening, forcing him onward. The lure was in his bones, tugging, contracting his muscles. The scent of oranges wafted from miles across. It was strong, enveloping, compelling. It beckoned him. How long had he waited to feel so much, to care about a nameless living organism?

Where are you?

"We're going west, Dad." Nico wanted nothing more.

"Why west?" Everything had to have an explanation with Kurt. He left nothing to chance. "What new idea has you thinking you can change our route?"

Nico ignored the man. He closed his eyes to take another whiff of ecstasy. His muscles hardened. The smooth fragrance shifted his insides over and over again. Internally, his body was on fire. His heart raced. His blood pumped. His gut ached. A pungent odor emerged. Iron, pennies, the smell overwhelmed his nose. It was strong, pouring, spilling on the pavement.

"Nico," Kurt complained, "there's nothing west."

"I smell her." Nico couldn't explain the urgency to his father. The man lacked sharper senses. "She's bleeding, Dad. We have to save her."

"What?" Kurt yielded Sable, not happy; he seldom was. "What in the world is the matter with you? Are you insane or—"

"I'm not going to argue." Nico flicked the reins and Bronte galloped. "I won't risk her dying, Dad. I need to find her. We're going west."

VOICE

Raven reduced her jog to a walk and bundled her sweat-dampened hair under the baseball cap, removing the fallen strands off her neck. Each step forward was as difficult as wading through a lake. She was thirsty.

Go back now.

"Shut up!" She sat on the side of the road, on the hot asphalt. Her head pounded with startling vigor. She rubbed her temples, needing to lessen the pain.

Don't leave her.

"Strangers are usually up to no good." She had a mission that did not include running back to rescue Ata. "I have to find my son."

She needs you.

Guilt set in before she could come up with another reason not to return. "Damn it!" Maybe Ata was still alive. Perhaps it was Zemi in rags back there. She needed water. Ata had water and oranges.

She pushed herself up and started back, cursing every single step that brought her closer to the rebel.

You're going to need her.

"Hold on there, miss," a gravelly, *real* voice said. "I'm going to have to ask you to turn around slowly."

"Don't shoot, sir." Raven raised her hands and turned, startled at how yet another person had managed to sneak up on her.

Maybe you should start paying more attention to your surroundings, the voice said.

If you stop talking to me, she told it, *I would.*

19

The man slouched astride a black horse, a rifle resting across his knees. He looked about fifty. Deep scars covered his bald head, framing his leathered face. His accent caught her attention; she recognized the drawl as native to the state.

"What's a gal like you doing out in the open?" He scratched his head, confused. "Are you alone?"

"Please, let me be on my way." She wanted to run into the woods, but suspected her efforts a waste of time. The man had a horse. She was tired. "I don't have anything to offer you."

"I don't need anything from you." He patted both sides of his horse's saddlebags. "I have more than I can carry."

"Can I please be on my—"

"Don't move, Miss. I wouldn't want to shoot you accidentally." He turned his sights to another rider heading his way. "Gosh, darn it."

The chestnut stallion galloped like a valiant steed straight out of an old book. The rider was a young man of sandy blond hair and sun-touched skin. His horse rode past the older man and stopped in front of Raven.

"Are you wounded?" The young man's peridot eyes shone, unblinking, too sincere. "Are you bleeding, Miss?"

Raven stared up at him.

"Miss," he asked again, "Are you hurt?"

The older man grunted, instructing his lazy ride to move forward. He seemed annoyed with his younger companion. "Tell me we didn't change directions so you could play knight."

"What happened, Miss?" the younger one persisted, not paying any attention to the older man. "What do you need me to do?"

"I . . . I was traveling with another girl, Ata . . . and—"

"She's in danger," he said. "Where?"

Raven pointed.

The young man turned his horse around and took off at a blurring speed.

"Well, come on up." The older man adjusted his rifle holster. He offered Raven his hand. "I guess we're gonna help your friend."

She stared up at him.

"Don't worry, Miss. I don't bite. My name's Kurt Lowell and that over there was my son, Nico." Kurt offered his hand again. "Or walk. I don't care."

"I'll walk," she said.

"Well, suit yourself." Kurt's horse galloped into the distance, but not as swift as his son's steed.

It took Raven some time to decide whether she wanted to go back for Ata after all. The girl no longer needed her help.

You can trust them.

Water would stop the hallucinations, or really just the voice. *Who are you?* She waited for a response.

No one answered.

Ata carried water. Raven was not ashamed to return, if only for the water.

After catching up with the others, she hesitated at the sight of Ata. The girl was lying unresponsive in the middle of the deserted freeway in a gruesome mess. Her blood stained the asphalt. The red trail ended a little over the shoulder lane, on the edge of the forest. If she had sought shelter in the forest, the trees would have hidden her.

Too late.

Nico was off his horse, attending Ata. He used the contents of a leather-skinned first aid kit. That he carried a medical kit was impressive. The father, a few feet behind, guarded his son with a rifle in hand.

"Is she okay?" Raven noted Ata's missing backpack. "That's a lot of blood."

"I've managed to clean the wound. I'm patching her up now. She doesn't need many stitches, not with me as her healer." Nico cleaned her up with the precision and care of a book doctor. It nearly brought tears to Raven's eyes. She couldn't remember the last time anyone did anything nice for a stranger—besides Ata and her oranges.

"What's wrong with you?" Kurt watched Raven with suspicion. "Why do you dress like a boy?"

She wiped her eyes and cleared her throat. "Why do you think?"

"Aren't you a smart mouth?" The old man unfastened one of the saddlebags, retrieved a clean rag, and threw it at his son. "The one you're using is soaked, Nico."

Nico caught the rag mid-air. "I'm done." He left his patient in less of a mess. Ata's shirt was stained, but her stomach gash was nice and mended. Nico lifted her up and carried her deep into the forest. The thicker grass served as a bed. Rising, he turned to Raven for the first time since playing doctor. "Ata," he said. "Her name is Ata, right?"

Raven nodded.

"Ata endured a minor stabbing, a thin slash. Not much else to worry about." He glanced at his father. "Change of plans."

Kurt shook his head. "Oh, no. There's nothing else we can do for them. Let's not—"

"Two unprotected girls won't make it anywhere on their own. You know that." Nico's white shirt was surprisingly bloodless unlike his blue jeans. "They don't have transportation. One is wounded. They need us, Dad."

"That sounds good and all, Nico, but we don't know where they're headed. Going out of our way—" Kurt paused and inhaled as if defeated by his son's imploring gaze. "Only if they're going in our direction."

Nico turned to Raven. "Where are you and Ata headed?"

"I don't share information with strangers."

Tell him. The persistent, all-knowing voice muttered.

On foot she and Ata were bait. It was foolish to think that without her backpack—stolen by children days ago—Raven had a shot at survival. The rebel who had attacked Ata was probably hiding somewhere in the forest waiting for his opportunity to seize them again.

"I'm going to Willowy Farms in Taylorsville," Raven said. Worst-case scenario, she could either steal the knives peeking out of Kurt's saddlebags, or ride off with his horse. "Spencer County."

"Great." Nico's sweet boyish smile, full of trust and confidence, made her nervous. "Taylorsville's only a couple of hours away."

"Yeah, fantastic," Kurt said, dryly. He dismounted his horse. "Let's rest up for a while first. We can't travel with that wounded girl still unconscious."

"She'll be up soon, Dad." Nico patted his father's back. Together they guided their horses toward the shade, away from the middle of the road—away from Ata.

Never dismissing the men's position, Raven approached Ata with caution. The blue-haired girl's frame was tiny, almost childlike. The girl who'd casually saved Raven from hunger looked dead. It was difficult to kneel beside her as a 'friend', hypocritical, really. At least Ata breathed steadily. Her skin still glowed, still emphasized the amber gaze.

"Ata, you're awake!"

"What happened?" Her eyelids fluttered like butterfly wings. "Why did you leave me behind?"

"Don't worry about that. I'm back now." Guilt was a persuasive motivator. "Tell me what happened to you. Why didn't you run?"

Ata struggled, but managed to sit up. She inspected her body for cuts and scrapes. "My stomach hurts."

"He stabbed you. I think. That's what Nico said."

"Who's Nico?"

Raven turned to the men brushing off the horses nearby, chatting among themselves. "You could have died if it hadn't been for them, Ata."

"I'm not supposed to die yet," she said. "I'm fine."

"Tell me what happened to you. Why didn't you run?"

Ata claimed the strange man had seemed decent. "He complained about his hurt knee. A brawl with other survivalists left him limping."

"Did he tell you his name?"

"Levi," the girl said. "He wanted to know why *you* ran. He asked me to find you and explain that he meant us no harm."

Raven scoffed. "And you believed him?"

"He said he wanted to take us back to his town where his people would offer housing and protection." Ata had refused to go and instead explained her mission to find Zemi. "Levi suddenly changed."

"How did he change?"

"He told me I had to go with him and find my keeper. He wanted me to take him home."

"You have a keeper, Ata?"

"I don't have a keeper." She got up on her feet and tried uselessly to wipe the blood off her top. "Levi wanted to know if you were a Carrier. He was looking for you."

Raven fought the rage tempting her to run into the woods in search of Levi. She wanted to bludgeon him to death. "He's one of the rebels." She had to reach her son soon, and if riding with Kurt and Nico spared hours, then she would travel with the duo.

Don't think anyone a non-threat, added the voice.

Make up your damned mind. Her cheeks burned with annoyance. *Either I trust the pair, or I don't.*

Trust him.

She rubbed at her temples, alarmed. *Which one?*

"They're coming over here." Ata hid behind Raven.

She met them halfway. "I didn't get the chance to introduce myself," she said. "My name's Raven Carrier."

"I already told you my name." Kurt shook Raven's hand and mounted his horse. "This here is Sable, my mare," he said about the overweight animal.

Nico smiled past Raven, tilting his head to catch a glimpse of Ata. "Hi, how are you feeling?" Ata blinked, silent. "I'm Nico. Would you like to ride with me?"

"She's still in shock from the stabbing," Raven guessed. She wasn't surprised a naturally trusting Ata would turn cautious after being attacked. "It's nice to meet you, Nico."

He reached for Raven's hands and gathered them firmly. "Likewise, Raven."

An electric current pulled at her insides, shocking and stretching her organs. She had to step back to gather her composure.

"Are you sure we want to travel with them?" Ata said. "Maybe I should go back home."

NO! the voice wailed.

"No, Ata. I think its best you travel with us."

Smart move, Raven.

Shut up. You're giving me a headache. I don't even know why I listen to you.

Ata bared the look of an abandoned child and she obeyed like one. Her lingering silence distressed Nico. He kept trying to please her. He offered her food, water, help mounting his horse. Kurt, unhappy with his son's chivalrous displays, insisted Ata ride with him instead. He cantered away with her before his son could debate the seating arrangement.

"Well, looks like it's you and me." Nico gave Raven a lift. The horse started in a trot. "I don't think your friend likes me."

"Don't worry about Ata. She's odd."

"Sable's wider," he said. "Ata's probably better off riding with Dad because of her injury."

"The injury you were nice enough to patch up," she reminded him. "I wouldn't mind her."

"I mind. Do you think it was my tone of voice? Was I not gentle enough?"

"Gentle? You saved her life."

Nico sighed, turning to Raven. His eyes dimmed. "How are you feeling, by the way?"

"I feel fine." The question puzzled her. "Why do you ask?"

"I wondered if you were still in pain."

The swell and soreness in Raven's throat was healing at a rapid pace, and already her saliva glands worked as if aridity had never happened. Sudden strength overwhelmed her. The fever was gone.

"Mind over matter," she told him. "She who thinks health gains health. I actually feel much better."

"Good for you," he said. "Why was Ata attacked?"

"Because that's what scum rebels do best. They steal women and hurt them. You can't trust the lot."

"Do you know why a bounty hunter would want Ata?" Nico's stomach muscles contracted after he had asked the question.

Raven let go of his taut waist. "How do you know he's a bounty hunter?"

"Because," Nico said, "Father was also a bounty hunter."

REBELS

Camden Sickles stared at the cerulean sky and wondered if the warm weather would linger. Fresh winds rarely ever caressed the variant shades of trees. Most summer months were typically too hot to endure outside. He usually read indoors, avoiding critters and the sun's beating heat, but not that afternoon. His mounting anger had driven him out to the porch swing.

He thought about his family and the land they once owned. His father and brother used to raise animals, while his mother and sister harvested crops. Camden had merely existed, abandoned to his reading, a hobby encouraged by his mother. She had understood there was more to life than growing food. A good woman, his mother. She fell ill one summer, and his father Pat refused to sell the property in exchange for medicine. He worried about the rest of the family's wellbeing—an excuse. Pat's negligence secured her fate. Mother died a week later. Appendicitis.

The garden quit producing right after the funeral, a blow to their personal economy. The losses turned Pat into a compulsive drinker. He married off his only daughter in exchange for a hefty dowry, and sent his oldest son on a search for fertile soil. Gad returned a day later with promising news. The Carriers from a few hills down had plenty of land, a creek, animals, and a beautiful owner.

Eliza Carrier's dead husband had surprisingly left his wife all of his property. She lived with her nine-year-old daughter, Mary, a six-year-old nephew, Bran, and her Father-in-law, George. Pat, being the dog that he was, claimed the widow immediately after selling his own fallow farm.

Camden tossed the book across the porch, wishing the novel had been his father. The volume landed on page twenty-five, twenty-one, three, one, eight, and then twenty-one again; the wind flipped the pages as if an invisible hand was speed-reading back and forth. He stood up to retrieve it, noticing for the first time the men coming up the hill, most in military garments. His father's warning whistle blasted a minute too late. The porch door swung open, and a blond man with a rifle grabbed Camden by the hair. He dragged him inside the house.

The furniture was pushed up against the walls, allowing ample room for the Sickles and the Carriers to kneel. Three men faced them. Two aimed assault rifles: one was a skeletal blond, and the other an old slob. The man in the middle sifted through documents while occasionally smiling to himself. His gunmen never broke steadiness. These men were rebels, expired soldiers.

"Okay," started the one holding documents. "If I'm reading the deed correctly, this property belongs to Mr. Carrier. Am I right so far?"

"Yes," George responded. "You're correct."

The blond rebel hit the old man over the head with his automatic rifle, not hard enough to knock George out, but hard enough Eliza gasped.

"Sorry about that, sir. What is your name?" the man with the documents asked.

"George." He hoisted himself back on his knees. "George Carrier."

"Well," said document man, "George Carrier—"

"What do you people want?" Eliza demanded. "Why don't you people—" The rifle hit her across the face and blood trickled down her nose. She wiped it clean with her apron and squeezed her daughter's hand.

"Let me explain what's happening here," said the rebel. "You're not allowed to voice your thoughts, ideas, or opinions. When I ask a question, you nod for yes and shake your head for no. If you decide you do have something to say, then either Bowie here," he pointed at the skeletal gunman, "or Levi," the slob, "will continue to use force. Am I clear?"

A loud gunshot sounded off outside the house. Another rebel entered the property through the patio door, also wearing military gear. "Umm, did you say you wanted everyone alive, Joshua? 'Cause Toady shot a guy outside."

The rebel frowned. "Describe him."

"About late forties, brown hair, dark eyes. He had a rifle. Said he was going to shoot us."

"That's fine, Dagan. Go back to your duties," Joshua said. "His sons will bury him later."

It irritated Camden that his father had found a way to conveniently die. There was nothing remotely sad about the parting of a drunken excuse of a dad. Pat should have died sooner, passed away instead of Mother.

"George," Joshua continued after a pause of observing paperwork. "You had two sons. One worked for the Sorrows."

George stared blankly.

"Both your sons are now dead. Am I right?" Joshua smiled or smirked. Camden couldn't tell. The man's lips seemed to have forgotten how to widen and twitched stiffly instead. "You have something I want, George."

Bowie and Levi shifted postures. They aimed their weapons at the old man.

"How long were you planning on hiding him?" Joshua moved to the kitchen table where he neatly placed the documents. He returned to the living room with a frown. "How long have you lived here?"

"About ten years," answered George before the blond man whacked him in the head again.

"Stop it!" Eliza covered Bran's eyes. "Please, don't hurt him in front of the children."

Bowie was about to whack her again but Joshua stepped forward. "No, Bowie. Don't touch her."

"I thought you said—"

"I don't need you to hit the boy, accidentally. I'm trading him." Joshua stooped to reach the frightened six-year-old.

Bran's large, dark eyes widened. He shuddered.

"I've been searching a long time for you." Joshua rose, bringing Bran up with him. "Do you know why that is, Bran?"

"He's a mute," Eliza said. "He never speaks."

"Eliza, please stop talking." Joshua guided the boy to the end of the drawing room. "Don't forget the rules."

"He's a child." Eliza ducked Bowie's rifle, avoiding another whack on the head. "Why are you doing this to us?"

"Bran is not your child." Joshua knocked on Eliza's bedroom door. "Ida, are you done?"

A redheaded girl strode out of the room, hands wet and sleeves rolled to her shoulders. "The tub is full of water and the chamber is perfectly clean, new sheets on the bed. I think this room's the master bedroom. Do you want it?"

"Well, since you worked so hard." Joshua handed Bran to the redhead. "Ida, scrub him clean. Make sure he's the healthiest looking boy on the planet."

"I'll get him good and ready." Ida took Bran's hand and led him to Eliza's bedroom, shutting the door behind her.

"Question," said Joshua when he returned to the remaining prisoners: "Where's the other granddaughter, George?"

George did not reply.

Joshua grinned. "Mary is the daughter of Phil, right?"

Eliza nodded.

"The oldest son, Cormac, has a daughter too," Joshua said. "Am I right?"

"If you know everything there is to know about us, why are you asking questions?" Gad hissed. "Your men killed my father!"

Gad was struck in the temple. He fell back, unconscious. The rebels had more men, more guns, and probably a strategy. Joshua, for one, seemed to know exactly what he was doing. It was pointless to play the hero. Real heroes didn't exist.

Joshua smiled at Camden. "I'm sorry about your brother."

"She's in Glasgow," the slob rebel chimed. "The other granddaughter, Raven, is living in Barren County, a couple of days away on foot, not nearly as long on horseback."

"And you know this how, Levi?" Joshua glanced at the heavy man.

"You said so." Levi's brown, loose teeth were rotting. His smirk was disgusting. "You told us."

"When did I tell you this?" Joshua turned to Bowie. "I'm guessing everybody knows this piece of information?"

Bowie cleared his throat, uneasy. "You said you wanted a team to go get her. I thought . . . I thought you'd remember."

"And who," Joshua asked, "did I say I wanted on this retrieval mission?"

"I don't know," Bowie said. "We didn't ask you."

"I want Orion on the mission. Wafer, too. He needs the practice." Joshua studied Levi. "Go. You're a former bounty hunter. Keep the other two in line."

"I'll make sure we bring the Carrier girl in one piece." Levi chuckled, trying to ease the tension between himself, Bowie, and Joshua.

The rebels shoved Camden into the basement with the other prisoners. His brother alone was forced to burn their father's body. They were given pillows and blankets, but he slept on the concrete floor—away from the Carriers. Joshua assigned them chores the next morning. Eliza and George were to spend most of their days working the land. Mary was required to assist Ida with the cooking and cleaning. Gad became the animal keeper, and Bran disappeared.

The country-style house had three small rooms and one giant basement. The rebels took the two smallest rooms and the living room for themselves. Camden's chamber used to be the basement, and so it remained. The lack of candles, a rule imposed by the rebels to keep them well rested, was the real misery. Camden could no longer read after dusk. His brain was turning to mush. He hated the cold, dark nights because he detested sharing them with the other prisoners: Mary cried herself to sleep. George complained of cramps, and Gad snored. But even he could admit Eliza had it much worse.

A few days into captivity, Camden brought the woman a bucket of water he had been instructed to dump over her head. It was supposed to wash out the grime from her day's work. Eliza sat on the floor of George's former bedroom, a mostly vacant room. She was stark naked, purple bruises stamped her figure. Her blonde hair was matted and beads of sweat dripped down her forehead. Her once captivating eyes were dismal. She looked old, shriveled. Eliza did not attempt to cover her body when Camden walked through the door.

Toady, Bowie and Dagan arrived at exactly the same time. The pack surprised themselves with the coincidence of their timing. "An orgy then," Toady said, and the rest agreed.

"No, please." Eliza pointed at the various discolorations on her mutilated skin, the ones still healing from previous assaults. "Let me heal . . . let me heal first." Her voice trembled, her body quivered.

Camden's hot muscles tensed, his skin prickled. Sweat ran down his back, dampening his shirt. His pants suffocated him. "Should I leave?"

Toady, reeking of tobacco and manure, waved him away with the hand not busy unbuttoning his camo pants. "Close the door behind you."

Camden wasted no time slamming the door shut on his way out the house. The rebels were stupid. They had accidently set him free. No one was left to guard the house. No one. In his blissful, almost sensual relief, Camden forgot all about the rebel leader until he crashed into him. "I wasn't escaping," he quickly lied.

"Are they done yet?" Joshua, unfazed by the push, took a scat on one of the deck's steps. He watched the darkening sky, staring at the stars as if seeking constellations, hidden meanings in every twinkle. "She'll bore them soon enough."

"Why do you allow it to happen if you don't ever join in on the 'fun'?"

"Answer me this, Camden." Joshua turned to him, looked him over. "Why is your cock hard?"

"I . . . don't know . . . what you mean." The growing bulge in his pants both shamed and surprised him. "I'm not like you people."

"Of course you're not." For a man without a gun, Joshua confronted every situation with unnatural confidence. "I hope you at least watched the show."

"You're sick!" He wanted to attack him, break him in half, but thought better of it. Alpha rebels were ruthless. "Why are you letting them do that to her?"

"You don't care about Eliza," the man said. "Your first instinct was to run away and leave even your brother behind. What does that say about you, Cam?"

"I don't need to, well, to—"

"Rape, you can say the word out loud."

"I don't need to assault anyone in order to feel pleasure."

"Let's not pretend you're one of the good guys, yet." His grin was evil. "Your turn will come soon."

"Don't you dare touch me!" Camden threatened—pleaded.

The man laughed at the accusation, and then was serious again. "Not me, but you'll see what abuse looks like, first hand, Cam. It needs to happen, or she'll never notice you. I need her to know you exist. Do you understand?"

"No. I don't understand."

"What year are we in? I might be ahead of myself." The rebel leader stared up the twilight, intrigued, fascinated, confused.

HUNTING

Raven relaxed in the warm afternoon air enjoying the pleasant clatter of the horses' hooves on the highway. The road's asphalt was not as worn or cracked as other roads she had traveled. Barricades were supposed to signify the government succeeded in rebuilding the region. Not the case. Rebels ruled Kentucky. When the plague hit the third time around, folks accused farmers of spreading the disease, causing panicked citizens to abandon rural zones. Later, it was believed the rebels started the rumors in order to steal fertile land.

"Eight days," Kurt said, shaking his head. "It takes two days tops to get from Barren to Spencer County. How did you get lost?"

"I lost the map the towns folk drew for me when the kids stole my stuff," Raven answered.

"You had a shitty map to begin with." Kurt fidgeted on his saddle, noticeably uncomfortable with Ata's grip on his hips. "Whoever drew that map probably hasn't set foot out of Glasgow."

In her suburb, which was really land protected by cunning farmers, people claimed cities up north were populated again, and that the government employed actual police officers to uphold the law, instead of crooked bounty hunters running amok. Supposedly, Northerners not confined to their homes or jobs, lived the life described in twenty-first century books. Raven didn't believe any of it. If the government truly controlled the north, why hadn't they sent troops to reclaim the southern states, lands ready to feed the starving survivors? Why were small villages making their own rules, their own versions of suburbia?

"It took me days to get from Barren to Graves County, and then four days to Hardin, and one here to Jefferson," Raven said.

"Why did you go to Graves when that's west, and you wanted north? Don't you have a compass?"

"I was following the map."

"Some map." Kurt coughed and Ata let go of his waist. "If you ask me, whoever drew it wanted you lost."

"I'm on track again, that's all that matters." And no one had asked the old geezer for his opinion. She balled her hands into tight fists, squeezing into Nico's stomach. He didn't make a sound. "What about you, how did you become a bounty hunter?"

"I don't do that no more, do I, Son?"

Nico slowed his horse a bit, guiding the stallion closer to the mare, closer to Ata. "How did you and Raven meet?"

"Do you want to tell him?" Raven asked Ata.

The girl stared into the woods as if longing for the leafy camouflage. "No," she said simply.

Any story that kept the details of Raven's past a secret was up for discussion.

It can't hurt. Can it? She asked the voice in her head.

Hurt to talk about the past or Ata?

I obviously mean Ata.

Knock yourself out.

Who are you?

Who are you, Raven?

I thought you were my subconscious trying to—

The old man is staring at you. He might think you're crazy.

I am crazy.

Tell them about Ata.

Raven told the men all she knew about the blue-haired girl. She finished with, "but the orange was what truly baffled me."

Ata jumped off Kurt's horse and landed on her feet. She ran into the woods. The abruptness of her sudden escape nearly knocked the man off his mare. He made no attempt to follow suit. "Ungrateful brat," he yelled.

Nico turned his horse around. "Brace yourself, Raven."

His stallion galloped into the woods, trampling on dead leaves and evading trees. Bronte quickly caught up with the runaway. Nico dismounted his horse and ran after the girl. He caught her arm, trying to slow her down. Ata fought hard. Kicking and screaming.

"Stop!" He pinned her against the nearest tree. "I'm not going to hurt you."

"Leave me alone!" Ata squirmed until he released her. She slumped to the ground. "I'm completely healed."

Did she? Raven asked the sibilant whisper. *Did Ata really heal?*

I guess she did.

Don't you know?

Why would I know?

Aren't you using me to help her?

What makes you think I'm not using her—to help you?

Help me do what?

Find who, you mean?

"Why do you want to leave?" Nico knelt beside Ata. "We can help you."

Ata tilted her head slightly to the left. "Are you Zemi?"

"I am not Zemi." He tried to inspect her wound; she slapped his hand away. "I could smell you from miles away. You were bleeding. Let me help you. Please."

"Who are you?" She narrowed her gaze. "Where do you come from?"

Nico sighed, slowly. "I came from my mother's womb. She's dead now. Dad and I were on our way to her grave."

"Sorry about your mother." Ata straightened her back against the tree trunk and crossed her legs. "I never met my mother or father."

"That's a shame."

She leaned forward and inhaled Nico's scent before she leaned back again. "You smell funny."

"Is that good or bad?"

"You smell—wild—like nature. You make my body feel uncomfortable."

"Uncomfortable?" Nico glanced around him, scanning the heavily wooded forest.

Raven did the same.

Towering old-growth trees permitted the entrance of a pale, gauzy light. The dark soil was still moist after a rare rain shower. No creatures in sight—large or small. The air was fresh, wind chilled. No immediate threats.

Nico glanced at Ata again. "How do I make you feel uncomfortable?"

"I don't know. My body feels funny, tingly." Her tone was earnest, quizzical. "I don't know how to explain it. I just feel strange."

"You're attracted to me." He offered Ata his hand. When she took it, he lifted her up, and sat her behind Raven. He took the reins and led the stallion out of the forest and back to Kurt, who waited for them in the middle of the narrow freeway. "Dad, I think I'll walk Bronte. Later we'll switch."

Kurt's laughter was a resentful sneer. "I didn't know you were such a gallant gent, Nico."

"We've never traveled with ladies before." Nico turned to Ata and smiled. "She likes me."

"Well," Kurt said, "pester someone long enough and they'll believe they do."

The orange sun reminded Raven of her hunger. Hunger prompted the old man to ramble. Kurt talked about food, the weather, and then elaborated for some time on the FOY pandemic, stressing how the label FOY was a street name. He tried to remember the scientific definition and failed. Ata, the only one interested in his stories, was amazed to hear that Earth had once harbored billions of people.

"But where did they all live?" she asked Kurt.

"All over the place—the whole stinkin' globe," he said. "But with the first FOY wipe-out, the poorest countries lost half their populations."

"Did the virus kill the animals, too?"

"Tons of endangered species died every year. After the third world war—"

"A third world war?"

"After our economy collapsed—"

"When did the economy collapse?"

"Just listen, kid!" Kurt snapped. "The country was suffering from a weak ecosystem, too many wars, a dying economy, and skyrocketing gas and food prices. Then the water shortages came about, loss of jobs followed. The whole planet was in the pits. Things got worse and worse, and the crooked politicians decided to blame it all on overpopulation."

"Then why not have less people?"

"That's easier said than done, kid." Kurt's mare slowed, struggling with the human cargo. Her rider was too consumed with his stories to notice. "No one wants to be a danged Nazi. No country wants to tell its people to stop making babies."

"China did." Nico's horse mimicked the mare's sluggish speed. "India did too, remember? A lot of countries tried, Dad."

"Well, they didn't try hard enough, but there was a team of scientists and doctors, same folks that was involved in the Puerto Rico—"

"What's Puerto Rico?" Ata asked.

"An island in the Caribbean."

"Does it still exist?"

Kurt breathed loudly, inhaling irritation. "How old are you, kid?"

"Twenty."

"And in those twenty years of your life, when was the last time you saw or heard an airplane, assuming you know what an airplane is?"

"I've only heard of them," she answered meekly.

"Then how would I know if Puerto Rico was blown to smithereens or not?"

"I guess you wouldn't."

"I guess I wouldn't!"

"Dad, relax." Nico smiled up at Ata. "I wouldn't interrupt him with questions. He takes history stuff seriously."

"You should too, Nico." Kurt kicked the mare, unhappy with her pace. "You have to know what went wrong in the past, if you expect to fix it for the future."

"There is no future," Raven muttered.

Kurt ignored her and continued, "The government paid cash money to anyone who'd go for permanent sterilization. Folks thought the program foul since it was mostly poor folks and the sick who needed the money and would volunteer—reminded them of Nazi Germany."

"What's a Nazi?"

"Never mind that, kid. Folks argued the subject for a decade before the program got banned. And wouldn't you know it, a year later, this new virus killed thirty-five-percent of the world's population. Killed the economy, too."

"Where did the plague start?" Ata asked.

"Here, in this once great country of ours, and it quickly spread around the world, abruptly ending global travel. It was years before we got out of the depression, before technology offered new ways to isolate and quarantine infected countries. The world was different. The world feared touch. Massive hunger wiped out most of the remaining animals. Most were already endangered, anyhow. Eventually though, scientists came to the rescue and saved the rest of us from extinction."

"Allegedly," Nico added.

"But the 'side effects' of the vaccine were far worse than your usual diarrhea," Kurt said. "There was no way to confirm this, but conception became almost impossible right after the vaccine came along. Most civilians were sterile, but no one really cared the first few years. They were glad to live even if it meant no one could naturally reproduce."

"But you have Nico," Ata pointed out, "and I'm alive and so is Raven."

"Barrenness only lasted for a decade," Kurt assured Ata, who clung to the man's every word. "New testing was later created. Fertility drugs were enhanced. If you wanted a child, you had to pay ridiculous amounts of money for expensive procedures. Basically, if you were poor or working class, you couldn't afford to breed."

"Is that still the case today?"

"The fertility prices dropped drastically after the second and third strain of the plague, especially the second one that took out half the planet. It's affordable to get the fertility procedures done now because we're an endangered species. Where are we in the millions worldwide? I don't know anymore."

"Can't anyone get pregnant from just having sex?" Ata glanced at Nico when she asked the question, expecting him to answer. Nico averted her gaze.

"Sorrows are barren," Kurt said, "but us down here do fine the old fashion way."

Raven had heard enough. "If you're going to ramble, Kurt, talk about your bounty hunter days."

"You start killing animals, become good at it, and next thing you know, someone will pay you to kill humans." Kurt's mare needed water. She decelerated to a shallow pace. "Nobody says it like that.

They tell you the payment is so you catch criminals, arrest them. I wondered where the heck they were going to put the 'prisoners'. We have no goddamned prisons, active ones, anyway. So, you get good at catching the crooks and robbers, get fine tricky with it. You see, capturing humans is exciting, especially when you know you're not going to get in trouble for it."

"What do they pay you?" Raven had always assumed bounty hunters killed for pure enjoyment. "What useful stuff do you get in exchange for a bounty?"

"Rifles and bullets," Kurt answered. "The items we catch the bastards with."

"Dad." Nico reached for Sable's reins and stopped her. "Don't ride her to death."

Kurt dismounted the mare, grunting in frustration as he did so. "What good are these damn horses if they tire so easily?"

"They've been riding for hours without stopping." Nico glanced at his stallion. "They need water."

"Well then, we better find a creek soon." Kurt unlatched one of the saddlebags and retrieved a steel flask. He shook it. "We're almost out of water, too."

"There's a creek at the end of this road, two miles ahead." Nico turned to Ata. "Are you thirsty?" He snatched his father's flask and handed it over to her.

"This chivalry thing is getting real old, Nico," Kurt said. "You keep giving these girls all of our supply."

"'These girls' no. Just Ata." Raven had only used the horse, the healthy chestnut one, not the fat, exhausted mare. "Don't generalize old man."

Nico's peridot eyes scanned Raven from head to toe. "I'm sorry. Have I been neglecting you?"

That he believed it was his duty to take care of her was infuriating. "You're not my keeper, Nico. I don't need you to un-neglect me."

"I don't think 'un-neglect' is a word." He smiled. "Ata needs more attention because of her injury."

"Ata's healed." Raven tried to dismount Bronte, showing her displeasure, but instead nearly fell backwards. "I haven't mounted a horse in a while, is all."

"Here, let me help you." Nico offered his hand. "I forget you're also very weak."

The nerve of this guy. She jumped right off the horse, scraping her left knee when she hit the ground.

Kurt relished the scene with smug laughter. "Well, then," he said, "everyone's walking except for Miss ask-a-lot."

Ata also jumped off the stallion, but Nico caught her and gently set her down on her feet. She pushed past him and pointed straight ahead, "Rebels!"

The hooded man with a limp was Levi. His companion, a darker man, advanced toward them with a confident swagger. Both men cradled rifles. Both men grinned.

FOCUS

A better hunter would have heard the rebels miles before they approached. Nico blamed himself. Ata's presence distracted him. *Focus.* Keeping her safe was important but so was her sweet smell. *Focus.* He found it difficult to put it into words. Her scent engulfed and surrounded him. *Ata.* Nico could never grow tired of repeating her name. *Focus.*

The meandering, sunlit path was no longer solely a highway but lots of overgrown plants on broken asphalt. Derelict and rugged ground lay ahead. He expected gravel or perhaps dirt roads further north. Nature was taking over, which was great for the rebels. Wildernesses meant stealth. The rebels—or the one since Levi vanished into the woods—had been tricky enough to avoid being spotted until Ata pointed them out.

"There's a boy out there too, a teenager." Nico shut his eyes to inhale the odors of his surroundings. The boy hid somewhere near a tree, out of the road and deep into the woods. He had stepped in his own excrement and stood wiping his left foot. The smell of oranges invaded Nico's nostrils again. It aroused him. He turned to Ata. She was too close, clinging to his shirt. "Step back, Ata." *Focus.*

"We can't kill them, Nico. You know that." Kurt waved at the rebel and yelled, "What do you want?"

"They want to kill us, stupid man." Nico heard Raven's heart thump faster than the rushed words leaving her lips. "They will kill the two of you, and then they'll take me and Ata. Is that what you want, Nico, for the rebels to take Ata?"

He hardly intended to keep his preference a secret and yet, Nico detested the way Raven used it to her advantage. "They can't kill me, and for as long as I'm conscious, they won't take Ata, or *you*." He would do everything in his power to protect the women. It was his duty as a true hunter.

"I'll talk to him." Kurt volunteered. "The rest of you stay put."

"If the situation looks bad," Nico said, "signal me. I'll figure a way to get us all out of this."

"Or, and I'm speculating here, why don't you kill them." Raven gnawed at her cheeks as if chewing gum. "They'll kill us."

Kurt headed toward the man twelve yards away from them. The man greeted him with a malicious grin, obviously up to no good. The rebels had come a long way for a female. *But which one?*

Nico turned to Raven. "Do you know them?"

"No!" she snapped. "Rebels are all the same. You know one, you know them all."

He doubted that. "They might try to barter for you."

"Or they might try to kill your father." She glared at Nico. "Do you have any sense at all?"

"My senses have always been sharp, not uncommon in animals but unnatural for humans." He related something useful about himself in order to have Raven do the same. He imagined the rebels wanted her for something specific. "Why are you going to Taylorsville?"

Despite the rags for clothes and the rough attitude, Raven was not ugly, although a dip in a lake would do her some good. While Ata's aroma wafted fruity fragrances, Raven reeked of spoiled mushrooms. "My family lives in rebel territory. That's all you need to know."

"I can reason with them, maybe strike a passage deal." Ata stepped out of Nico's shadow. "We can barter with them. I have plenty of goods back home. I don't know if I want to go home. He may not let me leave again, but he does have plenty of things, maybe, maybe we can trade."

Two details bothered him about Ata's offer: one, she believed he would allow her contact with the rebels. And two, someone had once held her captive. Her scent was potent, strong enough to summon him from miles away. If Ata had been kept in some dungeon, it explained why he never found her before.

"No," Nico said. "I have a better idea."

Raven cackled, nervously. "Look at that, Ata, you have a new keeper."

"Keeper?" Nico had avoided looking at Ata from the moment she first spotted the rebels. Wary, he turned to her. "Do you have a keeper?"

Her beauty resonated and much of it kept him dull to coherent thoughts. *Focus.* Her soft skin was a rich tawny similar to that of the extinct lion, and her chalky blue tresses gave her the aura of a deity. The hue was an optical effect, an amazing one. And those eyes, those large, honey-glazed eyes were unreasonably carnal. *Focus.*

She wandered over, sensing his uneasiness, making it worse by wrapping her hand around his shoulder. "Are you tingly, too? What's that about?"

"You wouldn't believe me if I told you—" He shoved her behind him the moment the boy in woods revealed himself.

"Hand over the girls." The shaggy-haired teenager aimed his rifle at Nico.

"Why don't you drop your weapon instead?" Nico was not intimidated by the puny kid.

Raven's hands began to shake. "We're going to get picked off."

"It's alright, kids." Kurt was all smiles. He waved from afar. "They want to bargain!"

"Not for the girls, I hope?" Nico answered back. "They're not for sale, Dad."

His father laughed and so did the other man. "You're a healer, Nico, don't ever forget that." Kurt's eyes twitched. He rubbed them. "Someone always needs . . . healing."

Nico took several calculated breaths, nodding at his father.

"Don't do that. Don't look at me like that. I'm your old man. I know all your tricks. Come here!"

It was an order Nico would obey. His father would never put him in harm's way. "Okay, we're coming."

"The hell we are." Raven took steps in the opposite direction.

The boy targeted her with his rifle. "If you run, I'll shoot you."

Raven stopped and glowered at him with an almost tangible hatred. "Filthy rebels, the lot of you! What do you want from me? You've already taken everything."

Nico sprinted toward the teen rebel, snatching his rifle and using it as a shocking device. "You're better off with me, Raven."

"I don't trust you." Her eyes darted from Nico to the struggling boy.

"You don't have to trust me, but I did scan your insides earlier when I healed you. I know what you've lost. I can help you find it."

She cursed him. "What kind of healer are you?"

"The only kind worth having," he said, flinging the rebel to the ground. The kid was gasping for air. "Get up and walk, rebel. What's your name?"

"Wafer," answered the scrawny kid. "Can I have my rifle back?"

"No. How old are you, Wafer?"

"Thirteen, sir." He smiled. Several teeth were missing.

"March, kid. Lead the way."

Ata followed, with Raven close behind. Nico admired Raven's stubbornness, which alone convinced him she too needed his full protection. Her previous appearance of strength was hardly a shield to protect her from vermin. It took a lot of courage—a hand with the silkiest skin clung to his arm and shifted his thoughts. Ata had touched him. *Focus.*

"They have a covered wagon, Nico!" She shrieked excitedly, but the wagon only cemented his suspicions. The rebels wanted the females, alright. "What do you think they have inside?"

"I'm pretty sure it's empty." The girls were the supposed cargo. Nico halted a good distance away from Wafer's friends. "This is close enough."

Levi sat in the front seat of a horse-drawn wagon, reins in hand. No one explained where the carriage came from. Nico supposed Levi had masked it in the forest in order to sneak up on the girls. The man's shirt was stained with Ata's blood, and Nico's anger exploded. Unable to repress his hatred, he aimed the boy's rifle at Levi's head.

"Easy there." Kurt's frame blocked the intended target. "All they want is the girl."

"I told you no, Dad. Why would you do this?"

"My name's Orion. Let's start there," the man said. "We don't look like much of a threat to you right now, but that's only because you think we're alone. Don't fool yourself, Healer."

"The girls are not for sale."

"They don't need both girls." Kurt pointed at Raven. "Just the one."

The man cocked his pistol, and although Raven wanted to run away, pounding fear held her still. "Yeah, I wouldn't dash off if I were you." Orion kept his aim on her, but he directed his words to Nico. "Your father says you won't give up the blue-haired girl. That's fine. We don't need her. Keep her. But I can't say the same about the Carrier lass."

"The girls are not for sale."

"Everything has a price tag." Orion was burly and over six feet tall. He spoke with the buoyancy of a man of no worries. "But suit yourself."

Wafer ran toward Levi before Nico had the chance to stop him. Levi reached inside the wagon bed and pulled out two rifles. He threw the boy one. Wafer pointed the weapon at Ata. He grinned. Fired one shot. Missed. That was all it took. Nico jumped the boy—Orion had run away. He grabbed Wafer by the neck and tossed Kurt the rifle. Levi, from his seated position, opened fire. One bullet missed Nico. The other skimmed through his torso. None hit Wafer. Ignoring the kid, Nico leapt inside the wagon. Levi reloaded. Nico knocked the rifle out of his hand. He grabbed the man by the neck. With his pocket knife, the one used to skin animal prey, he slashed the man's throat. Blood sprayed everywhere. And Levi died within seconds in a pool of his own essence.

Wafer fled to the woods. Nico could hear him trampling on twigs and leaves, hurrying away. When he was satisfied the rebel was far gone, he regarded Raven. Her unwavering stare marked her approval, and he was pleased to see she no longer trembled with rage and fear. No words were exchanged. Her nod was good enough.

Nico would have glanced at Ata first, but since he could always sense her presence, he never needed to reassure himself of her exact location. However, he faced her apologetically as Levi's blood dripped from his face, staining his shirt. Ata was not as understanding as Raven. Unable to face the carnage, she hid behind Kurt.

Kurt, still holding the boy's rifle, was equally disturbed. "What the heck is the matter with you?" he growled. "They'll return with more men. We're not supposed to kill them. We won't be safe now, and we won't be able to roam freely, not without always looking over our shoulders. You know Kentucky belongs to the rebels. Where do we go now?"

"Father—"

"No!" Kurt said. "Where do we go now?"

"Willowy Farms," he answered. "If we want to—"

Ata made a run for the woods. Nico sprinted after her. Her attempt to flee again upset him, but he also understood her motive. Nico had decided to end Levi's life the moment he found Ata in the middle of the road, bleeding to death. He would never apologize for killing the man, but he could apologize for doing so in her presence.

It was a momentary hiccup. If Ata allowed him the chance to prove his worthiness, he could set things right again. Her scent faded for a few seconds, and the stench of the rebels returned. He couldn't afford to play the running game anymore.

"Stop, Ata." He pinned her to the nearest tree. "I'm sorry I have to do this to you again, but you can't keep running away. The rebels are out in the woods. Father and Raven are unprotected. Please, come back."

"No, I'm fine. Let go." She shoved uselessly. "I want to go home."

Nico didn't intend on using his full strength. He released some of the pressure on her shoulders. "You can't go back. You were a prisoner."

"I want to go home." Her eyes glossed, darkened. "Please, don't make me yours."

He was taken aback by her words. She thought *him* the oppressor. Wrong. Nico was a hunter, yes. He was a healer too, but never a slaver. "I would never hurt you. I can't. I need you. Ata . . . Ata, is that your real name?"

She glanced up at him, tears streaming down her cheeks. "Atabey."

"I'm sorry, Atabey." He truly meant it. "Let's start over, huh? Tell me, are you named after the goddess?"

"Let go." She shoved him.

He released her. "I'm sorry if I hurt you. I was—"

"What goddess?" A bruise the size and color of a single wine grape marked her left shoulder. She rubbed at it, absentmindedly.

Nico winced. "Your name, you mean?"

"Yes. You said 'after the goddess'." Her previous scent of oranges faded, and her natural scent replaced all of his common sense, his urgency.

"Zemis are gods according to *Taìno* mythology. Is that what you were referring to earlier? Is someone named Zemi related to you, the one you're looking for?"

"Oh, thank you!" She wrapped her arms around him, squeezed him. "I didn't know what I was looking for, but now—" She gripped him harder.

The experience of total body involvement, the complete awareness of living and breathing, was brief in physical time. Time, space, and his usual sense of self disappeared for the duration of her embrace. The attraction was strong, stronger than any other sensation. She belonged to him. She was made for him. Atabey was his transcendent better, and he would never, ever give her up.

A hard blow to the back of his head sent him into a black oblivion.

WAKE UP

Every time the oversized wheels rolled over a tall bump everything in the wagon jostled, and due to lack of rain, dust sprang up with every bounce. Descending sharp ridges always led to near crashes. It was jarring to the teeth. The rebels had punished Raven and Ata by binding them to the bed. The bonnet kept them hidden. Wafer drove, and Orion monitored the girls from horseback, trotting behind the wagon.

Raven and Ata's arms and legs were shackled, a disaster when trying to keep from swaying. Raven's body smashed into Ata on several occasions. The girl said nothing. She knew better.

Cut her some slack, the voice said.

She shouldn't have run into the woods, then. Raven refused to accept Ata's stupidity as anything other than plain stupidity.

Raven, you're only angry at your own shortcomings.

The voice—*It*—knew nothing about her.

Call me 'It' all you like, but what I said is true.

You're wrong. If Nico hadn't chased after Ata—

Where do you think you're going?

What do you mean?

Where do you think the rebels are taking you?

She shrugged. *They'll sell me off or something.*

Ask. Orion. Where. He's. Taking. You. Its words floated in her mind, bouncing from cortex to stem.

No way!

You'll be okay—

Its quick absence disoriented her. Goose bumps erupted all over her body.

"I'm sorry I let us get caught," Ata said.

"No talking!" Orion snarled at her from his horse. "You, Blue, no talking."

Raven blamed herself for the rusty shackles, and the long heavy chain, bounding her to Ata and the old wooden wagon, but she could not help but also hold the father-son duo partially responsible. The ardent fire in the healer's wise eyes had her believing—in him. *Stupid.* Rule number one: never trust anyone. She was, however, rash to assume Nico approved of Kurt's barter. The old man had requested to have his son pardoned in exchange for the girls. Nico, absent during the exchange, probably had nothing to do with the trade.

The rebels stopped to rest for the night right as a fever began to attack Raven. Her inflamed tonsils clogged up her airway. Swallowing was difficult. The cold air dried her skin; she scratched the inflamed patches on her forearm, neck, and stomach. Oh, how her stomach hurt. Her body burned. She trembled, in desperate need of a blanket. No one listened to her moans unless she counted the wolf howling in the distance. Her head throbbed. She broke out in a sweat, her entire body drenched. Death from overheating awaited her or the delirium induced from her high temperature.

She awoke chilled as the dark, starless night lingered in silence. Why was it still dark out? She shivered. Hours moved slowly. The freezing weather was unbearable. Cold, so cold. She could feel the ice forming on her feet. Numb. She hugged her body and wished for a quilt.

You have a high fever. The voice chimed soothing music. *Wake Ata.*
I can't speak. Her throat burned.

I'll wake her, then. A sigh of impatience accompanied its words. *Hold on.*

Raven wanted to drink from the fountain of imagination, a place where the only poet she remembered lived. *I will lead you away to a beautiful land, The Dreamland that's waiting out yonder.* She sang the

53

beautiful lyrics from Child and Mother by Eugene Field. *We'll walk in a sweet posie-garden out there, Where moonlight and starlight are streaming, And the flowers and the birds are filling the air with the fragrance and music of dreaming.*

Snap out of it!

She shuddered.

The night rode to eternity.

"Raven, are you sick?" Ata sat up, rubbing her eyes. "Can I do anything for you?"

After much shuffling and rustling, the broad face of Orion appeared. He was drowsy, angry. The glare was directed at Ata. "What did I tell you, Blue, about talking?"

"Something's wrong with Raven. She's sick."

"Is she now?" Orion climbed on board, shaking the whole wagon with his heavy steps. He pushed Ata back to her corner, sending her sprawling. He settled on top of her before the girl could sit upright. "Where're you from, Blue?"

Ata struggled to free herself from the big man. The shackles didn't help. She mostly wiggled. "Get off me!"

"No, no yelling now." He covered her mouth with a callused hand, pressing her head against the wooden planks. "Why are your eyes so yellow? They're bright even in the dark. You see me, Blue?"

She shook her head.

"Am I that black?" Orion laughed. "Let's see what your kind hides in a skull."

Raven's rage centered her, pulled her out of the sick haze. She wanted to kill the man, but her weak muscles were useless. Her head throbbed. Thought alone required effort. The vicious cycle of hot, cold, sweat and pain continued with no end in sight.

Orion wrapped his hands around Ata's tiny neck and squeezed. The girl writhed underneath him. He leaned closer, listening to the gurgling moans escaping her throat. Unsatisfied, he brought her head up, his hands still snug around her neck. He smashed her head against the wooden floor. Once. Twice. The brute cackled. "I know what you really are, Blue." He released her after another loud thud and staggered backwards. "You pissed yourself, filthy freak!" Orion pushed his foot between her legs and shoved, hard. He left after promising to finish cracking her skull if she uttered another sound.

Ata sat up, rubbed the back of her head with what little mobility the handcuffs allowed, and studied her palms. No blood. She hugged her knees to her chest and hid her face. Without shedding a single tear, she fell back to sleep. Raven envied the girl's ability to dismiss the beating, but offered her no pity, not when her own life was a nightmare.

Plagues of mosquitoes hovered around them the following day. The sun pestered, relentlessly. The asphalt's heat penetrated the soles of their feet. Raven and Ata walked cuffed together in hot chains that also linked them to the wagon.

Wafer drove the prairie schooner, while Orion took a nap inside the bed.

Ask the boy for water, the voice said.

She scoffed. *No. Where were you last night when I almost died?*

Get over yourself, Raven.

Who are you, and how did you wake Ata?

Did I wake Ata?

Don't pretend—Raven doubled over, the sensations of gargling gravel left her breathless. *I think I'm going to pass out.*

You'll survive.

I'm barely breathing.

Raven, it insisted, *the kid won't deny you water.*

What the hell do you know?

We can argue all day about this, or you can get hydrated.

"I'm thirsty." Her scratchy throat made her sound like a frog. "If you want me to go anywhere, give me something to drink."

Wafer brought the wagon to a full stop. He climbed down and headed toward her with a canteen. "Drink before Orion wakes up."

She chugged the whole thing down almost forgetting Ata. "Ata also needs water."

"No, I'm fine." She looked perfectly fine, too. "Take it all. You need it more than I do."

The voice inside Raven's head rambled on and on for several miles. She listened. The alternative was to surrender to the hatred and pain, but anytime her feet stumbled, the voice steadied her pace. The canorous sounds always reminded her to rise above the worst. Where had the voice come from? Maybe it was her own voice, keeping her sane.

If you're not Zemi—

Its vibrating laughter resonated in her mind.

What are you laughing at?

You're trying to figure me out. It cackled, quite amused. *Women never change.*

You're a man?

I'm an ancient man.

Ata was the first to notice and greet the brown dog following the wagon's trail. She named the creature Maple. Maple huddled close to the blue-haired girl as if always knowing Ata would do her no harm. The lanky mutt had a broad head, a thick nose and long, black droopy ears. She went from licking herself, to chasing flies, and critters, to simply barking at the horses. At times, she spun around her own wagging tail.

"Dogs communicate with humans better than any other species. Without dogs," Ata said, "humans wouldn't have evolved."

"What makes you think we ever evolved?" Raven took a good look at the mutt. Maple was a humdrum product of terrible times and so was Wafer, silently sweating and panting, leading the tired horses over cracked pavement.

"I was told dogs followed hunter gatherers for meals." Ata knelt to pat Maple. The mutt rolled on her back, expecting a full massage. "She had owners."

"Her owners are probably dead," Raven said, "and we're next."

Bourbon County was a day away. Families throughout the region offered the rebels flour, bacon and salt in exchange for their safety. That night, Orion built a campfire. He made a farmer's wife cook them supper: beans, rice, venison, watermelon, carrots, and freshly baked bread. They washed it down with lemonade. Everyone ate, including Raven and Ata.

The route the rebels took led them back to Fayette County. Raven woke the next morning with a wild fever and a red rash on her neck and shoulders. The skin on her stomach burned, but she never complained to the rebels for Ata's sake. Orion was disgusted with everything about the girl. Ata appeared to frustrate him in every possible way. He wanted to kill her, but something about her frightened him. Instead, he used any excuse of disobedience as a chance to strike her.

"I'm watching you, Blue."

Ata marched quietly under the sun and often smiled down at Maple, her faithful companion.

"Do you hear me, witch?" Orion released his rifle from its sling and shot at the mutt. "Do you hear me, now?" Maple yelped and fell over, her coat splattered in blood.

Ata's hands trembled, and her lips quivered. If a gaze could start a fire, she would have burned Orion alive.

"That's what you get for not—" A sudden gust of wind rushed from the west and nearly pushed the man off his horse. "Where the heck did that come from?" He held on to the reins and glared at Ata with suspicion. "You two better get back inside the wagon. Stay there for the remainder of the trip."

The flat, rectangular wagon bed also stored big barrels. Raven sat in a cramped corner among the heavy cargo. She needed to lie down. With her fever untreated, her health only worsened. *Let death come quick.*

You're fading fast, Raven.

She wondered about the greater things in life. *What are they, Voice?*

I don't know, he whispered.

What are we talking about, again? She closed her eyes and begged to die.

Stay awake.

I'm obviously awake. She sneered. *Do you even see me?*

You're not conscious.

He was wrong.

Raven lay on a moist bed of thick lush grass, a meadow among dozens of oak trees. The steady sound of a nearby flowing brook eased her mind. A ground rainbow of flowers bloomed in all shapes and sizes. The sky shone blue, and the birds flew free, tweeting familiar songs. The breeze caressed her naked skin and the fresh, crisp air invigorated her mind.

A blackbird landed on Raven's foot.

She sat up, baffled by the yellow-eyed creature's bold stance.

You're in a fallow state. The bird scurried up to her thigh.

Unclenching her tight fist, she offered him nutmeats. *Are you talking to me, Birdie? Your beak isn't moving.*

Raven, this isn't real. Wake up. You're no longer on the road. The bird then ate, lightly pecking her palm.

Hmm, you sound like the voice. She stroked the small, plumaged head with one finger. *How do you know what's real and what's not?*

Ata lets me in from time to time.

Are you Ata's keeper?

The bird responded with an expansion of the wings and a high-pitched chuck: *Wake up!*

ARRIVAL

Ida joined Camden down the hill at the creek. She told him about the rebels' simple plan to establish a great monarchy. Her father, Isaac Mullin, believed societies were incapable of ruling themselves, and that the collective force within a republic was the real reason more than half the world's population had died out.

"A monarchy is no different," Camden debated. "The mistakes of a nation with many leaders are just as easily committed by one. What your father is doing makes him a dictator."

"My father's a pioneer," the redhead announced proudly. "He's well-known and greatly respected."

The creek was long and narrow, surrounded by barren trees, and specks of grass. The murky water roamed over rocks in a slow current, bereft of fish. Camden filled his two buckets. He made the trip several times a day.

"Why does your father allow you to stay with these savages?" It was ludicrous for Ida to enjoy cooking and cleaning for the rebels. "Why doesn't he marry you off?"

"Father's punishing me," she said. "He wants me to appreciate how easy I had it."

"Are you all staying?" Camden asked. "Is Willowy Farms your new headquarters?"

"We own every single farm in Prune Creek, and Father has already sent for more men."

Prune Creek farmers grew a considerable amount of crops per season. The high ground enclosed by a multitude of trees kept the fertile land well hidden from threats—or so the theory went. It was foolish to assume rebels would not come someday. They always came.

"Are you ever planning on marrying?" he asked her.

"I wish." Ida's throaty giggle made her sound ill. "Father insists I find the best man, but you see, he thinks he's the only flawless man alive."

"You don't believe that, do you?" Camden hauled the buckets up the hill with Ida by his side.

"Less talking and more walking!" Dagan approached them on horseback. "You hear me, prisoner scum?"

"Shut up, Dag. Move along." Ida waited until the horse ambled a few yards away before she glanced at Camden with a smirk on her face. "I wonder what it would be like to bed another man."

"Who's the man you've bedded?"

"Father," she said. "I've considered Joshua for my second, but he's a strange man. He goes into sabbaticals, and we don't hear from him for days. When he does come back, he's always a different person. Like right now, he's Joshua the Leader but sometimes, he's violent and crazy. Often, he doesn't know where he is at all. The day he decided we needed to come to Willowy Farms, he actually told me that if we didn't find Bran here, he was going to set himself on fire. Isn't that the weirdest thing?"

Camden avoided the obvious question, the one on the tip of his tongue. Instead, he asked, "Why do your people want the boy?"

"What do I know?" They reached the house and readied to part ways; she needed to cook dinner, and he had to refill the well. "I'm glad Joshua finally found Bran. I hope he keeps the kid alive."

"Why wouldn't he?"

"I already told you, handsome." Ida leaned close, her soft lips brushed Camden's damp cheek. "Joshua changes like the wind."

On another monotonous evening, Ida surprised Camden by visiting the basement. He and his brother were the only ones there.

Gad was asleep as he usually was after a long day of labor. The other prisoners were dealing with a commotion outside. The basement was windowless, but Camden could hear the shouting of rebels, the squeak of wagon wheels, and the neighing of horses. Either a new prisoner arrived or Joshua finally returned from his sabbatical.

"Are you going to ask me why I'm here, or are you going to daydream some more?" Ida placed her hands on her hips.

He watched her without uttering a sound. Ida's delay was her special way of exuding importance.

"My brother Wafer's back and so is Orion," she said. "I'm so happy, Cam."

"Oh, I thought your leader might've come back."

Joshua had allowed Camden the easy labor of water hauling, a task Mary could do blindfolded. The leader treated him well enough and chose to ignore his moments with Ida, even though the man reprimanded any of the other rebels—Toady in particular—who interacted with the redhead.

"Levi's dead," Ida blurted out.

"Good," Camden said. "I never liked the slob."

"Orion and Wafer brought two girls with them."

"What does all this have to do with me, Ida?" He was sure she had been fishing for that exact trout. "Why are you telling me this?"

"The new prisoners are going to share your basement." She grinned at him. "Are you upset?"

The windowless basement had always been a few degrees cooler than the rest of the house, but not anymore, not with the amount of people living there. Two box mattresses occupied the farthest corner of the room; George slept on one bed, and Eliza and Mary used the other one. Gad and Camden miserably rested on the concrete floor, too close to the stench of old urine. Mary had accidents every single night, and her soiled laundry lay in a pile near Camden's side of the room.

There was no more space for new prisoners.

"Yes, I'm upset." Camden wanted to strangle Ida for playing her silly feminine games of seduction that were more annoying than enticing. "Why are you trying to upset me?"

"Upset you?" She gaped, feigning disbelief. "I wouldn't dream of doing such a thing."

"Why do you play these games with me?"

"Are you angry?" Her malicious grin hardened him. "Am I being naughty?"

"You're being very naughty." He rose from his corner of the room, headed her way. "Have sex with me, Ida."

She giggled and sauntered away. "Your brother's awake."

Gad observed the scene with snooping, lustful eyes. Ida moved past Camden. She stood above Gad as if expecting another beggar. "I bet you also want to have sex."

He nodded, shamelessly. "You're too good for my bookworm brother."

She drank the compliment with a smile. "Probably, but I do prefer him. I have someone else for you."

"You do?" Gad sat up. "I doubt Eliza would please me any."

"No one's touched the new girls yet," she said. "I'm supposed to clean them up. Blue's with Bowie now, but the other one is still unconscious. You'll have a limited time span to take her first. Ask me why I'm doing this for you?"

Gad smirked at her. "Why are you doing this for me?"

"I see the way Toady eyes me. I want to leave this place before he takes me, and so I need someone to help me escape. You're stronger than most—"

"Wait a minute," Camden said. "*I* can protect you."

She and Gad laughed.

"What's so funny?" He grabbed her arm. "Don't laugh at me."

"Don't touch me like that, barbarian." Ida shoved him and left the room.

Camden considered fighting his brother until the ridiculousness of it all sank in. When it came to brute strength, Gad bested him every time. Besides, Ida was not worth the quarrel. He needed to find out what Joshua wanted from him. The rebel leader hardly spoke to Camden, but often brought him books to read. Camden suspected the man had big plans, and until he discovered what they were, he would ignore his urge to conquer Ida.

Ida returned with a gait of superiority, her head held high. Dagan followed, carrying in his arms a girl wrapped in a towel. He dropped her on the floor near Eliza's mattress as if discarding extra cargo. Dagan glanced at both Camden and Gad.

"Toady has first dibs, and if any of you two try something while we're gone, we'll have you killed for treason." Dagan squealed like an ignorant pig instead of coming across as stern. His corkscrew hair, prominent nose and crooked posture were laughable. The short man was only ever dangerous when he carried a rifle. His insecure fingers gripped the trigger at the faintest sound. "Do you hear me? You'll be killed for treason." Treason was the wrong word.

"We hear you loud and clear." Gad sprang up. "What else do you want, *Dag*?"

"It's Dagan, prisoner scum." Dagan removed the rifle from its sling. "Why don't you sit back down, big boy."

Gad obeyed.

Camden glanced over at the toweled girl. Her twitching was unrelenting. "What's wrong with her?" he asked Ida.

"What do I know?" She examined the wretched girl for a mere second. "I think she's sick, but she looks real nice after the scrubbing I gave her, doesn't she?"

The girl's dark hair draped down her shoulders like fine silk, her porcelain complexion neared perfection, but it was her rose petal lips that made Camden's pants itch. Many women suffered from malnutrition and sun-beaten skin. But not the new prisoner; she was somewhat healthier than others.

"Joshua will arrive soon, and Orion needs help unloading the wagon, Cam." Ida swung the door open as if angry with the hinges. "Drool over the prisoner another time."

Joshua's jet-black hair was peculiarly disheveled, and even from a distance, his stern gaze overwhelmed his men. Ink paintings covered various parts of his skin. The sketches mentioned and resembled revelations from another era. Joshua's clothes always consisted of dark jeans and weird T-shirts with logos ranging from vicious animals to bizarre diabolical hells and terror striking apocalypses. Some shirts exhibited simple words, phrases and sentences, none familiar to Camden, at least none he had ever read in a book.

The man arrived from a two day sabbatical carrying an acoustic guitar. No one remembered seeing the leader's musical instrument before; Joshua never bothered to explain where he found it. Instead, he settled on the porch swing and played a tune.

Orion concluded the leader had returned to his original self. The rest of the rebels gave a collective sigh of relief. Toady, in particular, had waited for the chance to go about his business without fear of punishment. He grabbed Ida and headed toward a private room, telling the other men the cocky slut had it coming. Orion reminded him that Ida was the daughter of General Mullin, leader of the North Central Militia.

"He's not Joshua's boss. Our leader listens to no one." Dagan also wanted a turn with the redhead.

Thirteen-year-old Wafer settled the dispute, arguing on his sister's behalf. He threatened to shoot anyone stupid enough to deflower the Mullin heiress. Camden had read enough books to know loss of virginity occurred when a female was fully penetrated but in rebel language, a Father had a right to his daughter. In the eyes of rebel men, Ida was still a virgin. There was no sense in it, and yet, Wafer won the disagreement with his flawed argument.

"Take the girl in the basement," Orion told Toady.

"What about the other one, the one in the master bedroom with Bowie?" Dagan asked.

"No." Orion was quick to respond. "Bowie's guarding Blue until Joshua takes a good look at her. Something's not right with that one."

None of the rebels wanted the daunting task of speaking to their leader. They sent Camden.

Joshua dropped his guitar the minute Camden entered his line of sight. He glared at him with a solid scowl of hatred.

"Sir, leader, I was told to speak with you." Camden avoided the piercing blue eyes and kept his gaze concentrated on the weird ink on the leader's shoulders.

"They're called tattoos, stupid fuck." Joshua slouched, extending his arms as if inviting a challenge. "I thought you were the smart one." He leaned forward in search of Camden's eyes. "Look at me, Cam."

Camden did as he was told.

"That's a good boy." He laughed. "How old are you?"

"I'm eighteen or nineteen, sir."

"Fuck me, you don't know your own age?"

"Father didn't celebrate birthdays."

"The prick, huh? Tell me, Cam, have you read all the books I brought you?"

"I have, sir."

"Get them out of whiskey town."

"I don't . . . I don't understand."

"Don't get too attached," Joshua continued. "The jackal will lead the way."

"Sir, I don't—"

"Listen fuck, while I still remember this shit."

Camden waited.

"I don't retain everything all the time, so listen carefully."

"I am listening, sir."

"Are you wondering why I favor you, Camden Sickles, age eighteen or nineteen?"

He nodded.

"Do you have a guess?"

"No, sir, I don't."

"I'll tell you as soon as—" Joshua's attention turned to the fallen guitar. He picked it up and without uttering another word, without finishing his own sentence, played a soft melody.

SNOW WHITE

Raven landed on her back; her head banged against enameled steel. Tired, so tired. She wanted to open her eyes and view her surroundings but couldn't. Her eyelids melded together in the common interest of languor. The faucet near her head clanked and screeched. A lukewarm dribble weighed her hair down.

Running water?

The liquid pool eased her aches.

"Let's fix you up," said a shrill voice.

The hot patches on her skin were raked with a bristled scrub. Fretful hands tugged and yanked her tangled hair. The wet strands slapped her face.

Do I smell rosemary oil?

"Nice rack," said a woman.

A prickly sponge massaged Raven's breasts, painfully hardening her nipples. Her thighs were forced apart. The shrill woman dabbed a cloth between Raven's legs. She flinched, fell away.

The water drained through a vortex underneath her bottom, slurping and groaning like a thirsty animal.

Raven woke again, but her eyelids remained glued together. Lethargy kept her dull, unmoving. Then loud knocks pounded on wood or a door.

"Well," said a man? Heavy boots stomped and squeaked on tiles.

Raven floated. A dry cloth enveloped her.

"I'm done. Take her," a woman said. Someone picked her up, carried her over a gaunt shoulder. Dark slumber followed.

I can't seem to stay awake, Voice.

You don't have to be conscious, right now.

Was I bathed?
She was cleaning you, for them.
For who?
The men who are going to hurt you.
Hurt? She detected the lie. *Rape, you mean. I'm not afraid.*
Life wasn't always like this, Raven.
My head hurts.
The rebel just dropped you.
It all hurts.
Do you want me to kill them for you someday?
No, I'll kill them myself.

Raven's eyes snapped open. She took immediate note of the room: two mattresses lay in a corner, loads of books stacked a wall, and piles of clothes carpeted the floor. She was in a basement, perhaps. Pushing her mind away from everything that hurt, she concentrated on the blonde woman and little girl standing on her left. The woman stared down at Raven with the stricken eyes of a person who had seen enough and gone through worse.

"I'm fine. Name's Raven." She headed to the pile of garments and grabbed a pair of jeans and a brown shirt. She dressed quickly, ignoring the aches, ignoring her tender hot skin. "What are your names?"

The woman sat on a mattress with the little girl on her lap. "I'm Eliza. This is my daughter, Mary. She's nine. Um, I don't mean to be forward, but you look so much like her father."

Raven glanced at Mary, a bony thing of brown hair and dark eyes. "Who's her father?"

"Phil Carrier," said the woman with a sudden sadness in her voice. "He was my first husband."

"Did he have a brother?" Raven asked. "Did Phil have a father named George Carrier, by any chance?"

"Yes." Eliza's eyes widened, her wrinkles eased. "Are you Cormac's daughter? I knew it."

"I am." She was finally where she needed to be. "Where's Bran?"

According to Eliza, her husband had contracted a disease. George had been unwilling to lose his second son after having lost Cormac, his eldest, many years earlier. "Your grandfather was on a mission to find a doctor," the woman said. "He heard about a traveling healer located in Logan County. George tried sending for him. The letters were mailed from farm to farm and county to county."

"Did you find the healer?" Raven asked.

"No," said Eliza. "But Glasgow's suburbia offered antibiotics instead. Phil still died two weeks later." She paused, pensive, staring at a black smudge on the wall furthest from her mattress. The tears filling her eyes never spilled.

"That's how Grandpa found me." Raven broke the silence, pushing to know more. "I've been living in Glasgow for years."

"Yes." Eliza wiped her eyes. She kissed the top of her daughter's head and gathered the little girl closer to her. "George was overjoyed by the news of Cormac's daughter, alive. After your home was invaded, you and your mother taken, and your father left for dead, we all assumed we would never see you again."

"But Father did find—"

"Cormac made George promise him to bring up Bran, hiding the boy from every known bounty hunter in the nation," Eliza said. "It was well known the highest bounty ever offered would go in exchange for a Northerner's natural first born."

Raven let the air out of her lungs slowly. "My son?"

"Your father worked for the government and so did George. They should have taken Bran to Barren County, a far better place to raise a child, and you, his mother. After the boy's rescue, someone should've given him back to you."

Mary crawled out of her mother's lap and grabbed the picture book near the mattress. She flipped through the pages as if searching for one particular frame. At last, when she was nearing the end of the book, she pointed at an image and glanced up at Raven, a wide grin on her face. She said, "Snow White."

"I've never seen snow," Raven told her. "Barren County has been my home for a long time. I can't remember much before my stay there, not after my mother was slaughtered, not after I was taken hostage by rebels, filthy rebels who did things to me, awful things. They took my baby away when he was only three months old. I haven't seen him since."

"Your father found your son, Raven." Eliza scooted forward and smiled, reassuringly. "He sent him to live here with George and Phil."

"The government men who rescued me from a rebel camp told me Bran was dead, that I was lucky to be alive." Her father had fed her the same lie. "Father sent me to Barren County and expected me to continue living as if I'd never given birth. I didn't hear from Granddad until a few weeks ago. His letter stated that Bran was alive and safe in Willowy Farms, and that I was more than welcome to come see him." That first letter had made Raven despise her whole family. "He told me Bran was six now, that he's a bright boy. Now that I'm here, I want my son."

"You look like Snow White." Mary's tiny finger tapped on a specific page. "See here, Mommy, doesn't she look like Snow White?"

Eliza studied the picture book. She looked up at Raven. "Did your mother ever read to you?"

"My mother's dead, and I don't know what Snow White is."

"Who," said Eliza, "Snow white is a princess in a fairy tale."

"Where's my son, Eliza? How long have you been a prisoner?"

"Snow White has skin as white as snow, lips red as blood, and hair black as ebony." Eliza took the story book to her lap and flipped through the pages. "Mary thinks you're Snow White."

Great, I'm stuck with a loony mother.

You're cruel, Raven.

I'm not, Voice.

They think you look like Snow White. It's supposed to be a compliment.

Who has time for compliments? Who cares about them?

His pause, his humming hesitance circled her head several times. *You must be beautiful.*

I think I'm sick again. The bile build up burned her throat.

You haven't stopped being sick.

What's wrong with me?

Butterflies in your stomach, maybe? Some girls need easing into flattery.

Why don't you just go away?

Amusement escaped his husky voice. He laughed. *Do you really want me to leave?*

No, no I don't.

Aww, I didn't think so.

Where's Ata, by the way?

She's alive.

Is Ata special?

She's a beacon for special. She attracts it to her.

Nico's special.

Your savior is probably dead right now.

Did she hint resentment in his words? *Can you get inside his head?*

No, and I don't trust what I don't know.

Are you saying you don't trust Nico because you can't eavesdrop on his thoughts?

She doesn't know.

Who doesn't know what?

The lady staring at you doesn't know.

Eliza rose with her daughter by her side. They held each other. "The rebels removed Bran on their first day here. I don't know where your son is."

"You have to know!"

"I swear I don't know what they did with him."

"How long have you been captive?"

"I don't know exactly. Days are all the same."

"Think, woman!"

Mary hid behind her mother.

"Bran's all I have in this world." Raven sighed, steadying her tone. Not trying to scare the child. "What if it were your daughter?"

Eliza took Mary in her arms. "I would do everything and anything for my girl."

"Then help me, please. At least try to remember where they took him." Someone had to know where her son was, and if not Eliza, then maybe her grandfather. "Where's George?"

"I don't know, perhaps in the field."

Ask for Ata.

"Does George sleep in this basement?"

Ask for Ata.

"When are the rebels coming back, Eliza?"

Mary shook her head. She tugged at her mother's skirt for attention. "Where's the other girl, Mommy, the one with the blue hair?"

"Why do you want to know, dear?" Eliza sat on the mattress. Her face flushed. "I feel lightheaded."

"Tell her where the other girl is, Mommy." Mary shivered as if ice blocks slowly slid down her back. "Tell her, Mommy. He wants to know."

Stay out of the girl's head. Don't bother the Mom.

Ask her about Ata.

No!

Don't make me extract it from her brain, it will hurt.

"Where's George?" Raven wasn't going to yield to the faceless voice in her head—or anyone. "Where's my son?"

Eliza bent over, sick. "Questioning . . . quest . . . Blue was taken for questioning." She gagged on her own vomit and then collapsed on the floor.

See what you forced me to do.

You're an evil man.

Ata can get you out of here. She needs to listen to me.

Why won't she listen to you?

She shut me out.

I don't blame her. You're a devious—

This conversation is over.

Four men stormed through the door. Raven recognized Wafer, but the rest were strangers. One of them, a blond man, fully undressed. The one with pockmarks all over his face kicked Eliza into waking. Mary was by her side. Pockmark glared down at the bile near the bed; he slapped the mother. The short man behind the other three men laughed.

"My sister cleaned this one up," Wafer said to Pockmark. "Are you gonna have her first, Toady?"

Raven shuddered. Pockmark was a hideous creature. She didn't know whether to gag or go ahead and tell him he disgusted her. Neither choice was a viable option, not with the blond, naked man staring at her.

"I don't want any problems." She hesitated as Toady approached her. "I just want my son."

"What son?"

"He's a six-year-old boy—"

The men laughed.

"That kid's traded and gone." Toady's tobacco breath dizzied her; Pockmark chewed the nicotine like a mule munching on hay. "Okay, Bowie, make it quick 'cause Dagan wants a turn."

"Why can't Dag take the other one, the one I was guarding?"

"Orion is being a freak about her. He thinks she's cursed or somethin'."

"Cursed?" Bowie said. "What's that?"

"Orion spends too much time in the sun." Toady turned his back to Raven, relieving her of his acrid breath. "He gets ideas that Sorrows are getting rid of folks like us."

"Is Blue a Sorrow?" Bowie's erection was like a long thick finger pointed at Raven. "What's a Sorrow, anyway?"

"I don't know." Toady said, mining behind his jaw for tobacco residuals, spitting out what he couldn't manually extract. He shrugged, and his shoulder muscles bulged. "Sorrows are fairy tales told to keep us all in line."

"I think . . ." The short man in the back paused and waited for Toady's nod before he continued. "I think a Sorrow is a mind reader."

"What the heck is a mind reader, Dag?" Toady was the only muscular rebel, the only real threat. Raven hoped. "People don't read minds, dummy."

"I think . . ." Dagan paused again, turned to Bowie. The blond man nodded. "Remember how you always say the lab people messed with Joshua when he was born and that's why he's a loony?"

"Joshua's crazy as shit," Toady said.

"As crazy as a starved vulture," Bowie agreed.

"My dad," started Wafer, "says we have to protect land from Sorrows, or they'll crawl down here and murder us all."

"True." Dagan took nervous steps forward. "But what I mean is, our leader is loony 'cause Sorrows got to him. He don't act right."

"When has he ever acted right, Dag?" Bowie laughed and the others joined him. "You're making my boner limp with all this stupid talk. Shut your mouth already, or I'll shut it for you."

Dagan took slow steps back.

"You're right, Bow, enough talk." Toady turned to Raven. A nauseating grin crossed his ugly mug. "Have all your holes ever been stuffed at once?"

Raven tried to fight, but Toady knocked her down with a single numbing blow to the face. Dagan held her while Wafer tied her wrists. The rope was attached to a meat hook on the ceiling. Her feet left the concrete. The men laughed, all of them pleased. Raven was meat. Toady struck her with his open hands until every muscle in her body vibrated and stung. She closed her eyes from time to time to gather her senses. Dagan spun her around, announcing that if Raven were dazed, she would never shove, kick or attack any of them while they fucked her.

Mary cried out. Raven concentrated on the little girl's sobbing, on the low voice begging the child not to draw attention. Bowie, distracted by the girl's cry, instructed Wafer to shut her up.

"Go ahead, Wafer. Get rid of the girl," Toady said. "Dagan, get rid of the mother. Lock them up in one of the upstairs rooms with the other prisoners."

Eliza screamed with so much agony, begged with all the persuasion of a desperate mother. Dagan knocked her out and complained about it. How was he supposed to carry her? Bowie smacked the short man upside the head. He called Dagan a weakling but still helped him drag the woman out of the basement.

Wafer struggled with Mary. The frightened little girl ran circles around him. Raven thrashed too, even if she knew they would beat her for trying. Her attempt to detach the rope from the ceiling hook was futile. Toady, who was no longer distracted by the chase, turned to Raven. He grabbed her. His fingernails dug holes inside her cheeks, craters as deep as the ones on his face.

"What do you think you're doing, Black?" Pockmark struck her. The thud was similar to the beating of a drum, and it hurt like hell.

Drums don't sound like that.

Voice!

Look into his eyes. His tone was so reassuring, smooth and calming. *Look at him.*

Toady took steps back, surprised. Immediately after, he balled his hands into fists, ready for another jab at her face.

Voice?

I'm helping you.

Toady sprang backward unable to control a sudden shaking. He pounded his head against the wall, mumbling incoherently. He shouted at Wafer, ordered the boy to leave the room. Wafer ran out the basement as fast as he could, not bothering to ask if anything was the matter. Mary coiled on the floor, trembling and sobbing.

Are you a Sorrow, Voice?

I am a Sorrow.

Do you really exist?

Yes, Raven. I'm more than just a voice inside your head.

What are you doing to Pockmark?

Does it matter?

BLACK AND BLUE

The mutt on the side of the road was no longer breathing. Nico dismounted Bronte, hoping to save the creature by using artificial respiration. His healing abilities had limits—bringing the dead back to life was one of them.

"Are you really gonna waste time on a dog?" Kurt complained. One quick glance from his son silenced the man immediately.

Nico was barely getting along with his father. Another senseless decision by the man would ensure they parted ways forever. That Kurt knocked him out was maddening enough. True, Nico should have scanned his surroundings, but even if he had, he would have never pinned his own father a traitor. The man carelessly bartered away what Nico had spent his entire life searching for.

Closing the mutt's mouth with one hand, Nico breathed gently into her nostrils. The dog, in shock, respired unevenly due to her low body temperature. He administered several breaths, sending energy through her system, repairing her from the inside out. Her chest expanded, once. He continued until the animal's pale gums colored, and she breathed without assistance. The task took seconds. With Kurt's reluctant support, they cleaned the bullet wounds. Blood soaked through the pads, reminiscent of Atabey's condition when Nico first found her.

"Atabey was here," he told his father.

Kurt gathered the medical kit. He straddled Sable. "I worry that you've become obsessed with this girl, Ata."

"I worry you know that and still gave her away like she was a meager thing." Nico walked to allow Bronte rest. "You knew how much I wanted, no, needed her with me."

"Why are you risking our lives to find them?" Kurt said. "I know I don't always understand you, but you are my son, and those girls are nothing but trouble."

"You're right, Kurt. You don't understand a lot of things. So do me a favor and trust me." Nico kept his eyes on the mutt. Her ears perked up. Wobbling, she stood. "She's a miracle."

"Your mother used to say the same about you." Kurt made no effort to slow his restless mare down. Sable trotted ahead of her own accord. "I'll give you some space."

Windstorms, tornados, and floods had misshapen the once level highways to uneven lines of concrete hunks spread with gravel, overgrown with vegetation, and covered with fallen tree trunks.

They followed the lines where the tarmac still showed. Ignoring the weeds growing through the cracks and the dirt layering the surface, Nico led a steady path to Willowy Farms. He never ate, slept or stopped. He refused to rest until Atabey was safe by his side. The rebels were cruel, and if Raven was the one they wanted, nothing would stop them from 'playing' with their other female. Nico winced at the thought of those dirty beasts torturing *his* Atabey.

"We need to eat," Kurt said after a day of silence. "We've traveled non-stop. Aren't you the one who always complains when the horses need rest?"

Bronte and Sable were tired, mostly Sable, and the mutt had developed an incurable limp. It was unfair to take his frustrations out on the animals. "I'll find a place to camp for the night."

Kurt monitored the grazing horses through the forest, while Nico hunted dinner. He returned with two small rabbits. Nico could have gone deeper into the woods. He could have searched longer and brought down a deer. But his worry for Atabey increased and so did his patience with large prey. The chocolate mutt accompanied him on the hunt, and no limp stopped her from chasing squirrels. He smiled. Nico became fond of the animal. And somewhere out there, he knew Atabey had too.

"Welcome back, Son. We have company." Kurt sat by a fire, and a twosome crouched beside him. "These two escaped a rebel group just this night. They were wondering if we—"

"You've come from Willowy Farms," Nico said. "Are you Raven's family?"

The bulky man glanced at the girl, expecting her to answer. The odd gesture confirmed her association with a rebel leader, a high ranking officer. The girl grinned at the man on her side. Her gaze then found Nico. "Oppressed for years—"

"Start over, rebel. This time tell the truth." Nico glanced at his father. "Get the baling wire and some wood stakes. I'm hungry." His father stared at him, concerned. "I can take care of myself, Dad. Let's cook these rabbits."

Kurt grunted curse words as he disappeared into the forest.

The bulky man rose to his feet, and his size alone could have intimidated many men, but Nico was not an ordinary man. The girl mirrored her guardian and also stood. The female's heart beat sporadically, and the male's adrenaline levels spiked. She told her companion to settle down. They needed the horses. "Play along," she whispered. "Let's tell him whatever he wants to know."

"My name is Ida and this here," she pointed at the man, "is Gad Sickle. We do come from Willowy Farms, and Gad really was a prisoner. Our brothers are still at the house." Her gesticulating hands wafted a familiar smell. Raven. "My rebel leader is messed up in the head. He can't protect me anymore, not until he changes back. In the meantime, I can't allow Toady or any of the other rebels to have their way with me. I was returning to my father." Ida sat down. She pulled on Gad's arm. He settled beside her. "You see, Nico. It is Nico, right? Gad helped me escape tonight. He's going to help me get home."

Nico dropped one of the sagging rabbits and gave the mutt a warning look not to touch it. "I'm searching for two females: Atabey and Raven. Raven was heading to Willowy Farms. Do you know if the girls are there now?"

Ida and Gad looked at one another. Ida asked, "Are you talking about Black and Blue?"

"Possibly, if you mean hair colors." Nico lifted the skin off the dead rabbit's back. He pinched it with his finger, dug a hole, and ripped the skin apart. He grabbed the knife from his back pocket and cut off the head and feet. Nico hunkered down, split the rabbit along the ribs and shook out the guts, tossing it for the mutt to eat. "I need the girls back, both of them."

"Good luck with that," Gad said. "If whatever they do to them is anything like what they did to my father's wife, you won't recognize the pair." And then as an afterthought, "Black was nice-looking."

"What about Atabey?" he dared to ask. "What are they doing to her?"

Kurt returned with baling wire and wood stakes. He drove the stakes into the ground on each side of the fire. "I brought salt and pepper too, Nico." The fire leaped and crackled. "We're going to have a feast tonight." He knelt and served broken pieces of wood to the flames before glancing up at his son. "What's going on?"

"I need you to pack it up. Go as far away from here as you can, Dad." The full moon and the open flames would likely summon unneeded attention.

"What are you talking about?" Kurt glanced at the ready-to-cook rabbit. "We're hungry, remember?"

Nico dropped the carcass and turned to Ida. "What are they doing to Atabey?"

"Blue," Ida said. "The rebels believe she's a Sorrow and if she is, our leader will . . . will gut her alive. That's assuming Orion doesn't get to it first." She paused, pondered for longer than Nico wanted to wait. "Are you a Sorrow, too?"

"No." He clutched Ida's arm and forced her to her feet. "You're going to take me to them."

Before Gad could think to defend the girl, Kurt butted him with his rifle. Gad passed out, cold. "I didn't hit him hard, I don't think." Kurt removed the hot baling wire from the fire and used it as a rope to secure Gad to the nearest tree. When he finished the task, he packed their belongings. He mounted Sable and glanced at Nico. "This is me trusting you, Son."

The house sat up on a hill surrounded by a field of gardens. Ida pointed at the brick home from afar once they left the woods and entered a clearing. The vegetation flourished as if someone had devoted all their time into cultivating crops: slave laborers. Rebels invaded fertile property, enslaved previous owners, and obligated the prisoners to nurture their own gardens. And if the plants faltered, the tomatoes didn't grow, or the squash felt mushy, death became the ultimate punishment. The ruthless oppressors worked the farmers into the ground, and good deeds were always unrewarded.

In the old days of country divide, the rebels offered the survivors of a crushed species a safe haven in the southern states, the states not mechanically corrupted by tongue-tied Sorrows. Yes, Sorrows were physically and mentally more apt than the rebels and farmers. The Sorrow immune system was stronger, and they seldom contracted viruses or diseases. But what the common folks retained that Sorrows simply lacked was free will. Sorrows existed to follow their one idol, an idol most of them would never meet.

The rebel's greeted Ida with sneers of animosity. They crowded around her outside the house, demanding information. Ida, glazed and resigned, stared into the eyes of the biggest rebel, one complaining of a mild headache; his hands came up to his head as many times as he blinked. He accused Ida of betraying her kind. Ida never bothered to reveal Nico's position. Her clandestine silence confused Nico and infuriated the big man. Wafer defended the girl. He informed the other rebels that perhaps a Sorrow had mind-controlled his sister, a possibility Nico also suspected.

"Forget about Ida. Let's find Black," Orion told the men. "Blue's no longer a problem." Orion, the only one who actively monitored his surroundings, perused toward the cluster of trees concealing Nico. And Nico wanted nothing more than to cut the man's throat. He was sorely disappointed when the rebel backed away, fearful of the coyotes yelping in the distance.

Nico stayed hidden as he approached the house, creeping on hands and knees. He concentrated on his sharp sense of smell. The inside of the house approximated the confines of an oven, dark, narrow and roasting with heat. The stench of blood and sweat hung like a heavy fog in the air. Many odors assaulted his nostrils, but Atabey's pleasant aroma reigned above the rest. Her fragrance came from the first door to the right. It was closed but not locked. A liquid dripped steadily, striking the cement floor. One drip, two drips. Three.

He burst through the door the moment Atabey drew her last breath. Her waning heat traveled across to him, her convulsive struggle for survival ended. Nico's heart smashed into his lungs as panic replaced his vision with white light. Ata hung like dead meat, a noose bound tightly around her neck. Her head resembled a bloated balloon waiting to be popped. Her disarranged clothes exposed the multiple scratches on her ripped skin. Blood escaped her slit wrists.

Nico forced himself to act as if Atabey was anyone else. He brought up her legs, cut down the rope, and laid her on the floor. He used his shirt as a tourniquet. With the ripped pieces of cloth, Nico staunched her bleeding wrists. He picked her up, cradled her in his arms, and rushed out the room.

He wanted to shout out his anger. A need to kill each and every rebel responsible for her hanging consumed him. He chose to keep his rage internal, taking into account Atabey's immediate health. He removed her from the house as fast and as far as he could before attempting to save her.

The woodland grass was stiff and dead. Nico laid Ata down. He inspected her marked neck. The rope had burned a deep groove on her skin similar to that of a cattle brand. Her face was bruised, the flesh almost black.

"I'm so sorry, Atabey." He held her in his arms, livid with himself for not finding her sooner, for allowing her to suffer. "Please, come back to me." The soft hissing, a tingling sensation, the erect hairs on his arms caused his inward energy to desire a merge with the strike of lightning. He shivered. "I just found you. You can't die." Dark clouds loomed above his head, the wind gradually picked up. *Calm down.* The first tumultuous thunder echoed in his ears. *Calm down.* Rain was forming.

One whiff of the air distracted him. Nico turned fast, ready to pounce on the daring coyotes. The pair observed from several feet away, their ears pointed, their fur stiff. The tails hung low, motionless. Each dog weighed about fifty pounds. Coyotes seldom confronted other predators, but these two feared nothing. Their intelligent eyes centered on Atabey.

A bolt of lightning ignited the sky, and Ata gripped Nico's arm, the sensation moved through his entire body, sharpening his brain cells, a breath of consciousness, and a blunt heartbeat. "They won't hurt me," she whispered to him, removing her hand from his shoulder. "They think you will."

Her skin's ugly discoloration started to fade, turning a sapphire blue, then a bilious green. She was healing. It amazed him how quickly the process continued. He placed her head on his lap. "Ata, I would have found you sooner if—"

"Raven, we need to find her." The words spewed from her lips with waning effort. "We need to find Raven."

"*We* are not doing anything right now." He smiled, despite himself. She could self-heal! "You've lost a lot of blood."

Her heart labored and pushed at her chest as if yearning release. "It's my fault . . . my fault they caught us."

"Atabey, I need you to concentrate on your inner wounds not the outer ones." He caressed her cheek and allowed his energy to leave his body in soft repairing currents, assisting her struggling organs. "I will send my father in search of Raven as soon as he gets here."

Her large amber eyes stared up at him. "Where's your father?"

Nico grasped Atabey's hand and pressed it on the rich soil. He wanted her to hear, as he did, the swarm of insects headed their way. The wind billowed through the leaves. The scream of a distant mountain lion pierced the air, squirrels soared from limb to branch, and native birds landed on the nearest trees.

The ground trembled with the beating of hooves. The horses galloped hurriedly. Bronte and Sable had sensed the danger, and willingly headed toward it. The mutt limped with the same desperate rush. Animals were coming from all directions to aid Atabey. Her near death had triggered something new in nature.

"Nico," she said, less fatigued. "Raven trusts you, but she'll never go anywhere with your father."

"I won't leave you alone." Nico tried to ease Atabey's disastrous attempt at sitting. "You're groaning, Ata. Stay down."

"No." She scooted away from his touch. "What happened? Why am I here?"

"Atabey." He reached for her. He needed to touch her. He needed to fuse, soon. "I'm growing weaker by the day. Being away from you, without fusing first, hurts, it literally hurts. It has always hurt." Her questioning gaze exhausted him. "I don't want to have to explain. I want you to feel it and know it, the way I feel it, the way I know it. The way nature intended."

"Please, help Raven. It's my fault we got caught." She glanced at the coyotes, they approached her shyly. "See, the dogs will watch over me."

Nico sighed. He would oblige her.

"I know you . . . feel like you maybe need something from me." She paused, gazed at him. Her honey eyes glowed in the dark.

"I don't need *something* from you, Atabey. I need you." He stood, and directed a warning glance at the coyotes. "If she's injured while I'm gone, I'll have you both for breakfast." One dog watched him from its rested post next to Atabey, and the other one, determined to lick Ata's every wound, ignored Nico completely. "Well, don't say I didn't warn you."

"You smell like Maple, Nico." Atabey said, petting the coyote near her lap. "I don't know why you would smell like her."

He smiled at Ata's look of confusion, at her animal-like attempts to sniff him. "So, the limping mutt has a name. I healed her. She's a good squirrel huntress."

Atabey's eyes gleamed with gratitude.

Nico started back toward Willowy Farms as the first drop of rain landed on his forehead.

"Wait." She tried to stand, but the growling coyotes wouldn't allow it. "Nico, wait!"

He was scanning the area, seeking Raven. "What is it?"

"Please don't . . . please . . . please don't get yourself killed." Her voice cracked, and the coyotes yelped. The pair recognized her distress. "I don't want you to die because of me."

He knelt beside her and cupped both her cheeks, trapping her tears. "Don't ever worry about me. Worry about them, all of them, your entire species."

PAIN KILLERS

Raven crushed foliage and snapped twigs. She ran as fast as she could, dodging branches. She avoided stumbling over rocks. Nocturnal predators also posed a threat: snakes, coyotes—who knew what was out there. The full moon provided light, but no place to hide. Guilt set in after an incessant mile.

I shouldn't have left Mary behind.

That doesn't matter right now, the voice insisted.

She's my cousin, and she showed me the way out of that house.

Not worth the risk, and she barely helped.

Mary just wanted to find her mother.

And you want to find your son.

I could have freed them. Raven had left her own grandfather behind.

They're not your problem.

But George has information.

Stop.

She halted to catch her breath, heaving loudly. There was no visible end to the forest.

Turn back.

They'll kill me.

It's pointless for you to pretend to care. If you had wanted to help your relatives, you would have.

What about Ata?

Ata's no longer your problem. He paused. *She attracts special.*

What does that even mean?

You have to continue forward, Raven.

She listened for sounds, noises not resonating inside her head. When she heard nothing except the howl of the wind, the murmuring of leaves, and the subtle movements of insects, she continued forward. Raven paid close attention to the sudden climate change, the turbulent winds. A lightning bolt pierced the darkness, startling her.

"Hey, Black!" someone shouted. "I know you. Help me, please." She turned to a barrel-chested man tied to a tree trunk. Farm wire was wrapped several times around his torso. "I was a rebel prisoner, too."

"How do I know that?" she asked, ready to continue onward. "If I stop for you, I might get caught."

"No, wait, please." He wiggled and groaned in defeat. No way to disentangle on his own. "You can't leave me here. I hear coyotes or wolves. Do wolves still exist?"

"I haven't seen one in years." Raven bypassed the man with no trouble—he wasn't her problem. "Find a way out yourself." Her heavy feet snapped a sharp twig in half. She was barefoot, her legs mutilated, the skin tender from the run. *Mind over matter, she who thinks health gains health.* But it was too late. Every muscle began to throb and burn.

"Black, we'll help each other," the man said. "I know the land. I'm from here. Please, help me."

"Did you escape the rebels?" She returned to the tree, scrutinizing the big man. "Why didn't you help Eliza and Mary escape?"

He wore raggedy garments unlike the rebel's usual camo gear. "Survival of the fittest, ain't that the way?" He glanced at a frog that leaped to the nearest bush for cover. "I'm a coward," he confessed.

"I'm not one to judge. What's your name?"

"Gad Sickles."

"What's your relationship to the Carriers?"

"My father married Eliza." Gad was not bound by blood. That he escaped without aiding any of them was sensible. "My father's dead now."

"Don't move," she said to him. Raven searched for the knot binding him to the tree. "I'm gonna try to make this quick, but if I hear rebels, I'm leaving you behind."

Leave him behind now.

"That's okay. Thank you, Black."

Leave him.

"It's Raven, actually."

Listen to me.

"Thank you, Raven. I owe you one."

"Yes, you do." She found the bundled wire stuck inside a crevice in the tree bark. "Who did this to you?"

"I was knocked out before I could see." Gad tried to shake loose. "Are you almost done?"

He doesn't want to help you. The voice's irritation intensified his pitch. It hurt her ears.

I know he doesn't, she told the loud static. *Shut it.*

You don't have time for this, Raven. Is this guilt for not returning for your own family?

There's time, and it won't hurt me to untie him. She would run if anything went wrong.

You're shielding your own pain. He'll run faster and hurt you.

Life's hard.

Fine. You deal with your own stupidity. He abandoned her again, leaving a gut-wrenching emptiness inside her.

"Got it." Raven pulled on the wire, spun it around twice. She let Gad do the rest of the unwrapping. "I have to go now."

Gad snatched her by the throat. "Where do you think you're going? I need you for insurance's sake." His hands squeezed her.

Raven thrashed against his grip, against the wire he used to choke her. *Why is he doing this? Never trust a rebel, a prisoner, never trust anyone.* The brute pounded her with his fists as if wanting to break her body in half. He took hold of an object he found near the tree, a boning knife. It tore into her skin. Warm fluid dribbled down her stomach.

Gad dragged her torn body along the needle-like foliage. "You're my ticket out of rebel territory, Black. I can't just let you go."

Thunder disrupted the clouds and lightning scarred the sky. In the air, the storm clouds blended, whirling in darkness. Strains of light illuminated the whole of the forest. No one was hiding in the shadows, waiting for a chance to save her. She would have to save herself.

Raven scrambled to her feet, her hand reaching for Gad's knife. He moved seconds before she could snatch the weapon. They both toppled on the muddy soil, scraping and tearing at each other. He plunged the knife deep into her rib cage, raking and skinning her like meat. An artesian well of blood gushed out of her. Her skin was ripped, clawed, diced.

Her uncanny gift of suppressing pain proved useful when she yanked the knife from her own body and drove it into Gad's chest. She pushed the weapon as deep as she could without having it completely disappear inside him. Gad's bellow was atrocious. His weight crushed her bones.

The man wrestled his way off her, fighting to breathe, falling lopsided. Raven crawled on top of him and wrenched the knife from his chest. She was amazed at how solid the human body could be, how hard it was to remove an object deeply inserted.

Before pity hazed her judgment, Raven stabbed him many times over. Dark blood covered his shirt, her body, their world. Gad's final moments were gruesome.

With her last dregs of strength, Raven staggered toward a clearing. Her legs buckled. She fell hard on the grass. Face up. She looked up at the sky, at the flashes of lightning, at the clouds spiraling wildly above her. Her vision fogged. She was so cold.

Someone approached, crushing grass with every step. "Don't you worry, Raven."

The voice echoed, but not from inside her head, maybe from the wind, nature. Her body levitated off the ground.

"Are you conscious? Do you hear me?"

Why can't I open my eyes?

"I'm going to try to heal you, but I'll have to send you to sleep, otherwise you'll die before I can finish. Do you understand?"

"Others," she said, or at least she hoped she did.

"What others, others at the house?"

Don't mind the others. The voice pushed his way back inside her head.

Tell . . . him . . . about the others, my family.

His silence lingered for a second too long as if it pained him to care. *There's a mother and daughter that need rescuing, but save Raven first.*

"Don't speak through her, Sorrow."

Heal, healer.

"How much pain is she in?"

She's numbing it. Her efforts won't last long.

"I'm going to put her to sleep."

The pain will keep mounting until she's dead.

"She has gaping wounds everywhere. And the Scarlett Fever, how long has she had it? Did she have strep throat, too?"

You're the doctor.

"I'm worn out. I used excessive energy on Atabey, and I'm still using it now to keep her connected. I can't inspect Raven right now, not without disconnecting from Ata. I need you to tell me how bad it is."

Don't you see?

"Inside, how bad is it inside?"

Bad, she's dying.

"Get out of her head. If I can reach the chemicals in her own brain, maybe I can release her body's natural pain killers."

Like endorphins?

"Get out of her head."

Hollow emptiness followed his departure: *Don't leave me, Voice.*

The rush of an unknown substance thrilled her. Anxiety melted away and so did her hold on the pain. *What was her motto? Mind over what?* She swam in a pool of feel good, sensitive silk caressed her body. An explosive wave of pleasure secreted somewhere deep inside her loins. Intense. The beatings of a body relieved of stress and pain were pleasant ones. Did the sensation have a name? Her body vibrated and trembled with desire.

Her eyes snapped open.

"Hi, Raven." His face was creased with worry, but his eyes smiled at her. "Do you feel any better?"

She needed him inside her, needed to kiss his lips. "Nico," she whispered. "You're so handsome."

"You're on natural pain killers. I'll put you to sleep and then come back for you. Is that okay?" Nico's warm embrace was comforting. "I'm going to set you down, Raven."

Her vision blurred as her body touched the cold, hard ground.

I don't want to go to sleep. Wait, Nico, don't put me to sleep.

Roaring thunder filled the sky.

Raven, you need to wake up. They're coming for you!

She woke to the sound of galloping horses and nearby coyotes yipping and yelping. Gun shots and screams almost muffled the noises of wagon wheels struggling through mud.

Go north. Don't stop running until you faint.

She tried standing. But not because the voice demanded she do so.

I'm trying to help.

She snorted at the claim. *Where were you when Gad was trying to kill me?*

You weren't listening to me.

You allowed him to stab me to teach me a lesson?

No. His murmur was tiny, insignificant.

Get out of my head.

He lingered, silent.

Once up, Raven ran west, anywhere but north.

I couldn't enter his head through you because you were too weak.

You could have warned me.

I did warn you. I need you to run north to safety. You'll get adequate help north.

Like the help you provide?

Don't look at the body, he said.

Two coyotes snapped at each other, savagely fighting for more room to bite, shake and munched on Gad's entrails, which were wrapped around his corpse. The man's stomach, torn and bloodied, served as a bowl for the spongy dinner. Raven bent over to puke, not just at the sight of Gad's intestines, but at her pitiful display of lust over Nico. She had desired the healer with a passion so unlike herself.

How pathetic.

That was the chemical release, Raven.

Get out of my head.

Do you really want me to leave you for good?

Y-es. The stutter surprised her. *I won't rely on anybody anymore.*

His rapid absence nearly jerked her to the ground. Raven held on for dear life, and she would keep holding on until her son was safely in her arms.

PART TWO

ENERGY

The coyotes chased the doe far away from her fawn. She grunted, searching for her baby, but stopped after coming across Nico. Her snort and stomping of hooves never came, and neither did she secrete the scent cues to warn other deer of danger. He was surprised. The doe raised her tail aware of an eminent attack but did nothing to prevent it. Nico seized the opportunity and slashed her throat.

He dragged the carcass to a clearing in the forest, convinced the meat would last them for several days, a pleasant surprise for Kurt whenever he returned to camp. His father disappeared for two days after having cursed Ata. Her need to sabotage everyone's attempts at hunting big game got the better of the old man.

"Father probably won't come back," Nico told the coyotes, who anxiously waited for their share of the kill. "You two are getting plenty. Relax."

He inserted the knife between the anal vent and the hip bone and quickly pulled the hide apart.

Oak and Ash licked their mouths.

He carved the cartilage between the ribs and the breast bone and pulled out the bowels. Nico took out the heart for one coyote to eat and tossed the other the liver.

Ash devoured his share, but Oak observed Nico warily.

"She's bathing, Oak. She's not in any danger." Nico could track Ata fast enough if he wanted, and the lake was only a few yards away. "But for your peace of mind, I'll scan the forest again."

A weeping, motherless fawn fell silent in the distance, and the bucks throughout the region scattered. The breeze wafted scents of wildflowers, fresh dirt, fish in the lake, and pine. Nothing alarming.

"She's alright," he told the coyote. "Now, if only we could find the missing Carrier."

George, Eliza, and Mary had settled in a new home in Glasgow Suburbia. Nico escorted the family to safety after having sneaked into Willowy Farms and rescued them from the rebels, who were too busy looking for Raven to think to leave a guard behind. Nico laughed. The rebel's incompetence—or lack of leadership—had worked to his advantage. Raven, however, was still missing. His search through Spencer County turned up nothing, not a trace. He would have given up if Atabey hadn't insisted they explore further out.

He cut the carcass in half with a hacksaw. Nico planned to use the hams for pot roasts, the rump for steaks, and the loin for stew and soup.

The sun had set below the horizon by the time he finished cooking. Intense oranges, pinks and crimson splattered throughout the sky.

Oak and Ash growled. Their agitation communicated the same message: Atabey was on the move. Nico took a deep breath in order to restrain his fury. He chased after her scent. Was she escaping him again? Some of Ata's garments hung on a tree by the lake, giving him the false illusion that she had remained in one place.

He found her half a mile away seated on a bed of grass, cuddling a spotted fawn. "Atabey," he said, adjusting his breathing, masking his anger. "Why did you leave the lake? Where's Maple?" Ata stared up at Nico with her amber eyes that further winded him. He wanted to touch her gleaming wet skin without needing to fuse, without having to transfer energy. "I'm trying to protect you, you know," he said. "If you constantly run off—"

"Is your supper ready?" She beamed a knowing smile and rose to her feet with the fawn in her arms. Maple emerged from behind a tree bush, limping. She stayed close to her mistress. "Tell me you were gentle to Pine's mother."

Nico liked her habit of naming animals, her caring nature toward them, yet he didn't regret slaughtering the doe. "Do the animals talk to you?"

"No," she said. "I sense them like I sense you."

"Why did you let the doe come to me?" He was pleased that she could sense him. "I thought you didn't want me to kill animals."

"You were hungry." She tilted her head slightly to the side. "And so were the coyotes. I promised the doe I would care for her fawn if she surrendered her life. She was already wounded."

"I could have healed her."

"You would have, but I don't want you to starve."

He approached Ata and resisted the urge to touch her. "That's very considerate of you. Pine will make a great addition to our pack." He laughed at the thought of horses, coyotes, a mutt, and a fawn all getting along. "How do you communicate with animals?"

"How do you heal?" Her proximity, her sweet perfume consumed his senses; her pheromones invited him to fuse with her.

Nico took several steps back. "I go into the body as light energy and repair tissues and organs. Most of the time, I simply provide depleted chemicals."

"I don't know how I hear animals. I just do." It shamed her not to understand what she was or why she existed. "How do you always know what I think and feel?"

"I've touched you often enough," he said. "Can I show you?"

Atabey laid Pine on the grass and glanced up at Nico. "You think I wore a white dress on purpose," she said. "You think the texture is too thin, and you can see the outline of my shape. You're always aroused, and you think I make it worse when I touch you. You're torturing yourself with the effort not to touch me. You hold back but in times like these, when I look beautiful to you, you think you're going to explode." She inhaled, exhaled proudly. "Am I right?"

"Sorrows can't read my mind, Atabey," he told her simply. "You're not one of them."

"What am I then?"

"I can only help you feel it and know it the way you feel and know animals." He took her hands. "Fusing is the only way to pass on enough energy. It enables you to see my world, what my limited human brain absorbed when I was born."

"What is fusing?" Her curious gaze bore into him with growing anxiety. Deep down, she knew what he needed. "Is fusion your fancy word for sex?"

He laughed and at the same time released light through his fingertips, invisible energy her body was built to absorb. "In human terms, sex is the word for it, but we're not really human, Ata."

"If it isn't sex, then what is it?" She shivered and moaned as his electricity tickled her nerves. "You smell like death." Atabey took her hand back and knelt to reach for the fawn. "Are you going to make me eat Pine's mother?"

"Of course not." He started for the lake. "I'll wash up. Stay close to me."

Nico undressed and waded to the middle of the lake. Had Atabey ever seen the male anatomy? *No.* Her answer came through thought. Ata entered his mind as often as he lingered in hers—a new development. There was still a lot he wanted to share with her. His body always begged and pleaded him to feel her. Touch alone would never suffice; the kind of energy needed to make them one entity would melt off her skin. Fusion called for sexual intercourse. The energy emitted from his groin would flow directly to her core. Her innards were better equipped to receive the voltage. Skin only soaked up small dosages.

He swam to shore and was greeted by an inquisitive Ata. "I forgot to bring spare clothes," he told her.

Her eyes slowly moved over his arms, chest, waist and hips. "Can I touch you?" she asked him.

"I don't know if that's such a good idea, just yet."

Her stare centered on his erection. "Don't you want to touch me?"

"I do, but . . ." Nico sighed. He found it pointless to lie. "I do."

"Can I touch you first and see what happens? See if I like it?"

"You could, but if—"

"Do you promise not to touch me if I touch you?"

He would restrain his primal mating needs for her sake. "I'll try."

Atabey placed Pine on the grass near an oddly maternal Maple; the mutt licked the fawn as if it were her own pup. "Can I go ahead?"

Nico nodded.

She reached for his shoulders, her breasts sweeping over his upper body. "Every time I touch you, I feel like I want to burst into a million pieces. Why is that?" Ata brushed her cheeks against his chest, kissing him once, trembling, and then trying it again. Sparks of energy flowed through her, and every caress sharpened her senses. Her hearing intensified. She paused and looked into his eyes. "Your heart's beating fast."

"I know," he said. "You . . . you should stop. I might hurt you."

She laid a palm on his chest. "It's stone-like. You're strong, aren't you?"

Nico's muscles strained with throbbing agony, battling the impulse to make them one. "Ata." She was too close. Her body heat seeped through his skin and energized his cells. "This was a bad idea."

"Your skin makes my tongue tingle." Her mouth came up to his neck. "I could lick you all day." She smiled, delirious with desire.

"I'll hurt—"

R.M. James

She draped her arms around the hollow of his back.

"Stop, Atabey."

Her exploring fingers ignited pleasure and pain, and she knew his body was churning inside. "What are you?"

He shuddered at her sexual thoughts.

"Are you reading them?" she asked.

Nico's primitive instincts begged him to bury himself deep inside her, deep where she could absorb all of his energy, deep where she could burst into millions, no, billions of tiny pieces of light, scattered all around the earth, initiating the rise and fall of a new dusk, a new dawn. He saw a bright light, a color no human had ever seen. "You can't do this to me, not right now." Nico imagined her soft mouth closing snugly over his erection. The images were hers. Her mind sought to squeeze and extract, flooding him with pleasure. "No!" It was too much too quickly.

Her expression was wild. Her need beat at him. "I'm tingly." Atabey circled his neck, pressing her body against his. "Can I ask you a question?" Her eyes held him captive.

"Ask." Nico tried to rein in his self-control. "What do you want to know?" The strings of energy flowing through his bloodstream threatened to tear him apart. The energy grew inside his core, demanding he fuse. His inner being bounced all over the place, trying urgently to stay as one. And it was necessary for him to take a moment and scan their immediate surroundings.

Get off me!

She stumbled backwards. "Pine, Pine doesn't want to see her mother's remains." His reproach upset her.

Nico took another deep breath, a deep gulp of air. He released it as slow as he could after gathering control. "I wasn't trying to hurt your feelings. I'm not used to having someone read my thoughts."

"My feelings are not hurt." Ata picked up the helpless fawn. "I thought you wanted me, is all."

100

"I do," he said, his body pleading for her to reach out and touch him again. "But you don't understand how dangerous a first fusion is. I have to be in complete control of my actions."

"Maybe you should cover up more." She measured him from head to toe, her eyes feral with lust. "You didn't have to bathe in front of me. That wasn't fair."

"Was I a temptation?"

"You shouldn't push people away, Nico." Her irises glowed and her pupils dilated, adjusting to the fading light.

"It's amazing what your eyes—"

You changed your mind about me. I knew you would.

Nico inhaled her thoughts, but exhaled his words. "I don't think you're beautiful only when I want to fuse. You're beautiful all the time, Atabey. I'm sorry. I should be more receptive of your feelings."

"What color did you see?" she said. "Can you compare it to another color?"

"Actually, visible light is—" A familiar whiff of blood smacked him in the face. "Dad." Nico grabbed his clothes, Ata by the arm, and raced as fast as he could through the woods in search of his father.

SORROWS

Raven turned the last page of the yellow book, which fanned the pungent smell of tobacco smoke and musty decay. *The First Sorrow* by Z.M. Sorrow had brown spots and a cracked binding. She originally picked up the dull read thinking it informative on the science and history of a Sorrow. The novel was really about a woman learning to love and live with a disturbed man. Chapters where the narrator delved into the mind of the lover, a man not always present in regular space and time confounded Raven. The book was the heroine's desperate plea for sanity from a relationship with a schizoid. She died in the end, the heroine, of either a broken heart or a disease. It was all vague.

"What a huge waste of time." Raven set the book aside. She rose from the bed to stretch her legs. "Saul!" Four wooden walls bound her to the windowless room. "Let me get some fresh air, for real this time."

She wasn't a prisoner, not with the layers of quilts on the bed, the dresser stuffed with clean clothes, scented candles, and an ever changing supply of books. She even had her own toilet bowl. Raven was a kept pet, restricted to the log cabin for having tried to escape. Saul had taken her to the outhouse the day she bolted in the direction of the dense trees, which concealed the reality that the cabin was sitting on top of a precipice. Raven had nearly fallen off the unseen cliff when her captor pulled her to safety.

"Sit down," he said, from the other side of the door. "I'm coming in." Saul Leon always barked his orders. He entered the room with an air of indifference. "Sit, girl."

"It's Raven."

"I know who you are, Carrier." He left, only to return with a wicker chair. He sat, leaned forward, and motioned for her to do the same. "I'm going to ask you one more time."

"And I'm not going to tell you again." She settled on the canopy bed, at her own slow pace. "I don't know where Ata is."

"I know you don't."

"How long have I been here?"

"About a week or so," he said. "You've been up for a few days."

"Are you ever going to release me?"

"You're not a prisoner."

"Is that what you told Ata?"

Saul stood, sighing heavily. "Ata is all I have left in this world, and you're going to help me find her."

"Ata's probably with Nico. She'll be alright." The only healer worth having, Nico had once said. "He wouldn't let anything happen to her."

"You've told me about him, and yet your thick head doesn't get it." There was something cryptic about Saul's dark eyes. "You really don't get it, do you?" His skin gleamed, too clean for the average woodsman.

"What don't I understand, Saul Leon?" She doubted that was his real name. "Why is everyone so obsessed with Ata?"

"Tell me, Raven. What was your first thought of Atabey?" His hair was close-cut, definitely not a woodsman.

"Ata's weird, delusional." The girl reminded Raven of cats, animals. "She carried oranges. Her hair was blue."

"Yes, blue, natural pigments. I don't have the equipment needed to test the follicles, but it's interesting that her body hair is dark."

"I always assumed the blue was dyed?"

"You should have seen her as a toddler." Saul lowered his head as if concentrating on the memory of baby Ata. "Her eyes, hair, and skin tone, none of it made sense."

"I agree there."

He looked up at Raven. "Were you attracted to Ata?"

"What?"

"Answer me."

"No. Well, I just wanted her to join me. She begged or something. Her eyes are so huge and hypnotizing. I figured it wouldn't hurt to have her by my side. She had water. Food. I don't know. She was good rebel bait."

"Ata attracts Sorrows and repels everyone else," Saul said. "Natural human instincts, a self-defense mechanism, will unconsciously warn the brain to get away or destroy her. She's a threat to their existence. Most humans are not smart enough to recognize why they feel instinctively repelled by her. Are you following me so far?"

"I guess." Raven couldn't imagine what Ata's history had to do with her own life. "I'm trying to find my son and every moment—"

"Sorrows, on the other hand, intuitively know she's different and are attracted to her chemicals, her essence. Scientifically speaking, Atabey is an anomaly."

"What are you talking about?" Did she want to know? "What is a Sorrow?"

"Human origins," he said. "Do you know anything about it?"

"Ape to man, scientifically speaking, but if you want to go the mythology route, with which myth do you want me to start?"

Saul's frown lines deepened. "Don't think you know anything about my existence simply because you read a few books."

"'My existence'? I guess you're also a Sorrow."

"And so are you," he chuckled. "You're gaping. I'm guessing Cormac failed to tell you."

"You're too young to have known Ata as a toddler, and you don't know my father."

"How old do you think I am?"

"Thirty, at most."

"Try fifty."

"You're not fifty."

"Ata's embryo is older than that, way older."

"Ata looks—"

"Twenty, at the most." He left the room, returned for the chair, left, and then returned again. "Groom up. We're going to find Atabey."

The wrap-around deck was a nice place to inhale fresh enveloping air. The cabin appeared cozy from the outside, nestled on the ridge of a mountain; a great angle to spot intruders, probably how had Saul found her in the first place. When he least expected, Raven would run in whatever direction took her away from the deep forest. Her days of weak muscles and hunger were behind her. She could run far.

Saul headed toward a black horse. Sable. She recognized the fat mare's saddle bags: Kurt's mare. "Where did you get that horse?"

"It came to me." He walked alongside the mare, never bothering to mount her. "Ata communicates with animals. I'm sure this horse will take us to her."

"Are we following the mare?"

"Yes, we are." He squinted at Raven. "Do you have a problem with that?"

If Ata's eyes resembled sheer brightness, Saul's exemplified woeful darkness. "Why would Kurt suddenly leave his horse behind?" she asked.

"Kurt Lowell is, or was, a bounty hunter." He led her through the slope of a marked trail. "I found a bounty document on his saddle bag, a bounty for your capture. It's an old one, but that's how I figured out who you were."

"Why would anyone want me?"

"The government wants to test you. Don't ask me why." Saul stepped over every dead leaf in his path, warning nearby creatures of his approach. *Crunch, crunch.* "Atabey is not safe if she's traveling with a bounty hunter. We have to find her."

"Why? She obviously escaped you for a reason."

With an impatient sigh, he said, "Has Ata ever mentioned Alexander to you?"

"No, but she went on and on about—"

"Let me tell you a story." Saul steadied the waddling horse. Sable was extra sluggish. "Do you know what evolution means?"

"I'm not an idiot." She disliked that he treated her like a moron—all the time. "Evolution's the change from simple to complex."

"Correct," he said. They continued down the mountain, down, down, as if heading to an underworld. "Human evolution has had many stages. Sorrows are the last, except we didn't occur naturally."

"What does that mean?"

"I left the Birth Project, taking Ata with me, because rebel territory is the only safe place for a Sorrow trying to hide from other Sorrows."

"What's the Birth Project?"

"That's not the point, Raven." He steadied Sable as they reached a stone bridge almost too narrow for the fat horse. "The rocks are slippery. Be careful crossing."

She was always careful. "I'm a Sorrow?"

"If you heal at an abnormal rate, which you do, I've monitored your recovery, and if you have superior understanding, can astral or mentally project, you're a Sorrow. There's the ability to perceive past events, telepathy, which is the ability to transfer thoughts and emotions to someone else. There's also energy healing—"

"Nico can do that."

"He's a Sorrow. This is bad news."

"How is that bad? He saved my life several times."

"Sorrows can mentally communicate with other Sorrows. If you open your mind to others, the wrong Sorrow will trick and manipulate you. They'll make you believe you're something you're not. They'll pretend to be your friends. They'll make you think you're 'special' or that you have purpose. A strong Sorrow with unlimited, uncensored access to your brain, the organ that makes up who you are, can control your destiny."

"It's hardly believable that a human, advanced or not, could control who you are," she said. "If what you're saying is true, then how do you know you're not being manipulated right now?"

"I know how to shut my mind from intrusions and so does Atabey, but anyone else in our company is a serious liability."

They neared a clearing in the forest where the laundering light invited her to bathe in its sunshine. Raven was thirsty. "Why is it so important to keep Ata safe?"

"The same reason it's imperative to keep her alive. Ata is more advanced than regular Sorrows. How much do you know about physics, chemistry, or even biology?"

"Can we rest?" She sat on a boulder covered in moss. "I only know basic science stuff."

"Do you know what makes up a human?"

"Chemicals, we're a bunch of chemicals." Her childhood was a blur, but she did remember the amount of books her father had forced her to read. "I don't remember them all."

Saul smiled for the first time since her capture as if pleased to learn that Raven was not a complete idiot. "A century ago, scientist found some new elements. These elements were as old as hydrogen and helium, and as essential as oxygen and carbon. Are you following me so far?"

The trees on the far left of the clearing weaved a navigable track free of oversized rocks. Raven would escape as soon as Saul's tall, overbearing figure became distracted in the details of the new and improved periodic table.

"They discovered these elements decades apart in different countries," Saul said. "But scientists were unable to combine them with the known elements. New technology spotted them, but nothing that existed at the time could isolate these chemicals. Some couldn't be placed into a category, really made scientists realize how little man knows about the universe or our very planet. These elements had existed for so long, invisible to the human eye." He paused to think and with renewed enthusiasm, "An element as similar to oxygen could potentially create life or one as close to carbon—"

"What's your point?" She grew tired of his jargon. He was staring directly at her with his knowing dark eyes. How was she supposed to escape with that kind of intense attention?

"A physicist in this country discovered a new energy source, while a biochemist in Germany was able to create a compound. Another scientist, a geneticist, discovered that one of those new elements lived inside a few humans. He continued to investigate, wondering how these chemicals were never spotted before. He tested a specific volunteer, a lowly woman. Her DNA or genes or chromosomes kept the chemicals restricted to her specific blood line. The subject was tested in a series of experiments. They confirmed those genes traced back to—"

"What you're basically saying is that Ata comes from a long line of an elite few, and I'm going to guess that her line gave birth to the first Sorrows, right? Is that it in a nut shell?"

"Remember that biochemist in Germany?" Saul's dead set eyes tested her resolve. "Remember the scientist who was able to create a compound with the new elements?"

"Yes, I remember."

"He was overshadowed by the USA's discovery of a new, unlimited source of energy, the one the whole world would soon fight over. Of course, you'll find no records of any of those new elements in books because the new arbitrary government, the one we now have, has done away with all record of Sorrow beginnings."

"Why wouldn't Sorrows want to know where they come from?" she said. "Why not share what *we* are with the world?"

"If you learn how something is created then you'll soon discover how to destroy it, and for obvious reasons a Sorrow government wouldn't want that."

"I don't understand something." Raven rose from the boulder, ready to run. "If Ata is so important to Sorrows, a direct bloodline to our creation, why would you have to hide her from other Sorrows?"

"A Sorrow tyrant rules the government. Alexander is powerful, and his blood is as old as his sister's. His body carries more chemicals than the average Sorrow."

"Sister?"

"Ata doesn't always protect her mind when she sleeps. She woke up one day wanting to find Zemi, and I am almost positive her brother was the one who implanted the need. She will eventually move out of rebel territory and go up north. If she does, he'll kill her."

"Nico wouldn't let anyone hurt her. He's obsessed with her."

"Raven, Sorrows unable to shut their minds are susceptible to influence. The mere idea that this Nico is 'obsessed' with Ata might not even be his own. And even if he does genuinely care, a quick calculated entry by Alexander, a few implanted feelings of sudden rage, could result in her death."

"What about me? How do I know I haven't been infiltrated?" Would the voice ever come back?

"You want to believe you found me on your own, accidently stumbled my way, but I know better. You were hurt when I first found you, and common sense wouldn't have made you climb up a mountain, continuing north—"

"North? I wasn't trying to go north."

"Well, well, look who was sent my way." Saul gave Raven his back and grabbed a hold of Sable's reins. He continued on the trail.

"If I'm not mistaken, rebels will take Bran to Ata's birth place for examination. I could've taken you there too, but not now, not when I know someone deliberately brought you to me. Someone will probably use you to kill me. Go on your way, run. I'm better off without you."

Raven couldn't make herself run away anymore, not if there was a slight chance Saul was telling the truth, not if he could take her to her son. "Will . . . will you help me find Bran?"

"Only if you help me find Ata."

"How do I know I can trust you?"

"You don't. I suggest you keep it that way." He returned to her, reluctantly. "Don't trust anyone, and don't act on weird impulses, or on a voice in your head. Anything out of the ordinary is outside influence, so if you really want to join me, you're going to have to learn to shield your mind from intruders."

"How do I do that?"

"You're a Sorrow, Raven. Figure it out."

FUSION

Nico was ready to lay his father to rest after several hours of digging. He got down on his knees and glanced at the grumpy face one last time. The wrinkled skin was still molded into a scowl. He bid his dad a silent farewell and edged him to the verge of the grave, pushed. The body tumbled into the hole. Nico shoveled soil over the old man and watched him slowly disappear under the cascade of dirt.

For the first time in hours, he sensed Ata's proximity and anxiety. "What's the matter?" He turned to her. "Are you tired?"

Her gaze was concentrated on the fawn in her arms.

"It'll be dawn in a couple of hours." Nico dropped the deer scapula, the shoulder blade used as a shovel. "You should get some rest."

"Are you coming, too?" she murmured. "You have a backache, Nico."

"I'm a healer," he said. "Did you already forget?"

"You've been digging all night, and not once have you attempted to heal your backache." She stared up at him, her eyes shimmered. "Are you punishing yourself for not reaching your father in time? Sable was stressed and only bucked to protect herself from fatigue. It's not your fault your father's head landed on a big rock."

"Kurt died seconds after hitting the ground, *Ata.*" He caught the dry way he pronounced her name. Had he been indifferent to her the whole night?

"You've been silent, actually." She studied his face as careful and concentrated as one would a map. "Do you blame me?"

"No." He moved in the opposite direction of the burial mound. "Let's head back."

Atabey found it necessary to hold his hand on their way to camp. She needed his touch as much as he needed her. Her restive mind curiously explored his thoughts in an effort to understand what generated someone like him. Not able to find the answer in his mind, she imagined Nico knew little of himself.

Visible light is the only electromagnetic waves human see. He brushed her mind with the knowledge. *The wavelengths are found in the colors of the rainbow. Combined they form white light.*

Are you white light in human form?

No. I am not. Humans are blind to many wavelengths of light. They are blind to me in any other form. I am energy. Humans are energy too, except their chemicals—Exhaustion hit him hard.

The campsite was located at the heart of the forest, a clearing surrounded by an abundance of trees and tall grass. He left Atabey the tent and rested on a quilt near the fire. The animal companions settled beside him. Nico waited for sleep to come, a few hours to recharge his internal batteries. Instead, he found himself gazing at the twilight, waiting for sunrise.

"Can I sleep with you?" Ata snuggled next to Nico. Her immediate warmth surrounded him. She whispered, "I'm sorry about your father."

He inched closer, inhaled the scent of her hair. "You read my thoughts, Atabey. You know it wasn't your fault."

"But if I hadn't left the lake, maybe you would have received him. Kurt died close to the campsite. If I, if maybe I—"

"Is that bothering you?" He turned her over so he could see her face. "Do you think if you weren't in my life my father would have never died?"

"He . . . he wouldn't have." Atabey's voice cracked, and her eyes watered.

"Listen to me, carefully." He brought her chin up. "My father could have fallen off his horse whether I knew you or not." Nico was close enough to taste the salt in her tears. "I will always choose you over anyone else."

She attempted a smile, a faint twist of the lips.

"It's true," he said.

Ata leaned forward, her mouth caressed his cheek; her breath was warm against his ear. "You're not aroused anymore."

He tried for a kiss, but she dodged him by tilting her head back. "That's not very nice, Ata."

"You're always aroused." An accusation.

"Come here." Nico bunched her soft, blue hair into his fist and brought her close. "Should I be aroused?"

She shook her head. "You should heal. Your back still hurts."

"True enough." He closed his eyes and traveled deep inside his body. He moved cells around, produced new ones. He fixed his cramped muscles. He alleviated the strain in his neck and shoulders. Nico was light, cruising along his circulatory system. He ignored his core, where pure energy was stored, and headed straight for the heart of his central nervous system, his brain. The billions of neurons there communicated with specific fibers and . . .

A burst of pleasure and muscular contractions distracted him. Ata's involuntary orgasm pulled Nico right out of his body.

He opened his eyes, vibrating in the aftershocks of her intense sensation. "Why didn't you say anything, Ata?" Her pelvis beat loudly.

She watched him with anxious longing, adjusting her posture, uncomfortable again. "I saw you naked at the lake."

"Do you want to fuse?"

"Don't do that." She was angry. Her glare amused him. "You're smirking, Nico."

"I wasn't thinking about fusing since my father died. But are you ready now?"

Ata sat up and scooted away from his touch. "I know your father died. I feel terrible. I didn't want to think about sex when you were digging his grave. You don't think I feel awful?"

"I didn't pay attention to your need." He resisted the urge to laugh. "I'm so sorry."

The chaos in her mind consumed her, a persistent need to cry out in confusion. Her abrupt sexual urges were beyond her control, and one image in particular drove her insane. She pictured herself on all fours while Nico savored her body, his tongue deep between her thighs.

"Stop reading my thoughts, Nico." She tucked her blue curls behind her ears to keep her hands busy, away from his.

"I can't help it." He could if he had thought it necessary. "Your body wants to fuse with mine. It wants to keep me alive. I can die from not fusing."

"I'll have sex when I'm good and ready." *I want to cherish you first.* "Why is fusing so important?"

"Cherish?" He smiled. "I like that word. It's simple, yet strong."

"I can shut you out, you know." Her amber eyes glowed bright in the dark.

"Do you see better at night?" Nico assumed she could since he could.

"Read my mind and you'll know." She grinned. "Go ahead, read."

Her mind had pushed his out with a mental block, a barrier too solid to remove without touch. "That's a clever trick."

"Are you sad about your father?" Ata rested her head on his chest, easing a tad. "I didn't sense your sadness."

He folded his arms around her, gathered her closer still. "I watch people die all the time, some in horribly painful ways. I've seen mothers mourn their children, fathers mourn their wives, and children mourn their parents. I've become used to death, and I had expected my own would come soon. There's only so much energy I can produce without it affecting my human form." He detected the emotional upset in her mind. "I'm not going to die, Ata, not now that I've finally found you."

In Nico's dream the wind supported Atabey, embracing her with an amorous caress. The breeze mussed her hair with great affection. It surrounded and enfolded her in the beauty of twilight. The clouds danced, guided, and outlined her skin with mist.

The afternoon sun blinded Nico the moment he woke. He blinked. Atabey was not by his side. Dread soon pinched his chest. He called out to her with his mind, before he realized she had closed her thoughts to him. Without touching or fusing, Nico had no chance of entering her head. *Where are you?* The dread grew worse until fear choked him.

He closed his eyes and shut out the summer shades of the forest, the shadows on bark and bushes. He concentrated on listening: Bronte grazed nearby. The coyotes were busy chasing a rabbit. Pine slept inside the tent, and Maple lay licking her paws beside him.

"Why aren't you with her?" He reprimanded the mutt. "Why did you allow her to leave?"

Maple batted an eyelid, unconcerned.

Nico strapped on his boots and leapt forward. He hammered past the lake, up the green forest, and over Kurt's burial. He trampled foliage, and bobbed and weaved below branches. *Why are you always doing this to me?* Dread turned to frustration. Anger fenced him twenty minutes into the search. She couldn't have abandoned the woods in the short time he slept, unless Ata found Sable, who had disappeared after dropping Kurt. He took a deep breath.

There.

Atabey was on her knees, carefully picking wild berries from a thicket.

His body went rigid at the sight of her; a rumbling sound escaped his throat, a dangerous growl.

Her head came up, her eyes searched for the threat, but Ata was as helpless as the fawn after Nico had slaughtered its mother.

He seethed with sudden rage; currents of violent heat pulsed through his veins. A primeval need to have her, to fuse, a roar of expanding energy emanating from his core, electrocuted his nerves. His anger had turned into a vicious need to claim her.

"Nico?" She set the basket on the grass and rose.

He emerged from behind a tree and approached her steadily.

"I'm sorry for not telling you where I was, but you were sleeping, and I didn't want to wake you." Panic escaped from her voice. "Are you angry with me?"

Nico gripped her slender arms, directing jolts of energy through her skin. She winced. His fingers glided down to her stomach. Her heart pounded. He got a hold of her shorts. Her scent engulfed him; he drank her aroma as he would water. He needed to remember what she smelled like so he could never lose track of her again. The energy in his core spread a billion different ways, strengthening his muscles, thickening his chest, hardening him.

"I was only gathering berries, Nico." She took several steps back, real terror in her eyes.

Nico pushed her against the nearest tree and yanked down on her shorts, pulling them loose from around her waist. He ripped at her tank top, exposing her breasts. Ata tried to push him away, but he trapped her arms to her sides and dragged her to the grass. His body covered hers completely. He tore off her underwear. She let out a cry. He inhaled the fear from her sweat. Her tender skin begged him to feel, touch, and remember Atabey. It was important he always remembered her fragrance. Nico took off his own suffocating clothes. He left goose flesh wherever he touched her. A gray haze of lust aroused him almost to the point of exploding, and he needed to make them one.

He pinned her hips to keep her steady for penetration. He pushed himself as deep as he could, tearing past the thin, delicate, translucent hymen. She cried out in pain, pain necessary for her safety. Fusing was supposed to be painful—for her. He ignored her sobs, hardly hearing them in the churning of his own body as it prepared to strike hers with lightning.

The smell of her blood goaded him. He spiraled out of control. He created and expanded the first energy bolt and released it inside her. Atabey struggled, thrashed beneath him. Rays tore her insides, but they too were necessary. The emissions united them. She fought the static sting by thrusting upwards, but the more Ata fought, the harder Nico pressed her down.

He bit her on the neck to hear a cry of readjusted lungs, releasing his cells, energy he could physically do without, in a gush of pleasure that allowed him to bury himself deeper. He plunged with a fury of exhilaration. The harder he thrust the more cells he released, alleviating his body from the strain of harnessing so much energy. Nico never wanted the feeling to go away, not when the shockwaves made him orgasm again and again. For a brief moment, he wanted her euphoria to match his.

Chemicals violently shocked every cell in her body. The water boiled, oxygen and hydrogen separated. Carbon molecules rearranged her structure. Nitrogen tampered with her acids, calcium crushed her bones, phosphorus sliced, and sulfur burned. Sodium regulated her electrical signals. Iron reduced her metabolism. Potassium slowed her heartbeat to a near stop, and every other element enabling a human body, shaped and reshaped her insides.

Nico caught a hold of his senses long enough to pull out. He glanced down at Atabey, and was instantly taken aback by how marred, battered and crushed he had left her. Her skin radiated a feverish red, blood and semen trickled down her leg. Her body pulsated with pain, struggling to readjust to the massive energy stored. There was no way for him to permanently end her suffering, not while she was unconscious. She was in pain, terrible life threatening agony.

Her every fiber and cell worked overtime in a fight with every other fiber and cell for a place among the new chemicals. A war erupted inside her body. The circulatory system jeopardized the nervous system, muscles furiously attacked bones. One battle after another excruciating battle achieved many losses, and no molecule would win or lose. The struggle would remain for as long as it took her insides to establish a new regimen. The pain would take days, months or years to fully fade.

Nico cradled Ata in his arms. Her body attacked itself when he moved her. Every step toward the lake caused her lungs to labor. He had scarred her. Ata's pain beat at him. The fusion had made their minds interchangeable. He could ease her soreness. He could send her into a profound, regenerating sleep. He could heal her. She was his, but they were not one. Something had gone terribly wrong.

GLASGOW

Camden was supposed to rise at five in the morning for the fourth day in a row. He woke at noon, completely skipping his morning chores. Milking cows and climbing up tall silos full of grain and silage were not his idea of fun. Picking corn, baling crops and assisting neighboring farmers took a large portion of his endless days. Camden was not built for manual labor. He was too slim, small, and anemic. Reading suited him best. But no, the old man would eventually come find him. "The cow stables don't clean themselves," he would say.

The rebels had allowed many villages to thrive and farm without the fear of a hostile takeover. Individuality was not encouraged. No single farmer had a right to own property, but towns, they were different. Communities provided the rebels furniture, wool, food, soaps, mended clothes and anything else the militia needed. In return, the rebels offered protection and bartered liquor; they owned every distillery in the state.

He sat up on the bed, glancing around the room. A few books were gone. He blamed Mia. Camden arched his sore back and let his feet touch the cool, hardwood floor. He stumbled out of bed and followed the smell of fresh baked gingerbread coming from downstairs. He looked forward to breakfast, his only motivation in life anymore. Mrs. Laymon might have been a simpleminded woman, but at least she could cook.

Ida disrupted the peaceful living room when she burst through the front door and waved a brown dress in front of the older woman's face. Mrs. Laymon sat on a rocking chair, silently knitting a large quilt of many squares. Her daughter Mia sat beside her, also knitting, adding diamond shapes to her mother's quilt.

"You said on my last visit to this dumb town that you would have the ivory dress detailed and finished for me, and if not, you were supposed to start on the sapphire dress. I find out you gave them both away. And your assistant instead gives me this brown thing." Ida threw the flock dress on the ground and stomped on it. "Do you have any idea who I am?"

"Mia had malaria. We nearly lost her." Mrs. Laymon was a soft spoken woman, a seamstress. She handcrafted elegant gowns for her costumers, but kept the simplest rags for herself. "Mr. Lowell was gracious enough to heal Mia for free. His lady companion admired both dresses, and I thought to give them to her. I don't regret doing so. If you don't want the flock dress, young lady, you'll have to wait until I make you another."

Ida glared at Mia, who hadn't bothered to look up from the quilt. "She seems fine to me."

"Thanks to the healer." Mrs. Laymon's kind eyes examined her young daughter, a pretty brunette of fifteen. She turned to Ida. "I will reimburse you for the fabric."

"Arrg, you're an impossible old hag." Ida turned sharply to Camden. "Bowie's waiting for you outside."

"Can I at least have some breakfast first?" he asked her.

Mrs. Laymon chuckled. "Breakfast is over, young man, but I do have some gingerbread in the oven if—"

"Bowie wants you now! Don't make him wait, Cam." Ida dismissed him just as quickly as she had acknowledged his existence and continued to argue over the two dresses.

Camden stepped outside. He was greeted by the glaring sky and the hustle and bustle of a close-knit community always on the go. Men of all ages wearing different kinds of sun-shielding hats, moved steadily to and fro, trading and farming. Draft horses hauling buggies and wagons to multiple destinations packed the streets. The windmills provided the energy needed to run the town. Wind and solar power helped expand a county full of small business men, each man had a different trade, and all trades were needed.

"There you are, Butthole." Bowie used his rifle as a pointing stick to show Camden the way. "Let's take a walk."

"Can I ask where we're going?"

"Start walking." He jabbed him in the back with the rifle. "If Joshua changes his mind about you," said the blond man with a delirious grin, "I have plenty of things I'd like for you to do."

Glasgow's town folks helped each other raise barns, build stores, trade products, nurse babies, and school children. School years were a short seven. When kids turned thirteen, they learned a trade, and most of the kids usually chose their parent's occupation. If Camden had been born in Glasgow, he would have aspired to become an academic, a teacher, mostly to indulge his own reading habit. Educators were the only ones allowed to read without having other town member's judge or scorn them. No one wanted to teach and the children, always eager to grow old enough to start working, deemed letters and numbers unimportant.

"Did you eat?" Bowie made it a habit to check up on Camden once a day.

"Ida rushed me out," he said. "I didn't get the chance."

The rebel picked up his pace, hurrying beside Camden. "I'll get you something to eat later on." He jabbed him in the ribcage with his rifle. "Butthole, did you hear me?"

"Yes, I heard. Thank you."

"Do you want me to feed you or not?"

"Yes, please, feed me."

"Yeah." Bowie's grin was ridiculously lewd. "That's what you want, me to feed you."

A group of men, far off in the distance, pulled together on ropes and raised a new barn. The restless town clustered around the plot of land, troubled by the rebel's unexpected arrival. Yet, they never demanded explanations.

Bowie had barged into the Laymon household on their first day in Glasgow and forced the family to make room for Camden. Mrs. Laymon had smiled kindly before instructing her daughter to give up her room. Her husband's clammy grip shook Camden's hand in a warm gesture. He greeted him as if welcoming a long lost son. No one protested his stay.

"Am I eventually going back to the Laymon house?" he asked Bowie.

Bowie put an arm over Camden's shoulder. He guided him past the new barn and toward the open fields. "Nope, your time with them is over."

"I wouldn't mind living here if I got to decide my career choice," Camden said. "I'd prefer something in the education field, but I also wouldn't mind the doctor role."

"Doctor?" Bowie had to bend over to catch his breath from laughing as hard as he did. "You know what, Cam? I like you."

Glasgow's herbal health system was top of the line. The women harvested from the fields plants proven to cure mild illnesses. A doctor served little purpose since most families treated their own injuries at home. The title doctor was basically given to anyone willing to preserve the town's medical supply. However, if families ever suffered real emergencies, they counted on a traveling man, the healer who had miraculously cured Mia. The man had visited the town—the Carriers in tow—days before the rebels arrived.

"Here we are." Bowie stopped beside a green hill. "You'll find your master up top."

Camden regarded the blond man with suspicion. "Are you not coming?"

"You look scared, Butthole." He laughed. "You'll be fine. I'll fetch you some food. You'd like that, right?"

"Right," Camden said quickly, not trying to get poked with the rifle again.

"There's a festival Saturday night." Bowie leaned close, his flushed face smelled like corn. "Our last night here. How about we get drunk and have some fun?"

"I'd like that a lot, actually." He could use a break. "I've been working my ass off."

Bowie smirked. "No, you haven't."

Glasgow weekends were festive, full of singing, dancing and a whole lot of courting. The young seized opportunities for recklessness, their attention on the opposite sex. The town let loose for two days of endless drinking and dining. Old men held folk gatherings, their musical instruments diverse. On some occasions, Joshua brought his acoustic guitar and joined the men in song. For a 'loony' rebel, Joshua was a talented musician. He produced beautiful melodies out of every single instrument placed in his hands. Women sometimes joined the elderly gatherings just to hear him play. They never wandered close, never spoke his name, but they did appreciate his talent.

Some of his tunes were alien to everyone, and his rhythm was unlike no other. His beats, riffs, and tempo hypnotized, and lured. His musical genius exuded artistry. Joshua held every single instrument as a mother might hold a child, with love, devotion and admiration. Town folks lionized his gift of song. And the man was never quite happy unless he played. But when he stopped, the town folks would slowly back away, grabbing their children, remembering the stark blue gaze belonged to a rebel leader.

"Do you know how many churches this county alone used to have, the ones built before the reconstruction of the state?" Joshua stood tall, up the hill's highest mound, gazing at the vastness of the land, at the farmers working tirelessly below.

The climb to the top of the hill had exhausted Camden. He doubled over, heaving. "Religion is the set of beliefs concerning the cause, nature, and purpose of the universe," he recited from memory, from a book he had once read. "It contains a moral code of governing the conduct of human affairs."

"Do you think we need religion to govern ourselves?" Joshua's limbs hardly ever moved. He was like a statue captured in time with one expression, one stance. "What is the point of goodness if you are not rewarded at the end of your life?"

"I don't know, sir." Camden had previously discussed many philosophical theories with the man, and not a single one had led anywhere. "I read the Bible you gave me, but I don't necessarily understand all of it. Isn't it mythology?"

"Everyone wants to see the fruits of their labor, Camden. If I don't murder a family of ten, I better get rewarded in the afterlife."

"I don't think man is naturally good. That's why I don't ever try to be something other than what I am." Camden hoped he at least sounded smart.

"Do you know what I miss about the olden days, Cam?"

"I don't know, sir."

Joshua's face always twitched slightly in amusement at the word sir. Camden encouraged the rare smiles.

"Touring, on the road, performing for the millions, I miss the thrill of it all. Sold out concerts, exciting music videos, downloads. I miss the theatrics, even the awards shows, which I used to loathe." The man breathed an air of patience, rankled with the breeze, irritated with the wind tugging at his clothes.

"Were you a rock star, sir?"

"That's a presumptuous question, Cam."

"I'm sorry, sir."

"Have you read all the holy books?" Joshua asked.

"I've read every book you've given me, sir."

"Are you sure?"

"I haven't gotten to the Vedas or the Three Baskets, but I will as soon as I finish the Bible."

"I need these conversations from time to time, Cam. They keep me sane." Joshua often pretended to come from the twenty-first century, which would have made him older than dirt. "I get tired of it all, of living. Do you know why I keep moving forward?"

Camden moved toward the rebel leader and also observed the land below. His stomach rumbled, reminding him of Bowie's promise to bring him food. "No, sir, I don't."

"Did you love your brother?" For a split second, Joshua's icy blue eyes bared a hint of pain and loneliness. "Did I ever tell you what happened to him?"

"Gad escaped with Isaac's daughter, a dumb mistake on his part," Camden said. "Bowie told me he found him dead by a tree. Is that true?"

"I wasn't fully in my head when Blue escaped, a good thing. I'm glad she feels safe wherever she is. Let Daniel get comfortable with the idea that he can protect her."

"What kind of bird is that?" Camden pointed to the man's right shoulder at a tattoo of a black bird. "Is that a crow?"

"You don't seem to care that your brother's dead?"

"Gad and I weren't close."

"Ha!" Joshua laughed. "I never liked my brother either."

Camden shrugged. "It happens."

"What a heartless nation we've become, Cam. It's quite the spectacle."

"Why did people believe Christianity, Islam, Judaism, and all those other myths were real?" Camden asked. "I don't get it, entirely."

"One god sounded more believable than many, but at least Greek mythology was interesting." Joshua glanced at his left hand, wiggled his fingers. He cracked his knuckles. "If you need reasons to use your hands for good, you're really not good. Why fool ourselves with the idea that if we don't rape, pillage, steal, and kill, we might be rewarded someday? What if there is no reward? Why care? Why pretend to sympathize? In the end, none of it will matter. Why bother to live at all? Why accomplish a feat? I can go on like this all day, Camden. But I won't. Do you know why?"

"No, sir, I don't have a clue."

"Because no matter how many books I make you read, you still won't comprehend what I'm talking about. No book is ever going to define the world for you. What a book will do, Camden, is make it easier for me to dump information. Here I am trying to mold a kid of eighteen or nineteen into considering the possibilities of a life he has never and will never live. The best I can do for you, Cam, is expand your mind. Do you want to lead?" Joshua had finally made his case. "I need a leader with a brain. Muscle is easy to find. Soldiers are everywhere, but leaders, leaders are scarce. I'm not saying you are one, or that you're particularly adequate to lead anyone anywhere, but I do believe you're ambitious enough to strive for more. Do you want more?"

"I want to stay in this town and teach. I like it here. You may think Glasgow trivial, but all I have ever wanted was an easier life."

"You were born a century too late."

"I don't particularly like the rebel regime."

"And I do?" he asked. "I aid the rebels to give you all a fighting chance. The Sorrows will come sooner or later and these farmers," he said, pointing at the folks down below, "won't survive unless they have decent leaders. You don't fight fire with rain, you fight fire with fire."

"I've read about Sorrows, about the revolution of the intellect." Camden found the books on the existence of advance humans just north of the country terrifying. Rebels were tyrants themselves, but ultimately protected their own people from a larger threat. Sorrows had long ago stripped Southerners of technology, handicapping them in many ways, all to make it that much easier to destroy them. "They're nearly unstoppable, stronger, smarter, and healthier. They read our minds and manipulate our actions. You yourself know what they did to Toady. I can't help you lead with those kinds of odds. How do we fight that kind of fire with fire? I don't even know anyone or anything resembling fire."

"Not yet you don't," Joshua said. "But you'll meet her soon enough."

HEAR ME SCREAM

Located near the mouth of a creek flowing into a larger stream, a thin, shrouded waterfall fell freely, undisturbed, splashing on boulders. Nico spread a quilt on the mushy ground and gently laid Ata at an angle adjacent to the cascade, hoping that when she woke, the beautiful scene would soothe her. He sat beside the fire and prepared supper. As for the animals, Maple slept, Ash licked away at Atabey's wounds, and Bronte drank from the rivulet, no longer groaning from the pain in his hind leg.

The accident had occurred while Nico was searching for Atabey. When he returned to camp, he found the horse injured, the dogs playing, and Pine gone. He wanted to find the cougar responsible for the fawn's disappearance, but at the time, Ata's heartbeat troubled him. He was not about to leave her side in search of a dead baby deer, or the feline savoring the remains. The scene would have been too reminiscent of his attack on Ata. The mere image of the defenseless fawn being devoured by an uncaring animal left him disgusted with himself.

Oak patrolled the new campsite. And both he and Nico listened to the approaching steps of two humans and a horse. The fire's smoke drew the trio. Nico would welcome Raven and Sable, but as for the man who accompanied them, he wasn't sure.

He stood and waited for the guests to find his location. To his delight, a healthy Raven emerged from the bushes, prettier and taller than he remembered. "Raven, we looked everywhere for you," he said, reaching for her.

Her hands trembled. "I'm healed. What are you doing?"

"Double checking. I could've missed something."

"O-kay, I'm going to pretend you don't have two coyotes in your campsite. Why is one licking Ata?" She scrutinized the other dog. "And is that Maple, the mutt?"

"I healed her."

"Of course you did."

Sable waddled to the stream, nuzzled Bronte affectionately for a minute, and then guzzled water.

The strange man headed directly toward Ata, knelt to observe her face, and extended his hand. He attempted to caress her ruby cheeks.

"Don't touch her." Nico was more protective than concerned. "She's badly wounded. Her body's still burning with a fever."

"I see that." The man glanced at Raven. "I thought you said there were two of them?"

"There was," she answered. "This is Nico Lowell. Nico, this man here is Saul Leon. He's Ata's guardian."

Nico examined and measured the Sorrow. Not a physical threat. He settled near the fire on a fallen log next to Ata. "Are you two hungry? I fried some mushrooms, there's wild berries in the bowl right there, and for the main course, we have steaks."

"Everything smells delicious." Raven sat across from Nico, calmer than he had ever seen her.

Saul sat beside her, his gaze lingered on Atabey. "What happened to her?"

"An animal attack," Nico said, truthfully.

"I thought Ata could communicate with animals?" Raven reached for the pan of golden brown mushrooms, grabbed them by the handful, and inhaled the succulent sweet flavors concentrated on the pan. Sliced, cooked in hot oil, evenly coated, and still sizzling. "Where were you when she was attacked, Nico?"

"Close," he said.

"Close," Saul repeated. "What type of animal was it?"

"A dangerous beast."

"Should I be grateful that you've kept Atabey safe all this time?" Saul Leon's thick eyebrows and dark eyelashes set the tone for the rest of his stern disposition. He wore a gray shirt with the sleeves rolled up to his elbows, and his pants were not as dirty as one might expect from a man living in the woods.

Nico stuck his piece of steak on a stick and brought it to the fire. "I don't make decisions for you, Saul." The flames leaped up around the meat and coated the surface. The raw pieces waited on one flat leaf, ready to cook, already seasoned with salt. He grabbed two more sticks and handed them to Raven and Saul.

"So, Nico," the man started. "I know why Sorrows like Raven live in a rebel state, but I can't figure out why you and your father would—"

"Father's dead." The meat's juices dripped and the fire hissed up around the steak. "He fell off his horse." Nico glanced at the mare. Sable's udder had been enlarging for a long time. Her teats were full of milk. Her hip and buttocks had relaxed, and her abdomen hung low. "Sable's restive and cranky. Father rode her hard, knowing how close she was to foaling."

Raven observed the mare. Her eyes welled up with tears. She said, "Your Father was an inconsiderate man."

Nico's meat crinkled and darkened. "Perhaps someday you'll forgive him for selling you."

"He's dead now," she said. "It doesn't matter whether I do or don't."

"In answer to your question," Nico said to Saul, "I am not a Sorrow."

"I feared you would say that." The man nodded at Raven as if to settle an earlier discussion. "You're a healer, Mr. Lowell. Healing is one of the advantages of a Sorrow."

Nico almost laughed. "How many real healers do you know?"

"None but—"

"I'm not a Sorrow, but let me ask you a question." Nico turned the meat over several times. He grabbed Saul's unused stick, broke it in half, and threw it at the fire. The flames danced. "Why have you kept Atabey hidden for so long?" He set his cooked steak in a plastic plate where mushrooms waited.

"What kind of meat is this?" Raven took a bite of hers. "This is so good."

"It's deer meat. There's plenty more where that came from."

She bit off another chunk. "I thought Saul was trying to poison me, at first. I didn't eat a lot of his 'offerings'."

Nico liked the new and relaxed, less harsh Raven. "I'm glad Saul eased you in a way I couldn't."

"Not exactly the case." Her hazel gaze moved from Saul to him, contemplative. "I'm just tired of feeling defeated."

"Well, whatever it is, I'm happy you're happy."

She quit gnawing the meat and grimaced. "Nico?" she said, around a mouthful of grease.

"Yes."

"Ata's in danger." She ate in less of a rush and wiped her face with her shirt collar. "Saul, tell him what you told me."

The stories of Alexander and the tyrannical government taking control over the land, over the people's minds, were already known throughout the state. Nico's curiosity geared more toward Atabey's origins. Out of all the truths he understood about the world and evolution, he had never been able to figure out how Ata lost herself in an organic species.

"Why did you make it your responsibility to rescue her from the Birth Project?" he asked Saul. "You abandoned your own people to keep her alive. Why?"

The question puzzled the man. He cleared his throat a couple of times. "Ten years of watching the government torture her was enough. She was put through brutal, inhumane trials, caged like an animal, depleted of blood, bone and marrow but still, she remained such a beautiful girl. Her eyes made you feel all the guilt and terror of her confusion." Saul's forehead creased when he regarded Atabey. "On her tenth birthday, they decided to prep her for the 'real' tests, another year of cruelty, worse kind of cruelty. I heard her screaming every night after I went to bed. I sometimes still hear her scream."

"And so you what, rescued her?" Nico tried not to let his own memories of a tortured Ata consume him. "Why did y-ou, you bring her—" His voice broke for but a moment. Shaking his head, he tried again. "Kentucky isn't the only rebel state. Why did you choose this place, specifically?"

"I didn't. The idea came from Ata," Saul said. "I took her to the sunny state of Florida and surrounded her with orange trees, but her sadness kept mounting every day. She grew anxious and angry at me for keeping her away, away from what? I never knew. She harvested a few orange seeds and told me we had to go north. We settled here in Kentucky. Been here ever since."

"Thank you, Saul." He owed the man a great deal. "Thank you for bringing her to me."

"I didn't bring her to you, Mr. Lowell." Saul spat his irritation. "And bringing her to this state was a colossal mistake. We're too close to the north, and Ata has this idea imbedded in her head that she needs to find her murderous brother. He'll kill her if he gets the chance."

Nico didn't share the same fear. "I promise you—"

Atabey's roused pain encased his attention. Her waking disrupted her body's molecules and alerted them to fight, another battle of the cells. Her core rumbled in terrible pain as she struggled into a sitting position, her face turned to the waterfall. The cascade did not soothe. To her, the fall plunged mercilessly into the stream. Her mind instead concentrated on the leaves whispering to the trees, the winds muttering sighs, and the birds chirping beautiful songs.

Atabey.

She dug her hands into the soil, inhaling the musty scent, listening to the crackling fire, to anything but him.

Nico sighed. He would leave her alone for the meantime.

"Elements as old as hydrogen and as essential as carbon have probably already created life. Has this ever occurred to you, Saul?" Raven interrupted nature's serenity with her robotic voice. "You said scientists couldn't see them, didn't have the technology to spot them until a century ago. If these elements have existed longer than we have, but were invisible, what makes you think an earlier, more ancient, stronger, smarter, more adept life form doesn't already exist?"

"I don't know." Saul glared at her. "Your face is twitching, Raven. Are you in there?"

A malevolent grin ignited her eyes. "Maybe they don't like how we've singlehandedly exhausted most of our own natural resources, how we're trying to mess with theirs. Maybe we've shared this planet like a pest to the higher life form. If I were them, I would wipe us out. Maybe they already tried. Maybe they're responsible for our near extinction, for the FOY virus. But what would they do about the ten percent left, the Sorrows, the humans sharing a few of their compounds?"

"Stop talking." Saul urged. "Block, now."

"I know!" She continued. "They would have to find a way to shrink to our level, downsizing into our smaller being like a whale becoming a rat. This life form would have to journey around, maybe releasing energy to many rats, enlightening them, but also temporarily alleviating its own want, its own feeling of needing to expand and enlarge to its actual form, a form which doesn't need the debilitating human body because, let's face it, we're just a brain, neurons sending electric impulses . . . wait, stay with me, child."

"Push him out, ignorant girl!" Saul's face flushed.

"The human body serves to facilitate the brain, but maybe this older life form doesn't need a body, doesn't die, which would explain why Sorrows live longer," she said. "Maybe this life form has existed for many epochs. We know one thing for sure, if it's willing to go through all the trouble of becoming human, imagine how much more energy it would invest in our demise." Raven gasped, struggled to breathe. She took gulp after gulp of fresh air as if trying to rattle her mind back into place, releasing the sudden information download to her brain.

Saul frowned. "Put up the wall. Alexander found you."

"I thought, I thought. I can't breathe." She shook all over.

Nico rose and placed a hand on her head. With an energy push, he created a dome around her brain, protecting it from another intrusion. "This will last for another day, but if he already knows where we are, we better get moving."

"Why would he make Raven talk all that nonsense?" Saul asked. "Surely, he doesn't think she'll believe any of it."

"If he wanted Raven to believe all that, he would have whispered it in her ear. He wasn't transmitting it for her benefit or yours, Saul." Nico glanced at Ata, who already regarded him. "Alexander wanted Atabey to know another life form will destroy the rest of her species. This is not true, Ata."

Atabey's silent stare tore at him. He could see her fear, her disorientation. If he apologized, her panic would turn into rage. Whatever affection achieved earlier was gone, and Nico desired nothing more than to fix it. He wanted to approach her, to touch her, and make her forget his one moment of savagery, but he couldn't, not with all three dogs growling.

Maple's tail no longer wagged. Her glower centered on Nico. Ash crouched and waited for a chance to lunge at his throat. The hackles on Oak's back were up; the coyote exposed his teeth, moved in for the attack.

"What are they doing?" Raven stepped away from the dogs. "I think they're going to attack you, Nico. Do Sorrows influence animals, too?"

"No," Saul said dryly. "But Ata can."

Oak would pounce first—and die. "Atabey," Nico warned. "If you care about these dogs don't sentence them to death."

A low rumbling sound escalated into a screech, from a screech it blasted into a cry so loud it created the illusion of originating from his eardrums. Nico covered them in vain. The noise came from inside his head, Ata's piercing scream. His stomach churned, his head pulsed, and his body convulsed with the vibrations of the magnified shriek. Compounds in his body partially separated as if wanting to escape his corporal form, wanting to avoid being tortured by such a horrendous cry of pain and anger.

He fell to his knees. Nico could have easily sent the frequency in the opposite direction, but the diffusion would hurt Ata. He had no desire to hurt her ever again, even as she intentionally caused his ears to bleed. He would allow her to stop on her own, allow her to slice him with amplified sound waves until she was satisfied.

"Enough!" Saul positioned himself between Nico and the dogs. "We are not savages, Ata." She ceased the transmission in an instant and leapt toward the man. He held her, soothed her, and told her, "Everything will be okay. I'm here now."

BORN

"I've been thinking about Alexander's download." Raven sat on the thick branch of an old tree across the waterfall. "If another life form does really exist, and does compact itself into a tangible being, how would the amount of energy that kept it going in a bigger size be contained in a small creature? I don't think it would."

"Not for long it wouldn't." Nico sat beside her, but instead of looking at the cascade, he kept his sights on the pawing, pacing, and urinating horse. Sable defecated a few moments before she found a comfortable place to lie down. "It would have to transfer cells, energy."

"In my theory, this life form would have to find a similar being. The second being would have to share some of the compounds that make up the first being, not all, but enough to help it store cells. This would work until it decided to change."

"You're assuming it could ever go back to its original form." Nico's face was an expressionless mask. "In order for this life form to compact itself into a smaller creature, he would have to cram vital information into a tiny human brain. This life form, Raven, couldn't tell you what it is. He doesn't have enough space inside his cranium for millions of years of knowledge."

"So he, since we're establishing it's a male, would have to what? Wend around, hoping to find his counterpart, assuming there is one, feeling there has to be. Otherwise why would such an intelligent being bother becoming human in the first place?" She looked at Nico. "It doesn't make sense."

"He was probably constrained into human form because his species needs a certain amount of compounds to exist successfully, like hydrogen needs oxygen to form water. He needs to fuse with oxygen, in a sense, to exist properly. I'm trying to use human terms so you understand."

"Okay, go on." Raven paid close attention to the way his brows furrowed and his lips tightened. She imagined he was deep in thought, grappling to find the right words to describe the unknown. "Soul mates?" She offered.

"Maybe, if you believe—"

"I don't. It seems ridiculous to me that someone on this earth was born to just me."

"That someone is his other half, born human," Nico said. "He had to reduce himself to a tangible body to find his other half, in a sense. He doesn't know why and how it works. The only thing he does know for sure is that if he fuses, correctly anyway, he no longer has to be a human."

"Why doesn't he fuse then?"

"He thought he did, but it didn't work. He doesn't think fusing will ever work, not while in human form. The best he can do is to merge their minds, permanently."

"So, if he can't fuse, how will he ever go home?"

The healer forced a massive amount of air into his lungs as if always aware that he needed to breathe.

"Nico, how will you ever go home?"

"I can't, not without her, and she can't go home because she's partly human." He turned to Raven and his eyes, his peridot gems, reflected a foreign distress. "I have to come to terms with that. She can harness energy. She can keep me from exploding. My energy keeps her body alive. I'm always dividing new cells, hers are constantly dying. That's how our bodies work. We'll balance each other out for the rest of our human lives. We need each other, but we can't go home. I don't even remember what home was like or if others like us exist."

"Yet you want to go back."

"I don't belong here, Raven."

"Would you go home if you died?" Her question tied knots around her stomach.

"Maybe, I don't know."

Raven tried to dismiss the despair, the sadness rattling Nico's voice, his demeanor. "But there's a chance you could go home?"

"Atabey would have to die, too," he said. "And that's not a chance I'm willing to take."

"Do you ever get the sense that you're here for more than Ata?"

"I don't remember what that other thing is." His attention turned to the quaking, stressed mare on the grassy pasture, lying on her side, still trying to deliver. "I don't know if I put the information inside my brain, or how I managed to make myself an embryo. I don't know how my mother got pregnant. I can't see that far back."

"You were born the natural way?"

"Is there any other way?"

Sable had been straining, pushing out her foal for more than an hour. A clear, milky sac appeared at the mare's vulva. Two front feet emerged from the sack. The mare rose, pushed, and became recumbent again. Her body quivered with each contraction, until the foals head pushed through. Within seconds, the foal's entire body spewed out enclosed in the sac.

"Let's go help her." Nico joined the new mother at the birthing site and crouched to free the damp newborn. "Being a mother is a tough job."

Raven scrubbed off the tears that fell on her cheeks. How she longed to see her son again. "And I thought giving birth to a seven pound baby was rough." Her strained voice deluded the joke.

The mare stood up again, breaking off the umbilical cord. She turned to sniff her foal and gently lapped its coat. "I'm glad you were here to see this, Raven." Nico smiled, and what a smile. He was a handsome man, a caring man.

"Why do you waste your time?" she asked him. "Why Ata, I mean? It seems like all you ever do is try to win her over, but she rejects you every chance she gets."

"Don't." Leaden frustration exposed itself for a moment. Nico shook his head and exhaled. "Don't take my side on this one. Atabey has valid reasons."

"She caused your ears to bleed."

"Yes, but I had it coming." He greeted Saul with a nod; the man returned to camp alone. "She actually held back, a lot back."

"Ata stopped frying your brain because he told her to." Raven pointed at Saul.

"I need to talk to you, Raven." Saul reached them and grabbed her arm. He dragged her near the stream. "We need to talk about the plan."

"The plan?"

"Yes, we're traveling to Crystal City, home of the Birth Project." The man's lengthy discussion on the subject was mostly about the safest route to Virginia. "The journey on foot, assuming nothing goes wrong, will take about twelve days. Questions?" Saul, as if expecting none, added another detail. "The three of us have a long road ahead."

"Four."

"I don't think it's wise to take a demented Sorrow with us."

"Ata, you mean? Surely you're not talking about the man who has rescued her over and over again?"

"He's wounded Atabey," he said. "Ata would never attack anyone without a legitimate reason. She doesn't want to tell me what happened to her, but I'm a hundred percent sure it has something to do with the healer."

Raven also suspected Nico's sadness revolved around Ata. "Maybe he lost his temper, once."

"Once is enough. Don't you think, Raven?" Saul's posture stiffened, the action lengthened his torso. "We don't need him to find your son."

"I prefer Nico over you any day of the week if I'm going to put my life on the line." Raven's life had fallen on Nico's lap plenty of times before. The healer was tried and tested, more than she could ever say about the woodsman. "How does finding my son even benefit you?"

"We're helping each other." He wiped pesky beads of sweat from his forehead, smearing, annoyed. "The facility where I used to work has the equipment needed to block Ata from Alexander, forever. We'll also be able to block him from you."

"And in the meantime, what keeps that tyrant from getting inside my head again?" A reasonable question. "We won't be safe in Sorrow terrain."

"We're not safe now."

"Nico can obviously shield my mind, and I'm pretty sure he can also shield Ata. Why do you think Alexander entered my head to tell her something? If Nico can keep us all from mind invasion—"

"I don't trust him."

Nico meandered toward them as casual as a full bellied predator, surrounding an animal for the simple joy of destroying it. He dissected Saul with his gaze, gnawing at the man without actually touching him. "I don't need you to trust me, Saul." His words came from a greedy sucking of air. "I go wherever Atabey goes."

"She doesn't like you."

"Irrelevant."

"Great," Raven said. "You two go have a pissing contest while I do something useful, like I don't know, pack up, get ready to get out of this state."

"Am I neglecting you again?" Nico grinned.

"No." Did he remember her one and only sexual burst, the one achieved by him? She waggled her head and glared. "Unlike Ata, I don't need a keeper."

"I beg to differ." He turned to Saul and said, "I'll pack up and gather the horses. We'll go as soon as I finish building rafts since we'll make better time on water."

"Why are you stalling?" Saul positioned his hands on his hips, commanding, pissing. "We're leaving right now."

"We need the rafts, and besides, the foal needs time to learn how to walk." Nico said, observing the newborn being lapped by its mother. "Two rafts won't take long."

"Two?" Saul scoffed. "I don't know where you get the idea that you decide anything. You were hardly invited."

The healer's laughter lasted a few seconds and then his entire attention shifted to the waterfall where a nude Ata bathed. The fall cast a veil over her figure. Saul blushed and marched into the forest away from the view. Ata's massaging rhythm, her delicate caresses gestured sexual desire. Nico looked on sadly, guiltily.

"She wants your attention, you know," Raven said. "Why else would she display herself knowing we're only a few feet away?"

"She's in heat again, the water soothes. I would touch her if that wasn't the last thing she wanted."

"In heat? What is she, a cat?"

Nico smiled to himself. "More like a water nymph."

"I wonder if part of the Birth Project included mixing animal species," she said. "If the scientist working on Ata knew she couldn't die easily, do you think they tried to insert feline DNA?"

"When too many of Atabey's cells die," Nico said, "her body warns her it's time to fuse."

"You don't communicate with animals." Raven had never seen anyone's eyes glow like lanterns in the night, or gleam as sunshine in the day. "Your eyes don't do what hers do, and your hair is not blue, Nico. Did someone mess with her genes at birth? Saul told me

Ata's embryo was old. Do you think she was kept unborn to be engineered as a kind of animal? Animals were not affected by the FOY virus. Scientists might have believed it had something to do with their DNA."

"Atabey is beautiful."

"And?" she said. "I wasn't arguing that."

"The urge to mate is part of self-preservation."

"What are you taking about?"

Nico ogled the sprite on the other side of the cascade with unyielding attention. "Ata needs—"

"You're not really listening to me." She found it difficult to swallow the lump in her throat, the frustration. "Are you?"

Raven had a terrible headache by the time she reached the furthest corner of the stream, away from Ata, away from Nico. She stood adjacent to a rock shelter layered with gray stones, a good place to collect her thoughts. The rocks protruded enough to make them climbable, reaching a peak with a large view of the forest. She sat on a serrated edge, trying to convince herself that going to Virginia was the right thing to do. If worse came to worse, Nico would get them out of trouble. Why did she rely so much on him? Maybe he was a demented Sorrow, tricked into believing he belonged to another species. If Alexander wanted Ata dead, what better way to accomplish the task than through the kind and striking healer? Nico epitomized splendor. His hair reminded her of the yellow shades of autumn leaves, and the grain color of his skin—

She spotted the cougar's slender frame, grayish skin, and yellow eyes seconds too late. Leaping from above, it delivered a deadly blow, knocking her to the ground. The cougar's weight crushed her, powerful paws pierced her skin. She gasped. The cat hissed, licked its lips in quick anticipation. Panic kept Raven dull. A guttural sound escaped the animal's hot mouth. Startled, she thrashed beneath its crushing force. Sharp incisors clamped down on her throat. Her clogged windpipes hindered her breathing. She was suffocating.

The man-eater hesitated, backed away, hissing, confused. Raven wasted no time. She rolled to her side and used one hand to cover her neck, the other hand to drag her weak limbs to safety. Her movements caught the animal's attention. It clutched her again, bit into her arm, ripping a chunk of skin. Raven's mangled arm pulsated. She stared down at the pink wound where skin should have been and cried out in pain. Muddled again, the cougar shook all over as if drying its coat. Raven sprinted off the ground and ran as fast as she could into the woods.

Her neck throbbed. No tourniquet meant excessive bleeding. Her first thought was to find Nico. Or scream his name. She stumbled on rocks, branches, anything and everything in her path. She tried to climb the nearest tree in order to avoid leaving a bloody trail. Her efforts were disastrous, her vision a blur. Blood gushed from her wound, a major artery torn. She needed to think, but instead fell on the grass. Exhaustion kicked in. *You're going to die, stupid.* With little energy left, Raven contrived a tourniquet out of her shirt. The whole shirt would have to work since she had not the strength to tear the cloth into strips.

Images of her infant son nursing innocently from her breast consumed her fading memories. The painful suckling had been necessary for the child's nutrition. While imprisoned, repeatedly raped, beaten, and angry with the rebels, with mankind in general, Raven had given birth to someone worthy of her affection. New life awaited her beyond rebel territory. She had needed only to escape, and once outside the barriers of her prison cell, Raven had planned to forgive and forget all the wrongs done to her. She was going to teach her child to love the way her mother had taught her, the way Raven was capable of loving. A better life awaited her. But then her baby was ripped from her arms at three months old, never to be seen or heard of again.

The flood of emotions stirred her mind, heated her body, and regulated her breathing. Hope grasped her lungs and tranquilized her thoughts. Static, buzzing noises, a familiar most welcomed tune erupted in her ears, a melody of a sort, a comfort like no other. Voice.

You're bleeding to death. He grumbled, irritated. *Why are you always in danger?*

Admittedly, she was relieved to be able to tell the difference between Alexander's aggressive out of body intrusion, the painful tug at her senses, compared to the gentle breezy static of the voice, her voice, his voice.

Where are you, Raven?

Forest.

The cougar is disoriented right now, but it will only remain so for another few minutes, minutes you don't have.

You stopped the animal?

Did you find Saul Leon?

The jailer, yes.

Saul can help you.

I'd much rather have Nico heal me than—

Is Ata around?

Yes.

Good, you'll be okay.

The disconnection was sudden and severe, yanking her into her subconscious, an almost lethal sleep.

TOUCH

The smell of spilled blood should have been his first warning, his first sign Raven was wounded, but instead, Nico was alarmed by the undetected way a Sorrow entered Ata's mind. The Sorrow's brief request for help was there before he could push it out. Atabey ran to the rescue without questioning the order. Not close enough to stop her, he chased after her, well behind. Strange emotions agitated him, some of insecurity, and some of anxiety. Unrepressed anger erupted in his core. In the past, the disgust of such a petty sentiment would have compelled him to laugh. He wasn't laughing.

Maple protected Ata with all the strength of her bark. But the quick cougar clawed her, mauling the mutt, leaving her silent. Oak and Ash tagged teamed the cat. Ash acted as bait. Oak sneaked from behind and sank his teeth into the animal's neck, trying to pull the larger prey down. Ash gnawed at a hind leg, tearing a hole right through the skin, angering the cougar. The savagery then inflicted on the coyotes was brutal.

Nico cursed himself for having to stop and heal Raven. He couldn't ignore her bleeding, her mediocre attempt at a tourniquet. She would die if he joined the dogs a few yards away. He acted quickly, inserting himself as energy inside the girl's body, probing her neck muscles, repairing cartilage. Mangled tissue needed patching. Raven's blood loss deprived her cells of oxygen which made her unable to heal herself. She was in shock. The healing took longer than expected, and Nico's inability to fully concentrate on the task prolonged the process. He finally managed to mend all there was to mend before leaving Raven on a patch of grass.

Atabey was cornered under an overhanging ledge, a desiccated cavity in a disorderly pile of rocks. The cougar snarled and hissed at her, moving in close but not with the intention to kill. Pine's slayer knew Atabey was in heat, and the desire to mate had brought it from miles away, a desperate attempt to mate with the only female it had seen in years. Most animal species naturally found Ata's scent familiar and inviting but to felines, she was a reproductive female. Except in reality Atabey was not a cougar, and the second the cat neared her enough to sniff her fragrance, Nico leapt from behind and broke its neck.

The animal fell limp to the ground after having fought daringly for its chance to breed. Cougars were going extinct like so many other large mammals, and it was shameful to have to destroy one. After all, a desperate animal would do anything to perpetuate its genetic code. Nico shuddered with the effort to control his emotions, to contain his rage.

"Are you hurting, Ata?" He tried to seem unaware of her internal pain. "Do you want me to heal the dogs?"

The battle of the cells had taken a toll and too many of them were dying. Her insides thudded with pain, excruciating, never alleviating pain. Blood vessels circulated slowly. Plasma transportation became a critical problem. Sex pheromone made it so all she could think about was his touch. And yet, she hated herself for desiring him. The compulsion was her body's way of warning her, telling her if she did not touch Nico soon, her organs would start to shut down.

"Your few cells have slowly separated your entire life, and now they can't anymore. Fusing worsened matters. Your body knows it doesn't need to hold on to dying cells. We were supposed to be one, but for some reason we're not. You'll need my touch all the time. You need me to live, Ata." He had shackled her to him.

Her mind caught his last thought. The violation of her right to choose made her despise ever meeting him. *I hate you.* The words were clear inside his head, and they tore at his heartstrings with a force that nearly choked him. He should have waited until Ata was ready, until he had won her affection before fusing, before forcing himself upon her. He was careless, blinded by lust, by the thought of losing her. It was selfish. But how could he ever again put himself through the agony of holding her in his arms as she slowly faded, as a noose around her neck branded her skin.

"Please, let me help you." He dreaded her refusal. "You're in pain, Ata."

Atabey's chaotic mind struggled to keep it all together. Concern over his uninvited touch distressed her more than her inability to breathe properly. She turned from dog to dog, trying to figure out which canine needed her most. She crouched by Maple. The mutt neither moved nor breathed, and her coat was matted in blood. Death stamped Ata's mind.

She brushed back her blue hair and raised her head to meet Nico's gaze. *Is she?* Her large eyes were amber spheres of confusion. Her nervous hands fiddled with the hems of her ivory dress, a silk dress that gave her the aura of a glowing deity. She exuded beauty.

"Yes. Maple's dead." He hated himself just as much as she hated him. "I'm sorry I couldn't get to her in time. I'll heal the other two dogs if you like. Ash is badly wounded, but there's hardly a scratch on Oak."

Saul Leon jogged up the rocky cliff in the most doleful attempt to conceal fatigue. The clear bright sky, sunshine of a summer day was a contrast to the man's dark features. He seized, almost yanked Ata, embracing her. His heart pounded loudly in his chest. The man had worried gravely.

Nico knelt by Ash and wasted no more time repairing the dog. He wouldn't leave the coyote incomplete like he had Maple, the always limping mutt. Truthfully, Nico had generated too much energy since he first found the mutt—or since he first touched Ata. In fear of transferring too many cells and killing Maple, he had avoided fixing the leg. Ash and Oak would see different results. He repaired meticulously. The coyotes would henceforth have a fighting chance, something he never gave Maple, something he risked his own stability to make happen. The results: Nico churned with excessive amount of energy, and his phallus pulsated with a need to connect with the body whose pheromones beckoned him.

He glanced up at Atabey. "The coyotes will be okay."

"This is all your fault!" Saul spat. "We don't have time for your rafts or your wild tales. You might have Atabey and Raven convinced that you are not a demented Sorrow, that you're something else, but guess what, there isn't anything else. All you do is lie. No more. I want you to tell Ata the truth."

"I'll bury Maple as soon as I'm done checking up on Raven." Nico's desire to strangle Saul nearly destroyed his years of perfected civility. "I suggest the two of you get back to camp."

"We will go to Virginia without you, Mr. Lowell." The man clutched Ata's hand. "We do not need you."

Nico kept his expression in check, kept his own frustration at bay. "Raven will need time to heal. Are you also planning on leaving her behind?"

"Of course not." Saul dismissed Nico with a wave of his free hand, the one not crushing Atabey. "We're no longer traveling with coyotes, or any other conspicuous animal. We're not trying to draw attention to ourselves."

She shook her head and whimpered a protest.

"You're squeezing her hand, Saul."

Saul gripped harder until her wrist reddened. "We do not answer to this man, Ata."

"Why don't you let go of her." *I'm not going to ask him twice, Ata.*

She jerked her hand free and glanced at the healing coyote. Ash lay on his side, lapping his coat. Ata smiled at Oak, who patrolled the perimeter, vigilant, stubborn. Lastly, and with a twinge of pain, she studied the mangled mutt. *Maple.* Regret constricted her chest.

"You should let the coyotes go," Nico told her. "Or they will risk dying in order to protect you." He would too.

The two log rafts took an entire day to finish. While the reluctant crew relaxed and healed—not Atabey, her aches and restlessness beat at him—Nico gathered enough logs from dead trees and began the hard work of cutting and assembling. He used enough rope to support both rafts, securing them tightly in case they hit rocky waters. The next morning, they started to Crystal City. Bronte, Sable and the foal would follow by land. The animals were intelligent creatures. Sable had found camp once before and if separated, Nico was more than confident the mare could do it again.

The narrow river broke into several channels. They took the current to Virginia where steep rock cliffs concealed everything but the blazing sun. Manufactured leftovers from the industrial era cluttered the brown, shallow stream. They traveled when the sun was at its highest to avoid unwanted attention. Hundred degree temperatures and similar humidity served as a nuisance to Sorrows, but to humans it was deadly.

Nico was mindful of the extra blood circulating around Ata's vital organs, the additional plasma needed to keep her functioning, keep her cool. Perspiration no longer worked. She lost chemicals needed to support her, creating a major imbalance. Her thick blood required added pressure to keep pumping. Ata's heart strained. She rested on the raft adjacent to his, weak, fatigued and mentally unaware that her body was close to shutting down.

"Do you need me to paddle?" Raven said. "If you stare at Ata instead of the river, we might hit something." Drift-wood, rocks and other debris littered the channel.

"No." He only found it difficult to row where the water receded. "We are lucky these channels are passable."

The river sheltered many nonworking locks and dams. Men from the past had blown holes through them in order to allow access to the waterways, a convenience for present rafters.

"Do you think those houses along the coast are vacant?" she asked. "I need to stretch."

An abundance of uncut trees constituted their scenic route and the tranquil river further confirmed the regions solitude. "Did you need a quilt, Raven?"

"You gave Ata and Saul everything." Her fingers traced the flat binds of uneven logs, the raft. "We have nothing. But you, I guess, an excellent carpenter."

"Among my many accomplishments." Nico tried to seem at ease, tried to convince himself that Atabey could do without his touch. "Is your neck still throbbing?"

"It must really suck for you," she said.

"What does?"

"You're a healer."

"I don't believe that was a secret."

"You're always conscious of the changes in Ata's body." Raven examined Nico's eyes as if searching for the appropriate words to say. "It must suck to know she's in pain and you can't do anything about it."

"I can if I please."

"But you won't," she said, "because Ata doesn't want you to touch her. You have this stupid need to honor her wish. If I were you, I would heal her whether she likes it or not. If your survival depends on hers, it seems unfair for Ata to risk her own health just to punish you for whatever you did. Don't ask me how I know these things. I'm intuitive."

"You're an intelligent woman."

"What did you do to her, Nico?" she asked. "What makes her dislike your company?"

"Good question." Saul observed both the stream and the conversation from his raft. "What did you do to her, Mr. Lowell?"

Fusing was supposed to make them one. "I don't know anymore." Consequently it had the opposite effect.

"Help me!" A terrified boy waded into the stream, splashing his way toward the rafts. "Please, help me!"

Gun shots echoed through the thick forest. Heavy footfalls followed suit. A gray-haired man wearing overalls emerged from the woods. He aimed a rifle at the desperate boy and warned him to stop running. The kid continued forward, swimming. The man fired twice. One round hit the water and exploded skyward like a geyser. The second round hit the raft. Ata's raft. The logs came undone.

Nico placed faith in Saul's ability to handle the sinking 'boat' while he dived into the river, swimming toward the boy. He caught the kid and submerged his head under water when the man fired again. Rounds disturbed the tranquil stream and two of them hit Nico. He ignored the stinging ache, his heightened awareness of disturbed cells shocked into reaction. There was no time to stop and heal. He closed his mind to the pain. He severed the connection between him and Atabey, sparing her the knowledge of his disability. She had enough to worry about. Her raft had come apart.

Nico tossed the boy aside once they reached the shoreline. He turned to the shooter and charged him, slamming him to the ground. He tumbled over easily, beaten. Victory lasted for seconds. The man was up again. The probable farmer studied Nico's two bullet holes: one imbedded in his chest and the other deep inside his left leg. He smirked, grabbed his rifle, and ran head-long. He managed to ram Nico's stomach and left him breathless.

The gray-haired senior possessed the vigor of a much younger man. Hard work built strong farmers. "This ain't none of your business, boy. That there's my son I'm trying to collect." He yanked Nico by the hair, pulled his head back, and smashed his face into the ground. He kicked him, targeting the bloody chest and the broken leg.

Nico clutched the man's foot and dragged him down. He pounced on top of him with repetitive blows to his face, attacking him with frenzied anger, one punch after the other, distorting his appearance. His hammer-like fist pounded on the friable structure. The beating didn't end until there was nothing left to witness but the gurgling blood of a human unable to breath.

"Why are you trying to shoot your son?" Nico panted hard. He had never felt so exhausted in his life.

Farmers borrowed children all the time. Manual labor was a chain of command, and kids were usually at the bottom. They worked harder than their parents, worked to one day inherit land. If a mother conceived a male, the father would sell their child's labor to weaker families, families lacking boys. Unlike the females who were used for sex favors, cooking and breeding, males were best suited to work their land, other lands, any land a father traded for. It was common for children to escape their own parents, but it was unusual for a father to prefer his child dead rather than free.

Nico staggered into a sitting position, lacking the strength to continue an interrogation. "I'll give you a chance to—"

A resounding boom echoed in his ears. Blood spurted across his face.

The boy held the rifle. "He was good for nothin'." The kid had shot his own father dead in the face. "Good for nothin', I tell ya."

Nico reached for the child. "Help me stand."

"I had to do it, mister." The scrawny boy, no more than ten or eleven, was dirty and half-naked. "Pa was no good." He supported Nico's weight, prompted him to lean on his shoulder.

"Kid, are you—"

"Name's Fry, mister."

"Are you sick, Fry?" He could tell the child suffered from malaria, an endemic, his father had suffered from it as well. "Do you have a large family?"

"No, mister," the boy said, "just me and my pa."

"Good, I might be able to heal you then . . . might."

For the first time in Nico's life, he wasn't so sure if he could heal himself let alone anyone else.

BOWIE

The town buzzed with music and laughter. Aromas of baked goods drifted from all sides of Glasgow, a rural community that celebrated like it was its last days on the planet. Giggling girls in colorful dresses pursued gracious partners in lively dances. Children ran free, mothers laughed and gossiped. Fathers displayed their skills in lawn games, their roars of triumph filling the air. Teenage boys drank and stumbled in the chaos of their mischief. Light from lanterns, torches, and candles flickered in the same lively spirit of the town, dazzling the sober and inspiring the introvert. Houses endured the dark and empty, but the streets, the music halls, bars, gyms, and stadiums were surrounded by floods of people enjoying their Saturday night.

Bowie called the caramel-colored jugs bourbon whiskey. He had already chugged down two bottles when he asked Camden to try some. The liquor smelled like cinnamon spices and vanilla, tasted like burnt wood. His throat still burned several minutes after swallowing a few sips.

"You have to get shit drunk, Butthole." Bowie kicked the back of Camden's knee, making him buckle. "Don't lock your legs and you won't fall next time." His laughter was muffled by the sounds of cheery folk songs. The town's people clapped and sang along. Joshua was missing among the musicians.

"Where's your leader, Bowie?" Camden's scraped knees ached from the fall, and he found it difficult to stand up again. He kept stumbling. "I thought he liked the festivities?"

Bowie offered a hand and pulled him up. "Don't know where he is, but we're leaving tomorrow. Isaac wants his kids back home, so let's have fun tonight."

"I thought we've been having fun since seven." Midnight drew near. "Do you think Ida's okay?"

"We don't need that cunt. Just me and you, Butthole." Bowie put an arm around Camden and leaned on him for support. "Let's take a walk somewhere quiet. This music's giving me a headache."

They left another outdoor barbecue, one of the many places Bowie and Camden had stopped by to drink and eat. Ida had spent most of the night with them and at one point allowed Camden the rare pleasure of touching, pinching, and kissing her. Bowie detested the girl and degraded her with persistent slurs. Ida retaliated by shoving him. He smacked her to the ground and watched as she ran away, massaging her cheek. She had promised to go to Joshua with the complaint.

"Why did, why did you hit her?" Camden rubbed his beating temples. "You antagonized her first."

"She's a spoiled whore, daddy's little girl. Thinks she has a right to disrespect men because of her daddy, but I don't care. I'll remind her she's just a cunt. Cunts don't have a say over cocks." The blond man squeezed Camden's neck, hard, possessive, as if to remind him that he too was a female part. "Did I ever tell you I used to be a farmer's son?"

"N-o," Camden slurred. "I don't think you've told me much about you."

He grinned, taking Camden's face and pushing it against his own. "I used to be Isaac's favorite." His breath reeked of alcohol. "Isaac liked me a lot, thought I was a cute kid, had me trained to be more than a soldier."

"What happened with that?" He needed room to breathe, but Bowie would not let go of his face. "Did he stop liking you?"

"I grew older, and his teeny girl grew tits." Bowie dragged his lazy feet, picking up dust along the way. "Isaac gave me to Joshua who hates everybody, half the time doesn't know where he is, or what he's doing. Joshua doesn't like me, Cam. He doesn't care for any of us except you, and you'll be the one he teaches."

"If I had become a rebel leader, you would've been my second in command." Camden lied and tried not to cough into the rebel's mouth. Dust mites scratched his throat.

"Is that what Joshua wants you for?" The man's bloodshot eyes shone with a strange joy. "He thinks you're smart, don't he?"

"I think he does." Camden was proud of the fact until Bowie raised a speculative eyebrow. "Or maybe not, perhaps he wants a replacement."

"Replacement for what? Joshua's twenty-seven and doesn't seem to get any older," he said. "You know, Orion thinks he might be a Sorrow."

"He's not, trust me, not the way he loathes them." Camden lowered his head and wriggled out of Bowie's arm lasso.

The drunken man hardly noticed the absence of his human cane. "You want to be a rebel leader, Butthole?"

"I don't want the responsibility."

"And what did Joshua have to say about that?"

"He said I'll change my mind real soon."

"Will you?"

"No. I don't think I want to lead."

"If you're a leader everyone has to follow your orders," Bowie said. "Why wouldn't you want subordinates?"

The word subordinates was too grand for a rebel. Camden wondered if Bowie was not as stupid as he looked. "I'm fine hanging out with you."

"You know, Cam, if Joshua says you'll change your mind, chances are you will."

"Why do you think so?"

"He knows things."

"Rebels won't ever respect me as a leader, Bowie. You know that."

Bowie grinned and then tripped on a rock, nearly falling. He laughed, turning to Camden with a plastered smirk on his face. "Have you ever seen a Sorrow, Cam?"

"Wasn't the Carrier girl, the one with the black—"

"The blue-haired one is something altogether strange."

"I never saw her."

"I did. She's as scary as an alien." He folded his arms, pretended to shiver. "Her big yellow eyes glowed in the dark. She smelled different, not human, almost like an animal. Before your brother knocked me out and ran away with Ida, the night I had to lock Blue in one of the bedrooms, I heard her murmuring to herself, right before Toady got messed up and the Carrier chick escaped. I went to warn Joshua about everything, but he acted abnormal."

"Abnormal?" Camden teased. "You say it like he's ever normal."

"He was crazier than usual, turning around in circles, mumbling phrases in another language." Bowie's voice lowered, ominous. "He cursed at the wind, stabbed at it. He knelt on the floor, and I swear to you, I heard him sobbing. I asked if he was okay, and he glanced at me with his cold eyes as clear as day, but it wasn't day time. He told me to kill Blue. He told me she had to die in order for us to live, and then he abandoned the house, desperate like he couldn't breathe or something. Orion ended up hanging the girl."

"She's not dead," Camden said. "Didn't she escape?"

"Oh yeah, you were locked up weren't you? She didn't escape. The healer came for her. We didn't see him enter the house or leave. Ida, the traitorous whore, served as a nice distraction. If she wasn't Isaac's daughter, we'd killed her that night." Bowie turned to a figure jogging toward them. He reached for the rifle strapped to his back and aimed at the shadow. "Hold it right there or I'll shoot!"

Dagan stepped into the moonlight with a long blade in hand. "It's ready, the Laymon home."

"Oh yeah, I almost forgot." Bowie looked Camden over, scrutinized him as if realizing his drinking buddy was a prisoner, not an ally. He shoved him. "Get up, Cam."

Camden stumbled. "What did I do?"

"Come with us," he ordered.

The Laymon household was on a quiet street ten minutes away from the nearest festivity. Dagan pushed the door open. They stepped into the light. Several candles centered on Mia, illuminating her slick naked body. She sat bound to a wooden chair, hands behind her back and legs spread apart. A gray cloth gagged her mouth. She twisted and rocked, trying to remove herself from the hand ropes. Noises came out of her muzzled lips, frantic grunts, pleading.

"Does anybody know we're here?" Bowie asked the short man.

"Nope." Dagan smirked, massaging his blade, leisurely unaware. "I told Wafer he could have a turn if he—"

"That twerp ain't getting a—"

"I know, I know, that's what I told him so he'd keep a look out." Dagan headed across the room and hid behind Mia. He tugged at the rope, checked its sturdiness. "She's good and ready." He gave Camden a peculiar grin as he clutched the knife's long silvery handle.

"Tell me." Bowie slapped Camden's back, jolting him forward. "What do you think of her, Cam?"

Mia was a homely girl of dark hair and brown eyes, slender and tall, a quiet and concentrated knitter. She had only ever addressed Camden whenever her parents lingered in the same room.

"I thought Joshua didn't want anyone messing with the locals." His pants itched. "Aren't we supposed to leave on a happy note?"

"We are leaving on a 'happy note'." Bowie laughed, pushing Camden forward. "Go ahead, Butthole. I know you like this one."

Dagan glanced at the girl and then up at Bowie. "The prisoner gets her first?"

"Look at that boner," Bowie said. He unbuckled Camden's belt and pulled down his pants. "Step out of them. You're going to need a liberated wiener if you want to fuck her."

Camden's upset stomach made him wary of the stale air, the nebulous living room. "Don't you guys want her first?" He turned to Bowie. "What's happening?"

"Your dick's a decent size for someone as stunted as you." The man gawked, intrigued. "Go feel her, Butthole. I know you want to."

Dagan's grin resembled a crescent moon; the curved lips tracked Camden's every move. "Sure, go ahead."

"I don't know about this." Camden tasted the bile in the back of his throat. "She's Mr. Laymon's—"

"Listen, Butthole. You can't have Ida. She's Isaac's daughter. You better forget about that broad and concentrate on the one in front of you." Bowie lifted Camden's shirt. "Let's get you good and naked."

"I think he likes you undressing him." Dagan's laughter was haughty. "Do you need Bowie to tell you were to stick it, too?"

Camden moved away from the blond man's exploring hands. He took off his own shirt, gasped, breathed, and staggered toward Mia. Her teary eyes begged for help. He had none to give her. Or himself. He was hot and uncomfortable, her sweaty breast and stiff nipples gestured to him, asked for his mouth. He reached for them, cupping each one. She squirmed. The feel of her soft skin, soft mounds filling his hands surpassed any other sensation. She heaved and Camden almost ejaculated.

He knelt and pinched her right thigh when she tried to close her legs. He had never seen the female part up close, or smelled the insides of a woman. He took a quick whiff of fresh muskiness. Not bad. She was wet, gleaming with moisture. It amazed him how much a female's nether region reminded him of ripe fruit.

"Are you gonna stare at it all day or what?" Dagan dragged the chair away, came around, and blocked the better view, pressing the sharp blade to Camden's throat. "Turn, prisoner."

"W-hat are you doing?" Camden's turnabout brought him face to face with a fully erect penis.

"Put it in your mouth, Cam." Bowie's glazed eyes stared down at him. "Don't make me have to push it in. Do it on your own and do it right. If you bite me, Dagan will slit your jugular. Do you understand?"

"Why are you—" His sudden fury gurgled, his mouth watered with foams of anger. "Don't do this! I thought you were my friend."

"Friends pleasure each other." Bowie traced Camden's lips with his fingers and parted them with his fist. "Open wide, swallow, tickle the balls too, and don't make me ask you twice."

Humiliation bubbled to the surface, the right insults couldn't be articulated properly and so he sucked hard, sucked from frustration, betrayal, and an incredible urge to hurt Dagan. He wanted to stop the man's mocking laughter. He wanted to break the arm that held the knife to his throat, a sharp blade that scratched his skin every time he pulled Bowie in and out of him. Irritation filled his chest and then his mouth overflowed with a gluey substance.

Dagan removed the knife from his neck. "It's my turn, Bowie."

"Shut up, Dag." Bowie's clammy palms found Camden's cheeks. "Open up. I got other places to go."

Camden opened his mouth and spat semen. "Can . . . can . . . I stand?" He tried to get up, but his knees trembled.

"No. Get on all fours, Butthole." Bowie yanked him by the hair, turned him around, and pushed him to the ground. "Guess where I'm going next?"

SHAME

In a thicket along the trail edge, shiny berry clusters thrived near sharp spines. Raven reached through the gaps, avoiding thorns, for a taste of the deep, black delicacies. She stuffed her mouth with as many as she could, her lips and hands stained purple. The sweet juices filled her mouth, the seeds she ignored, not bothered by the crunch when thirst and hunger could be satisfied with a single patch of berries.

"Do you think you're the only one who's ever hungry?" Saul nudged Raven to the side and viciously tugged at the stems as if pulling irritating ticks. "How many do you want?" He turned around. "Darn it, Atabey!"

"She's probably off to the forest again." Raven sat on the mushy ground. She strained her eyes to look up at Saul. The glaring sun nearly blinded her. "This journey has been tiresome for everyone. Leave her be."

"Where are the healer and the boy?" Saul paced up and down the dirt track. "We shouldn't be wasting time."

His purple lips made Raven grin. "We lost one raft, yours. Nico and the boy are searching for logs."

"We should travel by foot, like I said." He reached for his back sling, assuring himself the rifle was still there. "He's burning daylight."

"He was shot twice with that rifle you now carry, Saul."

"He's a healer."

"Healers still bleed."

"He should have minded his own business."

"You see, Saul, that's the difference between you and Nico. He cares about people. You don't."

"Let's be honest, neither do you, Raven."

"Honest, yes, let's be honest—"

The bushes to the right of the trail shifted.

Raven sprang to her feet, on guard. Fry emerged, panting and carrying a handful of lumber. "Jeez, kid. You scared me. Where's Nico?"

The dirty boy wore nothing but torn, denim shorts. He smirked at Raven. "Nico was a finding his horses. He was tired, ma'am." He dropped the lumber to wipe his brown-stained cheeks. "Is that there blackberries?"

"Yes, help yourself, Fry." She smiled as the boy savaged the bush and stuffed the berries into his mouth.

What an odd name. Fry—fried mushrooms. Raven mused to herself.

Beats Bake, the voice said.

How about you? She asked, *what's your name?*

If you go to Virginia, you'll find your son. That's all you need to know. He paused for a brief moment as if considering his words. *Listen, I'm not asking you to trust me. I'm asking you to trust that your son will be there.*

How do you know this?

Right now, I don't.

Then why do you need me to get to Arlington?

Saul's the only one who knows where the facility is located. I've never been there myself.

Of course you haven't, she said. *That would be too convenient.*

Raven, keep Ata near you.

Ata appeared from the woodland quiet and unconcerned, prancing about like a furry creature. She hadn't spoken in two days, and no one asked her to do otherwise.

Saul's frown consumed his face in a twitching of muscles that resembled a stroke. "Atabey, where have you been?"

She ignored him and scurried to the blackberry thicket. Fry growled at her like an untrained dog. Ata smiled at the boy. He continued to stuff his mouth with berries and offered Ata the squashed fruits in his other hand. The offer resembled an afterthought, an involuntary act of sharing. As soon as Ata reached for the blackberries, the boy jumped her. His puny body managed to knock her to the ground. Once down, he scratched at her like a cat, clawing at her eyes and face, a savage boy, angry, and desperate. His hands balled into fists that furiously struck Ata's face.

Raven towered over Fry and pulled him as hard as she could. The child was small, not weak. He swung at her and scraped her jaw. She stumbled backwards, returned, and grabbed him by his feet. Fry kicked. His right foot connected with her stomach. She doubled over, gasping for air. Raven breathed, recovered and searched desperately for a useful object. She grabbed the nearest rock and weighed it in her hands, assuring its density was just right—not big enough to kill the boy.

A deafening shot blasted Fry backwards on top of Raven. She scrambled to her feet and noticed the open wound. Blood gushed out the dark hole in the middle of the boy's chest. She pressed on the gouge with both hands, resisting the urge to scream. Ata disregarded her own bruises to assist Raven. She took off her shirt, tore it to shreds, and covered the gash, replacing Raven's shaky hands. Raven asked Ata the silent question. Ata answered by shaking her head. No. Nico would not arrive in time to save the boy.

Damn you, Voice.

I told you, he said, *to keep an eye on Ata.*

You should have told me to protect Fry. His lack of compassion nauseated her.

Raven, I didn't know Saul would actually shoot.

But you suspected as much.

He prolonged a sigh meant to buy him enough time to form an excuse. *The boy's not my problem, and I'm not making excuses.*

Fry was a kid, a kid!

He's not your kid.

Get out. She bit the inside of her cheeks until the pain traveled to her head. *You should have warned me.*

You can't order me out every time you get angry. He responded in a piercing pitch, agitated. *You're being dramatic and ridiculous. Why are you growing so soft, Raven? A few days ago you wouldn't have cared.*

I care now.

Let this one go. You need Saul.

No! I don't. Tears clouded her vision, her mind.

"You cold imbecile." She regarded Saul with scorn.

The smoke of the man's rifle was evidence enough. "That boy was a liability, Raven."

She stood. "You had no right."

"He would have slaughtered us all."

"I had it handled."

"Slaughtered us in our sleep," he insisted.

"A kid?" Raven heaved with a fury she had never known before. "You were afraid of a damn kid?"

"This is not about—" Before he could finish his sentence, she lunged at him, striking, kicking and scratching, trying to rip his eyes out of their sockets, blind him, the spineless coward. Saul struck her with the butt of his rifle, pushing her back to the ground, aiming at her head. "Try that again and I will shoot you, too."

"You would, you coward." She wanted to snatch the rifle and waste the last of the bullets on him. "I'll keep coming at you until one of us is dead."

"I guess that'd be you." He targeted her forehead.

Ata stepped in front of Raven, not saying anything but watching Saul. The boy's blood dripped from her hands. She inhaled, gazed at her palms and then accusingly stared back at Saul.

He lowered his rifle. "I wasn't going to actually do it, Ata. Don't judge me. We will dig the kid a grave."

"His name was Fry." Raven spat. "You killed him. You bury him."

"It will take all day if I do it on my own. We don't have—"

"I'm going to wait for Nico at the camp. We'll go when he's ready to go. You, Saul, are the guide and nothing more."

"This whole thing was my idea and if—"

"Guide and nothing more."

The crowding trees hid the dwindling sun, and the dark earth came alive with the bugs attracted to the fire. Nico huddled near the flames, his sun-washed face glowing. His lips were drawn and the weight of his hunched posture rested on one leg. He struggled with the task of breathing, taking gulps of air infrequently and rarely exhaling.

"Do you mind if I huddle next to you?" she asked.

"I'm sorry about Fry."

"You're not the one who needs to be sorry."

"Is Saul digging a grave?"

"Yes. Alone. The bastard." Her anger lessened as her concern switched to Nico. "How are you? You don't look so good."

He studied the fire, concentrating on the cracks and specks of the orange flame. "The bullets are out, outside wounds are closed."

"What about the inside?"

"The inside needs some more work, but I can't fully . . . I'll heal in due time." He teased the swaying flames with a stick.

"Nico," she said. "If you need to release energy or something, you can give me some. I don't know how it works, but I'll take however much relieves you."

"You can't," he whispered.

"Does it have to be Ata?"

Nico's peridot colored eyes focused on her with all the passion of a permanent craving. "Raven." Her name was a gentle stroke, and her body shuddered in response. "I need to be alone right now."

Raven couldn't disregard the intensity of his gaze, the pain his words carried. "I don't think that's what you really want." She held his hand, tight.

His body ached and burned for her. He wanted to undress, feel, touch, and caress her. The urge, the desire to lay her on the grass while exploring her insides for hours on end was primordial. The need to forever mix, crave, and feel her silken skin, taste her honey lips, her other lips, roused him. His tongue salivated at the thought of savoring her breast, lapping each nipple until they hardened to dots of chocolate. He would lick every hollow, every ridge of her body. She was his and he needed her, wanted her with a force that could summon lightning, with potency capable of creating rain. Their bodies would sweat in a contact of endless fusing, endless sex.

Raven gasped and cried out as the burst, sparks of mini-shocks, consumed her body. Her orgasm was a result of Nico's need to rid himself of an insatiable thirst for Ata. Their minds had merged. His thoughts had become hers and the shame, the intrusion of having experienced another human's primal urge to mate was embarrassing. Raven couldn't make herself look at the man whose stare set her body ablaze.

"Raven." His hoarse voice grated her skin, dominated her mind. "I couldn't help that."

She cleared her throat and kept her eyes on the dirt. "I shouldn't have touched—"

Her pale sapphire dress, a short lacy thing, hardly covered her thighs, and clung to her shape, to the swell of her breast. Her soft tawny skin was luminescent. Her blue, wild hair shifted with the wind as sea waves. Her eyes were the color of dusk, vibrant, large, consuming him with a twinkle of knowledge, an air of a fairy tale, a nymph, beautiful and ever-present in his mind.

Raven jerked her hand away from Nico and stared up at Ata; she had wandered over to them from the stream. "Is Saul done yet?"

She shook her head with the exaggerated movements of a child.

"Are the quilts dry?" Raven's cheeks burned red. She suspected Ata was scrutinizing her with distrust, disgust, and maybe hate. "Ata?"

Nico continued to tease the fire with his stick. "You know why I can't heal, Atabey. And no, I can't think about anything else."

The girl had not uttered a sound.

He mimicked her silence.

The tension in the air grew hot and oppressive. Raven couldn't take it anymore. She rose and walked away, not giving the humiliating event another thought. She would sleep it off, forget.

He doesn't want you, you know.

Shut up.

You know he doesn't, Raven. He makes you act different, humane, but I call it weak.

She refused to listen. *I was trying to ease him.*

Keep telling yourself that.

Just stop.

You like him. He took advantage of that.

I don't like him. Her son was the only person who mattered to her. *And no one is taking advantage of anybody.*

Oh, really? Seems to me like he was horny and you knew it.

Don't do this to me right now.

I'll shame you until you act right, until you realize what's important.

Raven reached her side of the camp, a dark side away from the others. She settled on a grassy bed in the middle of a circle of trees.

Are you hiding?

You need to stop heckling me, Voice.

Do I? His taunts orbited around her mind like a pestering fly.

She sighed. *I should just leave him, them, all of them.*

No, you still need Saul, and Saul won't go anywhere without Ata.

Does Ata know?

Know what?

Don't pretend you don't know what I mean.

He laughed. *Of course she does.*

Does she hate me?

Do you care?

I think I do.

Well then, ask her yourself. She's looking at you.

Ata towered over Raven and watched her quietly.

"Did you follow me here?" Raven said, studying the girl's glowing gaze. "You know, those orbs of yours seem to hover in the air when it's dark out. Did you know that?"

Ata's mouth remained closed, but her eyes roamed as if absorbing a view larger than the one beneath her.

"Are you still not talking?" Raven adjusted her damp quilt and stretched the fabric into a decent sleeping size. "I'm going to snooze now."

"He's fond of you," Ata said. "Did you know?"

"Listen, you must wonder why—"

"I saw him in a dream once, but in my dream he wasn't a man, he was a bird, a raven."

"Okay, are you perhaps talking about Alexander?"

She shook her head. "He helped me once. Now he wants me to help you."

"Ata, you are aware that I don't know what you're talking—"

"I promised I would," the girl insisted. "This is why I left Saul."

"Did Saul ever tell you about your evil brother, the one trying to kill you?" Raven was not going to even try to process the girl's crazy tales. "Are you so gullible anyone can tell you where to go and what to do, Ata?"

She narrowed her eyes, dimming the surrounding light. "Are you?"

"I know who I'm looking for," she said. "You simply go with the flow."

Ata's smile was ingenuous and full of riddles. "I still need to find Zemi, for your sake."

"I suggest you worry about yourself." Raven made no attempt to conceal the bitterness in her voice. "You're the one who's going to get us all killed."

"Do you blame me for Fry?"

She glared at her.

"I'll obey next time and maybe," Ata paused as a whimper distorted her words, "Maybe no one else will die because of me."

"I'm not trying to attack you, Ata." Raven hated everyone responsible for her son's disappearance, his absence. She hated the rebels more than anything else on the planet, but the blue-haired girl was just a girl, another survivor. Despising her accomplished nothing. "You don't have to listen to Saul, Nico, or the voice—"

"What voice?" Her eyes widened.

Raven glanced up at the pale moon. She wanted the day done with. "There's a voice that talks to me. I used to think I was insane, but if Sorrows and all that other crap exists, why not a voice inside my head, right?"

"Oh, yeah, him." Ata wiped her tear-stained cheeks. "He's the reason I brought you oranges."

"You know, Ata, I've never thought to ask you before. I think he peruses your thoughts just as much as he does mine, and I just never really thought to ask. Who is the voice, Ata? What do you know about him?"

"The Sorrow—" The girl stopped, internalized, her eyes scanned the surroundings. She glanced behind her as if hearing something far off, something no one but she could recognize.

Raven ignored Ata's abrupt dismay. "I know he's a Sorrow, but what else—"

"No. No. No." Tears spilled down her cheeks, drowning her face. "I have to go," she said, desperate to head toward the imaginary noise.

"Ata, I need you to tell me what else you know about the voice. I already know he's a Sorrow."

The girl was racing away when she yelled out, "He's not *a* Sorrow, Raven. He's *the* Sorrow."

GROTTO

She hurried because the waves and particles, the vacuum of power pulling and pushing against all the forces in existence, slowly disintegrated. His total mass energy would always endure, but his human vessel would not. Nico could transfer energy by touch. Every force emitted, every particle consumed was thermal heat, electromagnetic radiation, a sort of kinetic energy, difficult to understand or put into words. Nevertheless, Atabey finally understood: what Nico stored inside his corporal being had at one point efficiently transformed into a human—a fading one.

Nico collapsed. He was too weak to shield his pain from her, his undoing, his slow and excruciating death.

"What do you need me to do?" Her tormented eyes struck at his humanity, and he should have never let her go. "Tell me what to do, Nico. Please . . ."

In his dreams, Atabey was the spirit of scattered red insects, the howling gray wolves. She was the voice of the green hills and the blue of the water. She reflected on the yellow corn, yellow because his sun reflected on her. She was nature's daughter and she rolled around in dirt. Her brown skin tasted like every succulent berry, apple, fruit, every orange peel. Jewels belonged to her eyes and minerals lived inside her skin. Coyotes, turtles, doves and olms were a part of her soul, her friends. She painted and decorated their home with flowers. She was every daisy, every rose. Atabey was Earth.

He woke remembering little of the previous night, yet his body lived free of the constant strain of binding energy. Nico breathed a gulp of dense air. There was a stream nearby. He lay inside a cave, near the mouth. Glaring morning sun bathed him and the dewy leaves of the adjacent trees, particles of rain, sparkled like diamonds. The soil beneath him resembled the rest of the cave, dark, damp. The blemished walls creased and layered in a multitude of earth tones. Nico inhaled again, taking in the aroma of the previous night's rain.

Ata's small body pressed against his, her top hand lay on his chest. She was warm, healthy. He turned to her, instinctively checking for her wounds. All of his were gone. She had cured them both, her kind touch. Ata had slept beside Nico for a full night, grasping him, never letting go. His energy had poured—was still pouring—into her, melting layers of her skin.

He sighed and pushed a gentle finger inside her mouth, choosing her parted lips as a new entry to heal her bruises and burns. Energy traveled into her system, naturally. Her body stirred in answer to his intrusion and before he could remove himself, she woke. Her large, amber eyes caught him like a rabbit trapped by the glow of a lantern. He pulled back, apologized with his gaze.

Her exasperation made her skin itch with a strange need, strange to her, not to him. She scratched the hollow of her neck. Her body was a snug and foreign place. She took back the arm that had enfolded him and inspected it for the burns she swore had marred her skin the night before. All gone. She sneered at Nico. Her breast ached. She blamed him for her racing heart, for her heavy breathing. Ata stifled an urge to scream.

"You had a bad night, Atabey. I apologize." His voice licked at her insides and she couldn't stand it. "Please, don't do this to yourself."

Why do you insist on reading my mind? The desire to rip his pants off the way she had removed his shirt on the previous night consumed her. *I don't want you.* She lied. *I hate you.* Another lie. Ata's inability to suppress the fear of losing him shamed her. She wanted to cry because she needed him and would forever need him whether he hurt her or not. *Raven will call me gullible and Saul . . . Saul . . .*

"You shouldn't care what he thinks," he said, reading her thoughts, unveiling her passions. "Ata, you're in heat. This is happening to you because we're together and because your cells are still dying. Don't torture yourself."

"I . . . want . . ." Her first lucent teardrop landed on her lip. He wanted to drink it, drink her. "I want you all the time," she whimpered.

"And I want you, Ata, a little desperately if you recall the incident with Raven." He smiled.

Her eyes brimmed with tears. "You wouldn't let me help you last night, then you passed out, you mumbled in my head, and then your body shut down. It rained. You were feverish. I couldn't carry you off the ground, I had to drag you to this cave, my back hurt, and you were cold, and I thought you were dead. I was so scared." She was out of breath by the time she paused. "I was terrified that you'd died."

He restrained the glee from his own mind. Nico was pleased she could feel so strongly about him. "I'm better now." He lowered his head close to hers, near enough to touch her. "I want to kiss you."

"No. Don't you dare." Her heart somersaulted, her insides turned to slush. Her hot bloodstream rushed through her veins in every direction. *Yes. Go ahead. Please.* "Should we go find Raven and Saul?" she mumbled instead.

Nico grinned and answered her spoken question with a mental shrug. The others were asleep. She knew it as well as he did. Before she could ask another pointless question, he kissed her. Her response was a compliant tongue. Time halted then, vanished. Her tellurian taste existed only to addict him, grounding him to Earth. Foreign harmonies boomed in his ears. His swollen muscles ached with need, his mouth watered with hunger. Bright colors twirled all around him. Electricity left his body in soft waves, torrents not meant to scrape but tickle.

He raised his head, held her eyes captive. "I dreamt about you."

Atabey batted her wet lashes in an attempt to regain a sense of self. "So did I." She adjusted her head, reliving her stiff neck. "I think I know what we are now."

Nico straightened his posture and cradled her head to his lap. "What are we, Ata?"

The sky and the earth, the energy all around us. We are energy. We are alive. We are the rocks, the trees, every living organism surrounded by We. We are the sand and the sea. We have existed for billions of years. We have seen the earth develop and grow. We have experienced human evolution, but we are not a species. I was born once. You are older than me. I was in love with Earth. You were bored with the breeze.

I was never bored with you, Atabey.

"I wanted you to remember how to feel again," she said. "I got lost in the chemistry of humanity centuries ago. You came down here to get me back, take me home. I don't want to go home, Nico. As a human, you feel again. You used to call them primitive sentiments, but they consume you now. That's all I ever wanted, for you to cherish me again."

Nico had clouted her with his winds, twisted her skin with every tornado, disturbed her with every typhoon and scarred her with every lightning strike, but still, he had always loved her. His human heart wanted to burst, all the organs blasting to the cavern walls. The reality that he could never take her home again, not for a long time, angered him. She was stuck in the chemistry of Homo sapiens. She was dying. For every . . . born, her stability suffered. They would never be able to abandon their mortal bodies, not until . . . the end of the . . . no more.

"What are you not saying?" Her hands moved over and behind her head, the only part of her body not craving his touch. "Are you disappointed in me, Nico? I stuck us here."

"I chose to come for you." It occurred to him: he had inhabited human bodies many times before. "There's a lot I understand now, Atabey. Your touch brings back memories. You should touch me more often."

You should maybe touch me. Trace me, Nicolas.

Ah, you searched my mind for a proper name. He allowed his churning energy to escape him through kisses that provoked her body to quiver, desire more. His hands ran up and down her arms, her buttery soft skin. Her breast pressed into his chest, a rubbing sensation. Her mouth gaped for him.

He stared at her chest, his mind failed to ask the question. He lowered the straps of her dress and gazed at her breasts, waiting for her to cover them up. When she didn't, he bent to kiss them. Her nipples hardened inside his mouth. He stiffened. There was no going back. "Stop me now if want this to end." He removed her dress completely, discarding it to the side, joyful she wore no underwear.

She shivered, writhing on the cavern floor, opening her legs to him. But her mind protested. Memories of teeth piercing her flesh, her lungs beating louder than her heart, the brute pounding into her body over and over again, tearing her insides, slamming her to the ground, disregarding her screams, not hearing them . . .

His mouth wandered over her figure, from chest to navel, to hands that gently traveled down her legs. His tongue found her trembling hips. He stroked her inner thighs, careful with his fingers. He touched her gently.

She bunched his hair, forcing him to look up at her.

"I'm not going to hurt you, Ata." Nico followed the trail to her lower lips, the ones eagerly waiting for his mouth to drink, feast, and celebrate.

Her sudden climax nearly severed his whole structure, and he needed to get away from the beatings, the aftershocks of her pulses. Nico dripped in sweat, taut with the need to have a turn, but no, not yet. It didn't matter that her orgasm rivaled anything he could ever have anticipated, or that her mind shared the experience with him. His body wanted a turn and he was afraid of himself, afraid for her.

Nico removed his jeans. They felt tight. "I need to fuse, now." He spread her thighs apart with his knees. *Don't push.* He plunged in a frenzy of lust and need. *Get out.* He tried to be gentle, pleading his body to ease up. *No more.* Her snug warmth egged him on. *Don't do this.* He stretched her insides, forced them to adjust to his width. *Slow down.* He was invading her again. *Slow down.* He pushed harder. *Pull out now.*

"Nico." Ata stared up at him, at his body towering over hers. "It's okay. You're not hurting me." Her trust was there, soothing, calming.

He breathed slowly, examined her eyes, not her mind. He wanted to see the fear gone from her amber gaze, and he wouldn't continue until she was ready. His body pinned hers down after all; his weight molded her to the soil. Atabey, however, responded by thrusting upwards, startling him for a moment. She had taken the first step to a sound fuse, driving into him, setting the tempo that would guide them the rest of the way.

His firm strokes had her moaning, aching with the same wild need. He moved his head toward her breast just as her hot muscles clenched him, extracting power from him, demanding he give it up. Nico couldn't hold back any longer. His body surged, his stomach churned. Energy flowed out of him in waves, restoring his stability and fixing her anatomy. Fusing was about equalizing, the need was always strong.

In the dark shadows of a murky grotto, traces of rock crystals bended on all sides of the compact walls. Sunlight poured into the stream from a slight opening on the cavern's ceiling, lighting the water like a candle so it was golden, boiling around her floating figure. The running stream echoed throughout the walls and the bats squeaked. He had crawled over rocks, mud, sinking further down and going deeper where he found the waist-high underground river. It amazed him how the water bubbled and foamed around Atabey, her temperature had risen to dangerous levels.

Ata had trusted him not to hurt her even as he heated her core. Her body had shut down. Nonetheless, the lapping tongues of water would ease her discomfort while he examined her insides. Practice makes perfect. He would get fusing right, eventually.

"What happened?" Her words bounced off the walls. She was startled by the sound of her own voice, frightened by the soil missing underneath her feet. "I can't see." She sank and needlessly splashed. The water was not high enough to drown her.

He realized her problem. "You can't swim?"

"No." She found his shoulders and held on to him like a scared cat, her fingers dug into his skin. "I can't see either."

"Are you sure?" He tried to shield the annoyance from his tone. "Maybe you should try opening your eyes."

She did so, not fully understanding why the suggestion hadn't occurred to her before. "Where are we?"

"Deep inside the cave you found," he said. "The water should be cold but it's warm. I thought you'd like that."

"Did . . ." The idea slipped away from her. "Do the others know where we are?"

Nico was not happy. "You don't remember, do you?"

"Can we 'fuse' again?" One of her hands reached under water and found him; he thickened in her grip. "I think sex is amazing with you."

He removed himself from her, from her memory lapse. "Do you know what we are, Ata? Do you remember our conversation?"

She examined his gaze, his thoughts, trying to extract the answer from him. There was nothing. He had shut her out. "Please don't do that to me, Nico. It scares me when you're angry."

"I'm not angry." He was furious. "How much control does he have over you?"

Her head tilted to the side, her amber eyes glowed in the darkness of the cave. They always shone in the dark. "Who are you talking about?"

"The Sorrow who enters your mind whenever he pleases," he said, swimming further away from her, knowing his rallied voltage could electrocute them both while in water. "Who is he, Atabey?" The question came across as an accusation and since he had closed his mind to her, Ata wouldn't be able to guess what troubled him. "You told Raven he was *the* Sorrow. Did he tell you that?"

"No, he—"

"What does he want from you?"

"Nothing from me," she answered. "He wants Raven."

Nico wanted him dead, the urge irked him. "What does he want from Raven?"

"Help her find—"

"Where can I find him, think?"

"He's not here."

"This is important, Ata. Think."

Her eyes watered and her hands came up to cover her bare breast. The stream was no longer warm to her. "Why are you interrogating me?" She bit at the inside of her cheeks in an effort to suppress a cry. "Why are you shutting me out?"

"Because you won't shut *him* out," he hissed. "You're giving me no choice but to close my mind to you. I won't let that thing have access to me."

"He's not a thing." Her need to protect the Sorrow incensed Nico to heights only contained when he stepped out of the water, which confused Atabey. "He was the only one who heard me scream when I was trapped inside a bubble. That's all I remember from my childhood. I screamed and he heard. He helped Saul hear, too. He's a good Sorrow, Nico."

"You don't know that."

"Why do you hate them so much?"

"Ata—"

"Why do you hate Sorrows so much?" she asked. "What have they ever done to you?"

"They shouldn't exist. They make it hard for you to do so, for you to remember simple actions like opening your eyes when you wake up. They boggle your mind and extract from it."

"Saul and Raven are Sorrows, too. They're just people." The cold licks of the water scratched like sandpaper. Ata wanted her clothes back. She wanted out of the cave. "We're not afraid of people."

"You've cared about these people for a long time now, Atabey. I allowed you to have your fun, but now it is time for us to go home. Alexander was right, you know?"

"No," she said. "I don't know."

"I have to get rid of them, every single last one of them." Nico inhaled the dense air of the cave and exhaled at the sight of Ata's trembling dismay. "All Sorrows have to die."

PART THREE

HELL

Bran was a peculiar little boy, short for his age and mute. After reading many medical books, Camden came to the conclusion the boy suffered from a developmental disorder. His brain illness affected his social and communication skills. But Bran did not exhibit the average tell-tale signs. No strange twitches or habits controlled him. The six-year-old conducted himself quite sane. However, his enormous black eyes never concentrated on a single face for more than a few seconds. The rare occasion Bran did look up, his gaze hinted to unknown knowledge, secrets he kept to himself. Mother would have called him a handsome young man.

Camden had not thought about his mother in a long time. He missed her, missed her more than he missed Pat and Gad. He missed his sister, too. Often, he wondered whether she enjoyed her new home, her arranged marriage. Was her new husband good to her? Some farmers and peasants still possessed strong values ingrained in them from centuries of practice. Pat and Gad had indulged in bad behavior, but Mother and Sister exemplified goodness.

He sat on one of the many twin beds in the nursery. Not far from him, Bran played on the carpet with a toy tractor. Their tranquil morning lasted a mere two hours before the door flew open. Ida walked in wearing a striking, beaded, red dress that carefully outlined the curves of her body. She was decorated in jewelry, and her cheeks and lips were rosier than usual.

"Father will see you now," she said. "Come, Cam, if you behave and Father likes you, he may let you marry me."

The bittersweet news stung him. If he married the daughter of a rebel general, he would have to commit to rebel life. He couldn't do it. "What about Bran?"

Ida glanced at the boy. "What about him?"

"How long have the rebels had him?"

"He was taken right after your house was . . . was invaded." She sauntered to the door and placed her hand on the knob. "He's going to be traded, I think. Father is trying to force a treaty with the northern government. They want the kid."

"Why would the rebels want to give him up, then? Shouldn't they figure out why the government wants Bran in the first place?"

"Maybe," she said, "but Father is more concerned about not having the northern army stomp through our land—"

"What makes you think they won't anyway?"

"I don't know, Cam. Maybe you should ask my father these questions?"

Toady apprehended Camden the moment he stepped out the room. He grabbed him by the neck and dragged him through the halls of the plantation mansion.

Luscious decorations, paintings, and vases adorned the house of many doors and stairs. Multiple opened rooms revealed suites with log fireplaces, sitting areas, and luxurious baths. The enormous beds and fluffy pillows welcomed extended slumbers. As they headed down to the kitchen, Camden inhaled the smell of eggs, coffee and bacon. His mouth watered.

Servants moved about the quarters doing all sorts of chores, from dusting and scrubbing floors to cooking and knitting. These healthy women concentrated on their tasks, eyes centered on the floor. Few regarded Toady as he ambled by, and the ones who did noted the rebel dressed in silk dresses. Younger, prettier girls did not clean or scrub, they merely sat around, eating and drinking wine. Laughing.

Toady escorted Camden to the dining hall where chandeliers illuminated the polished table and chairs. The stone, wood-burning fireplace was immense. The large windows showing off the stunning view of a river and mountainside inspired amazement. The mansion was meant to resemble the wealthy south, images taken from the few books Kentuckians owned. The long wooden table accommodated ten lovely ladies. They gathered gracefully near the man in the big cushioned chair: Isaac Mullin.

"Everyone is here, perfect." Isaac's opulent voice resonated around the room, piercing the ears of those listening. "Come, Daughter, sit by your father. I've missed you."

Ida ran into Isaac's arms. She kissed and hugged him. "Father," she said between sobs. "I'm so glad to be home. I have learned humility. I won't ever disobey you. Promise me you will never send me to live with filthy men again."

Toady growled under his breath, his distaste for the general's daughter loud and clear. Out of plain spite, he elbowed Camden in the stomach, making him double over in pain. Dagan, on the other side of Camden, laughed loudly. His glee caught Isaac's attention. He instructed his daughter to sit on his lap. The man was about to welcome his soldiers back home.

"Joshua, tell me why are you leaving us again?" the general asked.

Camden immediately scouted the room for the other rebels: Orion stood weary beside his leader, his red eyes half-closed. Wafer ogled the young maidens at the table; he giggled with juvenile fascination. Toady and Dagan, both on either side of Camden, appeared quiescent and attentive. All of Joshua's squadron, all but the deceased Levi, formed a perfect straight line, all had their hands behind their backs and heads held high, all clean and showered, something they hardly ever did while on the road. Bowie was absent.

Joshua's unique appearance separated him from the other rebels. He wore the oddest clothes, had the longest hair, the bluest eyes, the palest skin, and the most contagious lack of interest. He, unlike the other men, did not bow to anyone—for any reason. His personality changed with his mood, and he actively ignored the beauties on either sides of the general. He yawned, mocking Isaac's role as a leader. He thought the whole militia a weak joke, but went along with the charade in order to advance his own secret agenda.

Camden had learned a great deal about the rebel regimen on his many talks with Joshua, but he could no longer look the rebel leader in the eye. He was sure Joshua knew the details of the rape, probably knew Bowie's intention all along, had to have known, because not one of his men ever took action without his consent. Mia was spared. Stripping her naked and binding her to a chair had been Bowie's way of distracting Camden.

"You have the boy, and now you have more land than you need." Joshua's dull reply held neither respect, nor mutiny. "I'm taking three men with me on a trip, and I'm also taking the little girl."

Camden overlooked Mary on purpose, ashamed to face the orphaned nine-year-old. Her grandfather had been foolish enough to charge Orion with a broom back at Glasgow. The old man's attempt to protect the women was taken as a death plea. Joshua obliged George by shooting him in the face. Eliza tried to flee the town with her daughter, but was strangled. No one witnessed the murder. Camden suspected Toady. Soon after, the rebels shackled the remaining Carrier to the wagon and abandoned Barren County, leaving the townspeople to deal with the dead bodies.

"Three men?" Isaac's attempted smile revealed a hint of contempt. His left eye twitched. "Why do you need *my* men? They just returned home. They should be properly rewarded for their service."

"I'm thinking Toady, Orion and Dagan." Joshua's request was more like a demand, a right. "Toady's strong, Orion's a great navigator, and Dagan's clever. You're right, though. They need a reward. Hmm, let me think. When they come back, they'll each be given a new girl, you know, from the ones seated around you, the ones not touched."

"These ladies are to be gifts to higher ranking officers like you. You've never wanted one, and now you think to hand them over to simple soldiers, men of no stature—"

"All three men will choose," Joshua interrupted, causing the men and women in the room to gape and gasp at the blatant disrespect. "Besides, your ladies-in-waiting have waited long enough."

The proud girls glanced at one another in dismay. They inspected their potential slavers and were appalled by just Toady, the hideously scared man, a barbarian, everyone knew. Some rebels learned to appreciate their slaves. Toady was not one of them. He often said girls stared at his scars in disgust, which only made the man more abusive toward them.

A red faced Isaac retained his angry eyes on Joshua. He hushed the murmuring ladies with a wave of his hand. "You have done a lot for us, Joshua. But if you're going to take any of the men, which I would be happy to allow, it should be men already here. I have a lot of soldiers without missions. Some have never seen battle. Why don't you take them instead? I'm sure Toady, Orion and Dagan would prefer to stay home."

"No," Joshua said, unyielding. "I want tried and tested men." The argument was a power struggle, both leaders wanted to come out on top. "Let's ask them."

Dagan's eyes found the floor; his corkscrew hair shielded his expressions. Orion looked Joshua square in the eye and nodded. He would go. Toady was not going to pass on the opportunity to pick from the untouchable ladies of the plantation mansion. His phallus, obvious to everyone, brought more dismay to the girls. He grinned. Dagan's reluctant nod came last. His gaze never left the carpet.

"Well, I'm glad we have it all figured out." The general's bitter tone sealed his defeat. "When are you and my soldiers going to head out?"

"Tomorrow morning. But don't you worry, Isaac, we'll only be gone for a few weeks." Joshua's troops, with the exception of Wafer, followed him out of the house. The rebels proudly shadowed their defiant leader, a bold leader who feared and was ruled by no one.

"Father," Ida said, once the men were gone. "I'd like to take a husband now that I'm back." Her father laughed. Isaac's armed guards, on all corners of the room, laughed as well. "You said if I found a smart man I could marry him."

"And you will, my dear." He kissed her cheek. "You have grown so much in two years. Your bosom has swelled. I have to experience more of you before I'm quite ready to give you up."

Isaac Mullin was a silver-haired man around fifty years of age with taut bulging lines all over his face, the healthy, ruddy face of a man twenty pounds short of obesity. His dark features contrasted those of his red-haired daughter. Her genes were more than likely inherited from her mother.

Camden loathed the man, not only because he sat pathetically in a cushioned chair, but because Isaac had probably read enough books to know bedding one's daughter was wrong. Yet, he showed no shame in his lustful affection for his child.

Furious with wanting to bring down the worthless general, Camden failed to notice Bowie's approach. His skinny fingers wrapped around Camden's neck in a caress that startled him into leaping forward.

Wafer poked him with his rifle. "Stay still, prisoner."

Bowie pulled the loop on the leather collar he had quickly fastened around Camden's neck. He attached a black leash. He then tripped him, placed his foot on his back, and commanded he stay down, kneel like a dog.

"What are you doing?" Ida left her father's lap and hurried to Camden, unafraid of Bowie's fist. She had the protection of her father. "You ignorant, scum! He's not a slave. He's my future husband." She glanced at Isaac. "I want to marry him, Father."

"Bowie has told me about your fascination with this boy." The general spat. "Joshua may have allowed you to fool around with him, but none of that nonsense will happen here. You disgracefully offer yourself to this thing kneeling before you, and let's not forget the brother you ran away with. He is dead. Correct, Bowie?"

"Yes, general, Gad's dead." Bowie shoved Camden forward with a kick in the rear. "I want Cam to be my slave."

"First of all," Isaac said, rising to his feet, "You will no longer call him by his former name. He will now be known as Cad, an ill-bred man who dishonors ladies."

Camden groaned, enraged by the irony of such a stupid accusation. But instead of struggling, he bowed humbly. Taking on a man as insane as Isaac Mullin was an easy death warrant. He swallowed his pride and his maddening need to spring off the floor and attack the indolent general.

He would wait for a holy miracle.

Camden couldn't help but imagine Pat and Gad laughing at him from somewhere in hell. Hell. How quickly had he come to believe in religion after but a few days of discovering it.

CRYSTAL CITY

Raven stewed in the fetid odor of animal droppings and the thick stink of wet rust. She sat inside an overturned transit bus, monitoring Ata.

The girl twirled in circles as one with the rain, spinning her dress, and lifting the ends like a blooming flower. Her arms stretched above her head as she balanced on the tips of her toes, reaching for the sky. She opened her mouth, tongue tasting the droplets. Her whimsical expression almost slowed the downpours intent on cleansing the soles of her feet, damping her body, and exposing her to a cold. Ata danced, ignorant of the environment's harsh conditions.

After they had entered the city of Arlington, they threaded cautiously through the decomposing chunks of skyscrapers. Unstable slabs plummeted sporadically, breaking apart upon landing and crushing anything beneath. Thousands of vehicles sat uselessly on almost every road and corner, abandoned, wrecked. Overgrown grass carpeted the streets. Rubble settled far and wide. Water drainage spewed from every gutter, forming ponds and puddles where large rodents gathered to drink. Gray skies of lightning and thundering clouds made the air humid, soggy like a marsh. The rusted city stank.

"Are they any closer to the facility?" Earlier in the day, Raven had electrocuted herself with the loose cable of an eroded pylon, prompting Nico and Saul to go exploring for a safer route without them—the *weak* women. "Ata, you're going to get sick!"

Ata twisted and nearly fell on her rump. She giggled with glee, hopping her way back to the bus. She smelled like rain, and her clothes clung to her as snug as a second layer of skin. "He doesn't let me read his thoughts anymore."

"What's going on with him?" Nico had been silent and random throughout their trip to Crystal City, especially after he abandoned the horses a few miles back without an apparent reason.

Ata slumped near Raven, strips of wet hair created patterns on the girl's face. "He's confused about a lot of things," she said.

"What does that mean, Ata? Be specific."

"He closed his mind to me," she said. "But my mind is open to him, so if something were to happen to us he would know."

"Why did he close his mind to you? I thought he liked you?"

Ata retrieved a blanket from one of their backpacks. She laid it out. "He only lets me inside his head when he wants to 'fuse'. I don't remember him being so selfish, but then the more he remembers who he is, the more I remember why I became human."

"Nico is only going to the facility because you want to go, Ata."

"That was his original plan," she said, lying on the bus floor, hands under her head. "He changed his mind."

"He's still going there."

"Yeah, I guess." She yawned. "That's the problem."

"Ata, everything Nico does he does for you."

"Don't worry, Raven." Ata closed her eyes and drew her knees to her chest. "I won't let him harm you or Saul."

The girl's gibberish had always been a bit batty. Ata, at twenty years of age, both looked and acted like a child. Her bizarre moments of heat added stacks against her normalcy. At times, on the trip to Virginia, she had disappeared into the wilderness saying she felt too tight in her own skin. Saul worried every time, but Nico never did, mostly he grinned as if hearing her thoughts, purely sexual, Raven imagined. They would both disappear for half an hour to then return to camp serene and satisfied.

Raven sometimes wished she craved somebody as much as Nico and Ata desired one another. Bran came to mind. Unfortunately, she needed her son more than he would ever need her. Love was just a word when no one to care about existed. The closer she came to finding her son, the more she doubted he would want her at all. She was a stranger to him. What if Bran preferred George and Eliza's company instead? What would she do with her life then?

Your son is more than lucky to have you. His voice, his mental push always eased her thoughts. *A different mother would have given up by now.*

Thank you, Voice. She needed the support.

No, you don't. Laughter erupted inside her head. *You're confusing the affection one has for a child with that of a lover. They're different and distinct. You know, Raven, just when I thought you were stone cold like me, it turns out you're a romantic.*

I don't know what you mean by romantic, but you've been my constant throughout this whole journey. You're not stone cold. A realization suddenly enlightened her. *Are we ever going to meet?*

No, Raven. He paused as if to give the question an appropriate amount of thought. *That would be impossible.*

The thunder and piercing lightning continued to stir the sky, rain poured and harsh winds roared. She observed the furious display silently, waiting for the others to come back. After the clamoring ceased and the slick streets absorbed the evening's shower, Nico returned alone. His set frown neared a sneer and he was wet. He gave no reason for Saul's absence. He disregarded Raven's presence and knelt beside Ata. Silent. Nico picked up a backpack and mined through the contents.

"Did you guys find the facility?" she asked, in hopes of changing his furrowed brow and wrinkled forehead into a more agreeable expression.

He found a towel inside the backpack, patted for dampness, and set it aside. He lifted Ata into a sitting position, removing her soaked dress and exposing her bare breasts. She was asleep. Nico gently laid her on the blanket, slipping off her white panty, which highlighted Ata's pubic mound. He wrung the cotton fabric and stuffed it inside the backpack. He watched the naked girl for a moment, his lips tight and his breathing jagged.

"I'm here, you know?" Raven reminded him. "If you want to—"

"How long has she been asleep?" he asked, never bothering to acknowledge her.

"An hour or so."

He wrapped the towel around Ata like a quilt, cocooning her for warmth. "She already has a virus. Cells attack her all the time. She can't . . ." He exhaled slowly. "She can't expose herself to a cold, common or not, not now. I can't concentrate on anything else when I know this is happening."

"I told her to get out of the rain. She wouldn't listen. Where's Saul, by the way?"

"He's on his way back." Nico regarded Raven with glazed eyes as detached as his words. "I was a lot faster than he."

"Please tell me you didn't come back because Ata's a bit sick." She tried to suppress the next question, but couldn't. "Did you abort the mission because your *girlfriend* has the flu? Are you kidding me?"

"The facility no longer exists," he said, gingerly cradling Ata. "I simply don't like to take any chances with—"

"She's not a child!" If Raven had compared the love of two grownups to the love of mother and a son it was because Nico treated Ata as both lover and kin. "We shouldn't stop to pamper her every time she decides to do something stupid like dance in the rain."

"Or get electrocuted by cable wires," he said. "We won't stop to help her when she decides to free a stranger from a tree, or when she gets her backpack stolen by children, or when she strays away from camp and gets attacked by a cougar."

"She's still more of a nuisance than I am."

"Is that what she is, a nuisance?" Nico laid Ata aside and glared at Raven. It was the first time he had ever regarded her with scorn. "Atabey sometimes forgets how to take care of herself because actions like breathing, waking, and swimming are stolen from her. A tricky mind controller has monitored our every move through you."

"The voice—" She wanted to defend.

"That voice is as real as you and me, Raven. He's dangerous. I strongly suggest you keep him out of your head."

"He's helping me find my son."

"Why?"

"I don't know."

"That's right, you don't."

"Stop, Nico."

"I've always considered you to be a smart girl, Raven. I have protected you since day one, and I will continue to do so until the very end, but the second I hint that you could be a threat or a danger to Ata, I won't hesitate to end you."

His words stabbed at her gut like a serrated knife and before heartbreak could crush her chest, anger surged and bubbled to the surface. Raven could fathom anger and hatred. Those feelings had guided her throughout her life. "The voice has saved me multiple times."

"If he hadn't he couldn't bring you to the city."

"What makes you think he wants me here?"

"Doesn't he?"

"My son is here."

"And you know this how, exactly?"

"Saul told me, and where is Saul? I don't like who you're becoming, Nico, and neither does Ata."

"I would do anything for Atabey. You know that."

"Because Ata believes in you so much, doesn't she?"

"She knows I would do anything—"

"She doesn't trust you!"

The flames in Nico's eyes evaporated.

Raven had stabbed him right back. "I'm pretty sure you're jealous of the voice, too. Ata listens to him. She probably believes him a lot more than she believes you. That must hurt, knowing you have sacrificed your life, your own father, to be with a girl who doesn't even trust you."

"I'm not jealous of this voice," he stated. "Ata doesn't want it, she's controlled by it. He's a clever puppeteer, and he's been using you and Saul. What do you think happened to this town, this lively, roaring city? It was here years ago and now it's gone. Where are the people, Raven? What happened to all the Sorrows who lived here? Who's powerful enough to take down a whole city of Sorrows, blow it up, vacating thousands, leaving a landfill behind?"

"Rebels?"

"The facility is destroyed, has been for years, and yet a pestering voice kept guiding you to the same place where a fleet of people were taken down. Someone strong and powerful enough to exterminate a whole town of Sorrows is more than able to kill three more. I have no intention of leaving Ata's side for even a second, flu or no flu, knowing what I know now."

"If my son's here—"

"Your son was probably traded or sold to other rebels. Bringing you here was a trap and you fell for it, and so did I. I should've realized the same voice that whispers to you, guides Saul, and controls Ata, wants you all here. Do you even know why?"

"No, but—"

"I'll protect the three of you as much as I can, but if it gets to the point where I can't—"

"You'll hightail out of here with just Ata."

"If I have no choice," he said.

"I just want to find my son."

"And we'll look for him, but not in this place."

"Where's Saul?"

"He wasn't that far behind."

Raven sensed the danger Nico sniffed in the tarnished air. "Do you think something happened to him?"

"I think *someone* happened to him. I'm not sticking around to find out who. Get up," he ordered. "We're trapped bait inside a bus."

"Are we going to look for Saul?"

"No. He was never my responsibility."

"But Ata—"

Ata sprang to her feet in a panic as if waking from a nightmare. She glanced from one end of the bus to the other, her eyes darting in every direction.

"I'm not going back for him," Nico told her. "If I leave you—"

"No." Ata towered over Nico. "We don't leave without Saul."

"Ata, please—"

"I'm not leaving without him."

"Fine." He exhaled hoarsely as if his lungs were cramped inside a container. "Get dressed. We'll look for him, but then we leave this place for good."

Ata's towel fell to the floor, revealing her glistening and damp nudity. Nico gobbled the scene. His gaze never strayed away from her as she fully clothed. "Let's go," she said to him.

"Promise me you'll stay by my side, please." He sounded fragmented, vulnerable.

"I promise." Ata smiled, kneeling to reach his cheeks, cupping them with her hands, inhaling his scent. She took her time caressing his jaw with her fingertips. She licked his lips. "You're jealous." Ata fell to his lap and adjusted until her legs wrapped around his hips. "You're very jealous."

He lifted her up and stood. "Maybe a little."

"I like your primitive feelings."

"Ata. I keep you out of my mind because—"

"Do you cherish me, Nico?"

"You know I do, but that's not what—"

She savored his lips with slow and thorough sweeps of her tongue. "I cherish you, too."

"Ata—"

"I know," she said.

Nico kissed her solidly on the mouth. "Good." He instructed the girls to hold on to the backpacks. He would carry the heavy saddle bags.

"This reminds me," Raven said. "Why did you leave the horses behind?"

He shouldered the saddle bags; a long sigh followed. "I was not going to expose a new foal to this sickening city."

Ata looked up at him, apologetic.

He bent and kissed her again. "It's not your fault."

Voice, are you there? Raven needed to know why the man in her head had never bothered to contradict the healer's accusations. *Are you still with me?*

"We'll go straight—" Nico paused. He stepped outside the transit bus and considered the area. "Someone's coming."

Dagan, a rebel, who along with Wafer, Toady and Bowie, had violated Raven, headed toward them with a bright weapon in his hands.

The beam blinded her.

DON'T LET GO

Ata's amber gaze trapped tears. Her stare was the first thing Nico glimpsed when he opened his eyes. He smiled at her, sat up. She dropped down and wrapped her legs around his waist, a gesture of foreplay, one which in different circumstances would have enticed him to fuse.

"Where are we, Atabey?" He scanned her body for damage, injuries similar to the ones he had suffered under the electro blast delivered by a short man. The rebel weapon had released a beam of blinding light that first paralyzed and then knocked Nico out. "He didn't hurt you, did he?"

She shook her head. "No. He said he needed someone to help him drag the bodies."

"I'm sorry he made you do that." Nico caressed her cheeks, sending energy, inspected her sore muscles, fixing them before asking, "What does he want?"

"Dagan, he says we have to stay in here until he gets back." Atabey quivered and then glowered at Nico. "Did you heal me?"

"Of course—"

"Heal yourself, now."

He liked her fretful reprimands and always took them as signs of affection. "Okay, give me a second."

First, Nico surveyed the surrounding four walls, the decaying, eroded chucks of old concrete. The ceiling appeared to have been trapped in a permanent melt, and the pungent smell of rust, a dingy air of rot, burned his nostrils. Dim, flickering light shone from beyond a hallway, a long narrow tunnel. Their holding cell was dark, but his eyes had already adjusted.

Ata's soft lips grazed his neck, her wet tongue brushing over his throat. She bit down. "Heal."

"Oh, aren't you spirited." He rose, lifting her up with him. "What's troubling you? And where's Raven?"

"They put her in another cell, I think," she said, pushing her hips into him in a lazy back and forth motion. "Nico?"

Ata's survival instincts kicked in, a misery to her but never to him, not until that very moment. She could no longer endure a whole day without fusing, an upsetting and terribly frightening realization. "As soon as we get out of this place, I'll give you what you want."

She slipped off him and glared. "What do I want?"

"Ata, I didn't mean—"

"I wouldn't know what you mean. You don't let me inside your head." She dismissed him and knelt near the thinly spaced iron bars. She tested the bars sturdiness by stroking them one at a time, slowly, with intent.

The desire to fuse was always in the back of Nico's mind, a constant mental urge to be inside her. Still, he chose to ignore her teasing. "I hear footsteps. Someone is coming."

She turned to him, caught his shirt, and clung to it like a scared child.

Nico sighed. "Ata—"

"Don't." She hid behind him. Her mind drew a blank. "Don't let him touch me," she whispered in his ear.

Two rebels came into view, carrying with them Sorrow weapons and a lantern. "Well, lookie here," said Orion, "If it isn't Blue."

"It's time." Dagan fidgeted with his linen shirt as if the material caused his skin to itch; he did it often, uneasy. "It's time for the girl to come out."

Ata's fingernails dug into Nico's lower back. He gripped her hand and brought her forward, to the light, where the men could see her. "Is this what you want?"

Her anxiety liquefied and gave way to a new arousal. She found herself admiring the men's bulges, their evident desire to possess her. Ata's yearning exhilarated her. She wanted a man, any man, and the two rebels looked good enough. She was ready for sex, no longer fusion, but plain sex. Maybe she would take them both at once. The rebels were eager enough. One admired her glowing irises, and the other rubbed his crotch. She sauntered toward Dagan with a smile of seduction. Her steps were deliberately nimble. She led with her breasts.

Orion unlocked the cell door and yanked her by the arm, snatching Ata before Nico had a chance to react. "Mine!" he snarled at Dagan. "I'll take Blue."

Nico's sudden fury, the churning energy boggling his senses, rattled his bones. He had to remain still in order to harness his power back into place.

"Watch the healer, and be careful." Orion's words drifted away as the static in Nico's ears increased. "If he tries anything funny, shoot him."

Nico had expected the rebels to want the pretty girl. He had displayed her for such reason. Orion was supposed to come inside the cell and have his neck broken. The original plan was clear, simple, until Atabey's yearning for the men stunned him into stupor.

The cell door locked and only Dagan remained on the other side, pointing a telescope-shaped weapon. The man paced at a distance, made it impossible for Nico to strangle him lifeless, bathe in his blood, slice off his face, chop him into unrecognizable pieces of meat for dogs to eat.

Nico shook his head. "What do you want, rebel?"

"Don't, don't ask questions." Dagan blinked with every syllable. "We wait for orders in silence." His heart thudded in his chest.

"Orion took the lantern. Do you see me?" Nico stepped forward and pressed his head in between the cell bars. "What does your leader want?"

"You dead, probably."

"That's not ambitious enough—"

"Don't say another word. I'll kill you, dead." His hands trembled, and the weapon rattled against the rings on his fingers.

Nico smelled the sweat dripping, dampening the man's shirt. "Where's Orion taking Atabey?"

"To the boss, damn it." Dagan waved his weapon around, pacing back and forth, touching one wall and then moving toward the other. "If you speak one more time, I'll—"

"Shoot me?" Nico laughed loud enough his voice resonated and bounced off the walls. "This underground tunnel is rather small, isn't it?"

Dagan's shoulder's drooped. "Could the roof collapse?"

"This whole dark city is collapsing. We may even run out of oxygen." The wiring throughout the cavern walls had the potential to light up the entire underground facility. Nico, however, doubted anyone had taken the time to make it happen—in recent years.

"You don't know shit!" The man pocketed his clattering weapon. "You're going to rot in your prison, Healer."

"Dagan," Nico said. "Are you claustrophobic?"

"Shut your trap!" He took several light-headed steps backwards. A misstep put him in contact with water. The puddle startled him enough that he hurdled toward the prison cell.

Nico pinned the rebel's head to the iron bars. He snapped his neck and grabbed the keys from his pocket before letting him fall limply on the damp, cold ground. He unlocked the cell door and raced toward the faint glow ahead. He followed the sour smell of Orion and the sweet perfume of Ata. Rusted lab equipment cluttered the tunnel's bends and stairwell system. He flew past many metal doors.

At last, he leapt toward the flicker of light coming from Orion's lantern, but Orion was no longer carrying the lamp. Nico crashed into Atabey, nearly knocking her down. He clutched her arm, steadied her, and inspected for bruises. "Are you okay, Ata?"

Her mind swam with incoherent thoughts. Words failed her.

"Where's the rebel?"

She pointed to the door on the right.

"Stay here." Nico shoved at the iron hatch until he crash landed inside. He toppled over Orion who had pushed from the other side.

They wrestled on the floor. Their bodies dented adjacent objects. Their skin scratched sharp edges. Nico wanted Orion dead. He got a good hold of the man's neck when a bright beam electrocuted him. The blast knocked him sideways. He struggled to maintain his heated core from expanding in response, a hard pull of energy could destroy his human form. He held it together as white bolts of light dazzled his vision. His tingling fingers emanated static that burned as he fell on a nearby machine. He tensed every muscle in his body and ordered his cells not to divide. He rolled and writhed on the floor, spasm after spasm of losing control.

Orion's weight came crashing down, pinning Nico underneath. The rebel hurled punches in the darkness. He cracked bones, broke skin. Pain gave way to a migraine. Nico lacked the strength to dodge the swings at his face. Orion broke his nose. His vision dawdled in white obscurity. He recorded the sound of fists cracking and splinting his skeleton. Despite the blows to his jaw, Atabey's safety remained foremost on his mind. He wanted to mentally reach out to her, but exhaustion handicapped him.

A loud, echoing clonk jerked the rebel off his stomach. Nico tried not to think about it. He needed to gather himself and find Ata. Wild, her scent was wild. Her tears filled his lips. He differentiated her salty liquid from the blood gushing from his nose. He tasted her anguish. Her voice was a distant squeak, but he could feel her warmth, her body pressing so tightly against him it hurt.

She was trying to wipe the blood off his face with her dress, a pretty blue dress, he remembered.

Nico attempted to soothe his troubled nymph by lessening her worry. He entered his body and initiated the healing process. He controlled the bleeding. His engorged and broken nose worsened his breathing, but he managed to repair the injuries. His force field drew his arched cheekbones inward. He performed natural surgery on his fractured jaw with the help of his dividing cells. Lastly, he worked on his impaired vision. Nico conjured up his erratic energy and begged his body not to detonate.

Bolts of electricity filled his biological systems, a steaming pot with a lid about to pop. Nico's injuries impeded his ability to harness his own energy. His cells multiplied many times over in an effort to aid him. The support was more damaging than helpful. Excessive cells guaranteed chaos—

Energy abandoned his body in small quantities. He no longer strained to keep whole. Cells left him rapidly, faster and faster with keen interest in staying out. Energy swam away in good will. He was aroused by the festivities inside his head, his groin, and his jubilant erection. His vision returned and with it, the awareness of the occurrence outside of his body.

A beautiful being with wild cascading hair, tresses that feathered his cheeks, rode him. Atabey smiled, yearned, and moaned for him. Her clenched, hot muscles gripped his erection. Her body received a steady flow of energy. Nico could never live without her. Her perfection astounded him, almost blinded him again. She made him feel alive. She gave him the buildup needed to skyrocket. He braced himself, braced her hips, brought her to him, and kissed her fervently on the mouth.

I cherish you. He opened his mind to her. *I always have. Do you hear me, Atabey?*

Her answer traveled in waves of desire that pressed him deeper inside her. Blood flowed to her pelvis. Her breathing became jagged, accelerating her thrusts. The intensity of her need robbed him of breath. He shuddered. She wanted him forever, wanted him always. She cried out. Together they freed one burst of utter pleasure. Utter happiness. Exhausted, Atabey collapsed on top of him, dreamily blissful, but also naked and cold.

Nico held her and give her warmth. He stayed inside her until she ceased contracting. "Thank you, Atabey." He lay satisfied on the hard floor of a dark and moldy room. "I feel much better."

She lifted her head and looked him in the eyes. "You shouldn't have entered my mind." Bending closer to his mouth, she bit at his lower lip, tugged.

He liked the bitty bites, they mostly tickled. "You don't like it when I shut you out, Ata."

"Those sexual thoughts for the rebels weren't mine," she said, starting a trail of kisses along his neck. "After *he* made me lust for them—"

"I suspected as much. You can't physically belong to anyone else and yet . . ." Nico had come close to fragmenting with jealousy and rage. "I don't know what would have happened if you had—"

"Nico, I figured a way to block him." She lifted her head again. "But when you entered my mind, he somehow slipped back."

Nico sat up and searched for his pants. "Are you speaking about the Sorrow?"

"He now knows our exact location." Ata picked up her dress and glanced at the human garbage nearby. "I think I killed Orion."

"Yes, you did." Nico headed for the door. "Let's find Raven and get out of here."

"Saul, we have to find him." Her mind lingered on Orion, on how she had smashed a metal pipe over his head, one of the many obstacles lying around the room. "I can't believe I killed him."

Nico stopped and turned to her. "I was fortunate the rebel only used the electrolaser once, and even then, he nearly beat me to death."

"We fused next to his corpse."

"Passionate lovers do," he said, offering her a weak smile, worrying Ata had become wholly dependent on his energy.

"I want to fuse often so you stay near, close." She leaned on him. Her eyes brimmed with tears. "I don't want to lose you, Nico."

He pulled her into his arms. "You don't have to worry. I'm not going anywhere without you." She squeezed him in response. And Nico was overcome by her strong feelings. Her love finally rivaled his. "I'm sorry it took me so long to find you, Atabey."

A current of vibrating electricity ignited every light bulb in the room, painfully forcing Nico and Ata to adjust their sight. He captured the immensity of the room in one quick sweep. They were trapped again. The iron door was locked. A long glass-like wall connected their room to one containing loads of hospital equipment. Nico heard the subtle steps of a person approaching them from the other side of the glass wall.

The Sorrow's loud, malicious cackle found its way inside Ata's head. It hurt her. She buckled from the pain. The severe throbbing only drifted away once Nico grasped her arm.

"Whatever happens, don't let go." Nico was no longer sure if he could protect Ata from every single mind intrusion, but he would protect her from physical harm. "You hear me, Atabey. Don't let go."

SODOM

Lawrenceburg was nestled in a discreet countryside, a place where slavery thrived. Rebel soldiers strutted about the streets with half-naked girls and boys on leashes attached to either leather or metal collars. The more obedient slaves were spared bondage, which still left them resembling dogs, animals forced to walk on hands and knees. The display of bare, chapped skin, dark bruises, and welted buttocks disturbed Camden.

Two men casually chatted at the end of a busy street. They leashed two slave girls who stared into each other's eyes as if communicating an unspoken message. Neither one could speak. Their mouths were gagged: the plump brunette wore a type of horse muzzle, and the petite blonde was silenced by a thin rope stuffed between her teeth. Both wore fingerless gloves and kneepads.

When the men finished talking, they traded females. One of the girls sighed in instant relief, the other let out a gasp that had her new master yanking on her hair and pulling her neck backwards. He told her to keep her mouth shut. Tears filled her eyes. Her master smiled, cruelly.

"I'm not going to trade you. I don't think." Bowie grabbed Camden's hands and tied them behind his back. "Stand up. It'll be easier to show you around if you're up. Don't do anything stupid or you'll end up crawling like those bitches over there."

Camden rose to his feet, knees burning from having crawled on the hardwood floors of Isaac's plantation mansion—no kneepads for him. "Why are you doing this to me?"

"I like your sweet little ass, Cad."

"I don't like you anymore."

"Too bad, 'cause I like you."

"I'm not an animal," Camden protested, against his better judgment. "Can't I be a rebel instead?"

"Don't get finicky. Stop moving. If others see you fighting me, they'll come over here and subdue you."

Camden's rage negated his will to comply. "I'm not your damn slave!"

Rebels in the area spotted the newbie with disdain. They fired angry glances at Bowie. "Open your mouth." Bowie retrieved a ball gag from his pocket, a leather strap with a tortuous ball large enough to contort Camden's mouth into a ridiculous gape. "If you yell like that again, I will hurt you. Now, I want you to be a good slave. Follow and listen."

He nodded and hoped if he obeyed the horrid thing would be removed. Camden's stretched mouth ached.

"Let's discuss your circumstance, our way of life," Bowie started. He pulled on the leash and pushed Camden in front of him. "You're probably wondering if all rebel militias have slaves. They don't. Isaac's an innovator. He's the only rebel general who puts his men first. Other militias fall apart because there's nothing to do. Hopefully, by the end of this year, we'll be able to conquer South Central Kentucky. We already have most of the north."

The high, glaring sun dotted Camden's vision.

"I heard the western general doesn't allow slaves in the housing area. He says it distracts the men from their duties. I don't think so. Having a slave gives us a reason to accomplish our missions a lot faster. We're always eager to come back home. The South Central general doesn't allow slaves, period. And if you're wondering about the eastern general, you'd be surprised to know we don't have one. Eastern Kentucky's unconquered. Nature has done away with that part of the state. Anyway, let's go get drunk. There's a place I want you to see. You're being good and obedient, Cad. Keep it up."

R.M. James

Isaac's town was near a riverbed. Spring water filtered when it streamed over limestone rock formations, perfect for the many bourbon distilleries in the area. The oldest Kentucky whiskey distillery was a large warehouse.

The young and old male slaves worked at filling and exporting oak barrels from one room to the next. Rows and rows of barrels were stored for aging. The slaves labored speedily, and not one of the young workers regarded Bowie as he and Camden roamed through the factory. Children ducked and worked harder. They moved as if afraid the bright-haired rebel might punish them. The older graying men monitored the young boys and scolded the ones who faltered or stumbled. Most of the kids had been stolen from their parents and forced to work.

"Once they reach seventeen we send them back to their families. We do it to prevent them from ever growing strong or smart enough to rebel. Ironic, of course." Bowie guided Camden through many rooms. He showed him the equipment used to make the liquor he so enjoyed. "The old men are enslaved for the same reason as the brats. They're too weak to fight us. As for the females, we don't worry about revolt with them. Girls are naturally frail, but because of personal taste, we keep them young. We free the older ones. Most either end up in the hands of solo survivalists, or starve before finding a town that offers shelter. On a different topic, did you know Bourbon whiskey was invented in Kentucky?"

Pulverized corn cooked at high temperatures in a mash tub. There were several stages in the whiskey process and each one had its own pungent aromas hovering over the stilted air. Some of the slaves added ingredients into a mix. Mostly rye and barley.

In a different room, giant wooden tubs fermented the lumpy thick yeast. The next room, the largest, housed the enormous distilling apparatuses: the copper stills in which the mixture was heated and the vapor collected. The mash would finish converting into liquid after several days. Slaves would then pour the liquor into white-oak barrels for maturing. Preservation would turn the bourbon a honey color. Bowie said the end result would only be appreciated after several years.

"But we have plenty ready, now. This town drinks on a daily basis." Rebel territory was a drunken haze of soldiers prancing about half-drunk, violent and horny. After a few drinks, Bowie was one of them. "Let me take you to my place, Cad. Cad. The things Isaac comes up with." He cackled.

Rebels lived in rows of tightly packed wooden stocks. The small homes had wire-fenced backyards and personal gardens tended by slaves. The men could own no more than two slaves, a rule set by Isaac. Rebels on a mission of several days or months or years had to lend a comrade their slave before leaving. If the female was one coveted by many, the rebel could sell her to the highest bidder. Liquor rations were always the highest bids.

Bowie took Camden to a house barren of pictures and decorations on the walls. The furniture was simple, wooden, and handcrafted. "I've had plenty of female slaves." The man yanked on Camden's collar. He dragged him to his bedroom. "Good cleaners, very obedient girls, but they bore me. Real shame, too. Slave girls naturally prefer me. They think me handsome," he said proudly.

Camden nodded in agreement, still hoping to have his gag removed. The strain on his facial muscles was severe.

"If you keep me satisfied, Cad, I'll never let Isaac sentence you to death ever again." Bowie turned him around and untied his hands. "I'll treat you better than I have in the past. Can you already tell how good I am to you? How proper I am in every way. With the others I have to act a fool, but I don't think I need to do that with you. I don't want to be a heinous brute. I'm going to untie you now, take that gag off. If you try to flee, I'll keep you bound. Don't get any funny ideas. Do you understand all this, Cam or Cad?"

He agreed with a nod, but planned to run away as soon as he was free.

"I see that look in your eye, Cad. You're not going to be obedient, are you?" Bowie let out a soft sigh and punched Camden in the stomach, a blow that left him so winded he fell to the ground, squirming. Bowie then kicked him in the testicles. The pain had him doubled over with tears in his eyes. He groaned, twisted and moaned. "I'm doing this to protect you. If I don't train you, someone else will."

Bowie disappeared for a few seconds. He returned with a large wooden paddle in one hand and a metal chain in the other. He kicked Camden in the ribcage, sending a second blinding twinge throughout his body.

"Take off your clothes, quickly." His low terrifying voice lost the drunken friendliness which had previously made Bowie a tolerable companion. "If you're not naked by the count of twenty, life is going to get very uncomfortable for you."

Camden could no longer remember how he ended up suspended with both hands hooked and restrained above him. All he could recall from his first days of torture was the torment, the kind his body learned to endure. He stopped clenching his muscles and simply went limp. Bowie noticed too soon, and before Camden could get comfortable in his languid state, blunt torture from a new object attacked his limbs with more vehemence. The paddle had hurt, stung his rear for what seemed like days, but the whip, the whip drew blood.

The device had several short braids made of leather thongs and many sharp pieces of bones tied at intervals. It spread and captured his entire back. His legs, buttocks, chest, shoulders and arms all experienced the merciless flogging. Bowie always saved Camden's penis for last. But it too throbbed red and erect because the master wanted it so.

Days existed where he longed for the rapes. He always preferred the sexual assault as opposed to the beatings. Bowie was kind when he raped Camden, forceful, but kind to the rest of his body. Camden also looked forward to oral sex. Sucking Bowie guaranteed time off the chains, time he used to stretch his cramped muscles. He learned to be good at fellatio. He took his time and made it last. Not just because his master wished it so, but because it was time away from bondage.

Bowie was pervasive for several days in a row, dreadful, miserable days he took to converting Camden into a submissive slave. Camden stopped resisting and started calling the rebel his master. He kissed his feet and begged for compassion, for food, for sleep. He was eventually allowed a shower, a break to clean and scrub the piss from the bedroom floor, the result of going hours without a bathroom break. He ate. He slept on the carpet, on the floor near the master's bed, shackled of course, but comfortable, as comfortable as Camden was ever going to be before the torture started again.

Camden lay intoxicated on the floor the first time she appeared, a beautiful girl with skin the color of sienna. Her dark hair curled in every direction and spilled down her neck, surrounding her oval face. Her large brown eyes entered his soul and asked he give her his undying attention. An angel stood at the threshold, leaning against the door. The bodice of her silver dress clung to her, enveloping her voluptuous breast. The rest of the garment spilled loosely, nearly to her knees. Silver dangled from each ear, loops that pierced her tiny lobes. *Did it hurt?* She was gone before he could ask.

On her second visit, Camden feigned sobriety. His master had left him drugged and shackled to the bed. Naked and limp. Yet, her sudden appearance hardened him. Most of his bruises had healed after his master stopped punishing him with instruments. He mostly raped him every morning and almost every night. Camden's new reality no longer embarrassed or angered him. He accepted his life. He smiled at her from the bed and tried to keep his stoned mind from wandering.

"Hello, are you ever going to come inside?" he asked her, his beloved esculent angel. Angels. Why would a digital era believe in invisible spirits from beyond? Religious stories were more ridiculous and backwards than any fiction novel Camden had ever read. "What's your name?"

She advanced past the threshold. Her eyes inspected the room. There wasn't much to see. The master's solid oak bed had a spring mattress that echoed in Camden's ears hours after his rear stopped hurting. No paintings hung on the walls, and the only dresser contained the few garbs his master wore every day. The closet held torture devices. And the one rifle his master did own, he took with him wherever he went. Light came from a handful of candles, scented to mask the stink of sex and feces. The green carpet accommodated Camden, but was too short to cover the whole room.

"Zemi," she said, "my name."

He was delighted to meet Zemi. "My name is Cad . . . Camden. Are you the master's girl slave?"

She released a sweet satirical chuckle. "You mean the rapist who keeps beating you? No. I'm not his anything, and I've seen enough. You need to get out of here."

"I can't leave my master," he answered her.

Her lovely smile vanished in an instant and he could almost cry. He missed it so much. "Bowie doped you pretty bad. You look awful right now."

"You're so beautiful, Zemi." He beamed. The joy caused his cheeks to ache.

"Listen to me, kid." She approached him with her intoxicating scent of wild blossoms.

His body throbbed, hurt, stung until he quivered and trembled. "Whoa . . ." His watery release stained the cotton blanket.

"I'm going to pretend you didn't—"

"But I did," he said. "You smell so succulent. Do you taste like heaven?"

She sighed, and her slow release of air hardened him all over again. "You're kind of a mess right now, but I'll keep checking on you until you can function like a normal person."

"Please, don't leave me." He would be alone for hours. "My master won't return until midnight."

"I can't sit back and watch you and the rest of the prisoners get treated like animals," Zemi said. "Do you understand that you don't want to be submissive? You feel a certain way because you live in a new Sodom. Enough pain can make anyone believe anything. I need you, Camden. I need you to advocate for the slaves. It's sad to see history repeat itself. Do you know anything about history? Are you a read man, Camden? Talk to me!"

Her inflated tone yanked him straight out of his dreamy wonderland. "Yes, I've read books."

The Sorrow government had eradicated and burned most of the books in the farming states. They allowed them access to classical novels, mostly fiction, none centered on the digital age. Educational manuals and How-To's had barely survived the wipe out. Illiteracy was high among the peasants, so keeping the books away was never a real problem.

Camden had read every fiction novel available to him simply because Sorrows overlooked the power imaginative authors wielded on the common folk. Authors of fiction inspired as many beliefs as any creed, a will to want to be and do more. Sorrows assumed dumb farmers and backward humans would never understand the read material. An untruth. Camden had a curious mind.

"Who are you?" He wanted to know more about Zemi. Did she belong to Isaac, one of the ladies-in-waiting? Her cheeks reddened—either she was flustered or impatient. "What do you think I can do for you?"

"You're going to do this for yourself," she said.

"What do you mean?"

"I help your people. You spare mine, Cam. That's the deal. Take it or leave it."

"I don't know what—"

"Take it or leave it."

"Okay, but what is it you want from me?"

"You, Camden, are going to help me burn this town to the ground."

How could he ever say no to her fiery gaze of passion? She exemplified leadership, exuded intelligence. Zemi was an Amazon recreating her version of a revolution. History always repeated itself and books or no books, men—and women—would always move around in endless circles.

BUT YOU SAID

Wake up, Raven. He's got you again.

Her eyes snapped open as her body landed hard on the floor of a bright room. Raven sat up. She spotted Nico and Ata looking down at her. Sighing, she eased her taut muscles.

"Well, at least we're all together." Nico's hand seemed to crush Ata's left wrist. He held her too tight. "Do you remember anything?"

She remembered being stung into oblivion. "Did a rebel bring us here?"

"Dagan," said Ata, with distress in her voice.

"Where's Saul?"

"He's part of all this," answered Nico.

"What is this, exactly?" Twice she tried to get up and twice her legs buckled. On her fourth attempt, she reached out for Nico's hand. Her body hurt. "What are you guys talking about?" The pain drifted away. She grinned up at him. "Thank you."

Nico explained how Orion, before his death, had led him and Ata to the bright room. "Saul then appeared on the other side of the glass wall in surgeon's scrubs."

"He ignored me," Ata added.

"Yes," Nico said, "but he did eventually tell us he was doing all this for your sake."

"Do you believe him?" Raven asked.

Nico turned to Ata with a half-smile. "I don't think he means her any harm."

"What about the rest of us, Nico?" She tried to keep the contempt out of her voice. "Ata's not the only one in danger here."

"He doesn't care about you, Raven."

"What does he want then, and where did he go?"

"If I knew, I would tell you." He glanced at the wall. "It looks like glass, but it's not. I wonder what techy Sorrow invention produced that type of insulator."

The white lab on the other side of the wall overflowed with technical equipment, unused devices, electronic screens, probing sticks, and a flat table. It was a patient's heaven, an old fashion doctor's vision—or wet dream. Nico moved about the place like an animal trapped inside a cage too small for its size. That stirred Raven's nerves. The healer was never nervous, concerned maybe, but never nervous.

"Do you think one of us is going on that operating table?" she asked him.

He rubbed his swollen temples. "No, I don't think so. We're in the wrong room."

A large freezer hummed in the surgical room. The cold vapor seeped through the door frame gaps. "Then why does—"

"Saul was cleaning up," Nico said. "I think the 'surgery' was over before we got trapped here."

"Do you smell her?" Ata asked him. "I already do."

He nodded, gripped her harder. "This is my fault. I should have taken her someplace else."

"Taken who? You two need to start talking like I'm here. I can't read your minds, and I sure as hell can't smell a person before he or she walks inside a room."

Saul entered the surgical chamber with a little girl by his side: Cousin Mary. A vicious urge to kill the man in the oversized scrubs seized Raven. He asked Mary to sit on the operating table. She needed a stool for the task. Saul feigned a fatherly gaze, what was really frustration. It exuded from his grimace. Mary struggled to walk, to stable herself. The yellow gown made her skin look sallow and her eyes jaundice. She bent over to gag, ready to vomit. But nothing came out.

"What did you do to her?" The memory of Fry's small body lying lifeless on the ground with a big hole in his chest came back to Raven. "We should have known you were no good. Where's my son?"

"You're always whining about something," Saul said. "I'll have you know it was not my intention to—" He breathed, softly, calmly. "I needed a fertile female to insert the frozen embryo. Pure Sorrows are unfit candidates. Mary Carrier, on the other hand, has the blood of a human mother and a Sorrow father. She was perfect for the procedure."

"Fertile?" Nico released his grip on Ata and came forward. "Did you impregnate a nine-year-old girl?"

"You sound shocked," the man said. "I'm sure your mother never asked to have you for a son."

Nico remained impassive, unmoved. "What do you know about my mother?"

Saul used the stethoscope hanging around his neck to listen to Mary's heartbeat. He addressed Nico. "I used to be a fertility specialist and I remember your mother well. Rosetta was one of the doctors who helped bring Atabey into existence. As soon as the embryo took to the mother host, your mother miraculously became pregnant at exactly the same time."

"I know this."

"Do you, Mr. Lowell? All Sorrow women are supposedly born sterile. Rosetta had to leave the city before she was found out. They sent a bounty hunter after her. She was beautiful, I remember." Saul smiled down at Mary as if to indicate all was well in her small chest. "I guess your father fell in love with her. He took her out of Sorrow territory and protected her." He paused. "She's dead now, I assume. Did Sorrows eventually find her?"

Nico took several steps back and reached for Ata's hand. "My mother's body was not built to carry me."

"You killed your own mother, then?"

"No, I healed her as much as I could."

"Like you keep trying to heal Atabey?"

"Atabey belongs to me. It's different."

"It seems to me that everyone you touch dies."

Nico's eyes dimmed. "I'm a healer."

"Let me tell you a story about the voice who asked me to rescue Atabey. This voice told me I could live in the woods without worrying about Alexander. You see, I was tired of being a slave of the mind, of knowing every thought was monitored by the king of us all. I hated working here."

"King?" Raven asked.

"I hated how we punctured and injured Ata for reasons we were never allowed to ask." Saul took a long breather and continued. "Sorrows are sheep. We're an abomination. I wanted to be free. The voice offered freedom for a reasonable price: rescue Atabey, wait several years for Raven to find me, come to Crystal City, and lastly, impregnate Mary. I'm officially finished. My mind is now mine. I wasn't expecting to find Arlington destroyed, but I guess all of this was already premeditated. The voice knew this would happen. He chooses what he tells us." Saul glanced at Raven. "Isn't that right?"

I'm not the one inside his head, the voice said.

Then who's talking to Saul?

I don't know, but it's not me.

How can I believe you?

Don't you?

The voice, her constant, she couldn't, or wouldn't, doubt him. *I believe you.* If only he were there in the flesh, tangible. *What should we do?*

I can't enter Saul's mind. He has a block.

What about Mary? There's plenty of sharp objects around her.

She might not be able to handle a mind intrusion.

She'll deal. She would have to.

Raven, I don't advise—

We all have our crosses to bear, Voice. If I start sympathizing, I'll end up dead and so will my son.

"Raven, he knows all." Saul clutched the needle in his hand. He pricked Mary, and the child fell limply in his arms. "This is why I initially told Mary to sit on the table." He tapped his own head. "The voice knows all."

"Can he read my thoughts, too?"

"Relax. He has no desire to harm you or your son." Saul laughed at his own words and then frowned. He turned to Ata. "I'm a free man. We can live our lives now. The voice told me I could take you back home where Alexander will never get us. The rebel militias won't allow Sorrows on their land. There's a war coming soon, and we need to be far away from it. Me and Ata—"

"Whoever told you I'd allow you to take Atabey away from me must have severely underestimated my abilities." Nico eyes darkened to mountain green.

His entire body glowed. His scent wafted across the room. What was the smell? Wild animal? No. An ancient beast: powerful metallic molecules of a being far superior to anything walking the earth. The old, corroded computers started up as if no one had ever unplugged them. The lights flickered. Static, a quivering amount of it reached Raven. She stepped away from the radiant, alien man. Ata jerked her hand back. His grip had electrocuted her, too. She looked up at Nico, alarmed and confused. His eyes remained on Saul.

"For your sake and because Atabey cares about you, Saul, I suggest you let us all go."

"You're a magnificent creature, Nico Lowell." Saul's smile was irrationally exaggerated. "I would never dream of picking a fight with you. You can't be killed by someone like me. Heck, neither can

Sorrows. This whole city was thriving with them. I'll have you know, Nico, my grandfather is also an incredible creature. He wanted something once, just as much as you want Atabey. He brought down this whole goddamned city because of it. Still, he never could find it. We all have our limits. A war on a city damages and destroys many things, but a sealed off room engineered of elements unheard of was indeed his limit. We've managed to generate electricity down here, but we can't open the room without your mother's password. Like I said before, my mission is over. But yours, Nico, has just begun."

"You think your voice dictates me?" Nico's confidence was as poignant as if he were sure he could dissolve into mist and penetrate the glass wall. "No Sorrow can read my thoughts or control my actions."

"Yes, true, but Atabey is an open book. I will protect her and take care of her. I love her very much. She's my only family. You need to give her up."

"And why would I do that?"

"Because if you don't," Saul said, "he'll kill her."

"No one is going to kill Ata, not if I can help it. I'll shut out whatever comes her way."

"You'll never be strong enough to shut out the voice."

"Atabey is a part of me. I will shield her." Nico reached for Ata, but she was no longer within reach. She stood beside Raven, terrified. The room's old computers beeped strange and foreign sounds, blaring sounds capable of rupturing eardrums.

Saul placed his palm on the glass wall, the thick barrier between them. "Atabey is a part of him, too. He's her father."

Watch your step.

Raven jumped at the sight of Orion's corpse shaking in every direction. The static, the electricity emanating from Nico, revived the dead man's limbs. The effect lasted for a few seconds before Ata told Nico to stop it, and he did.

What the hell was that? Raven asked the voice.

The healer's frustrated. This could be deadly for you and Ata. Get out of the room. His words reached her in fragments, far away echoes. *Toady will get you out.*

Can you get inside his head again? she asked.

I can try.

What about Nico?

I think Saul's trying to stir him up.

Is Saul's voice really Ata's father?

If he is, he's a mean dad.

Ata ran then. She ran around the room until her head hit a solid wall. Her body bounced back. She fell on the floor, got up, dazed and muddled.

Nico headed toward her and the room's animations and electric activities stopped.

She screamed when he laid a hand on her as if his touch was death. Ata rose, floated. She ran again, her head butting another wall. She quivered. Her nose bled. She was immobile, but conscious, wide-eyed and speechless. Her mouth opened, and then shut down so hard she bit her tongue.

"Make it stop!" Nico pounded on the glass wall.

"I'm not doing this to her, Healer. You know I'm not." There was despondency in Saul's voice. He didn't want Ata hurt any more than Nico did. "You need to give her up, please. I beg you."

"She's mine!" The words were hissed, and Nico was like a dog fighting for a bone. He was dangerous and cruel. "I will never give her up to you."

"Please." Saul shook, his voice trembled. "He'll kill her."

Help her. Raven found herself telling the man in her mind.

I can't get inside Ata's head and neither can the healer. Whoever that voice is, he's shut everyone out. He's powerful. Get out of there, Raven.

She couldn't, not without her son.

I'm not so sure your son is in this city anymore. His words were only a confirmation of what she already suspected. *Ata is getting back up. He's going to hurt her again if you don't do something.*

Me, what can I do?

Restrain her. I don't think Saul's voice cares about you.

If I get in the way, he might start—

Raven, I don't have much time with you. They're going to take me away soon. You're going to have to stop debating everything I tell you.

Who wants to take you? Don't go! Her own voice inflation dazed her.

Ata's heading for the wall again. Stop her.

Raven grabbed Ata's dress and yanked on it. The girl stumbled to the ground. "Stay down, Ata."

"It hurts my head." She shuddered. "My head!"

"Nico—" He already regarded her. "I don't think Saul means Ata any harm. Let her go."

"No." His simple and cold answer amazed her.

Saul went nuts with the surgical equipment. He tossed heavy items at the glass wall. "What is the matter with you? Are you going to sacrifice her? Why? Why would you let her suffer like this?"

"Tell the coward to show himself." Nico towered over Ata and lifted her up against her will. She fought him. He ignored her small fists but never tried to dodge them. "I'm going to send you to sleep, Ata. Saul's 'friend' is not stronger than me."

A pissing contest if Raven ever saw one. "Damn it, Nico. I want to get out of here."

Ata sagged in his arms. He set her on the floor, observed her for a few seconds with longing and regret, then his expression changed into a vindictive glare. "That voice can temporarily injure her mind, but I'll keep fixing the damage. I won't let him break her. If your puppeteer wants me or Ata dead, Saul, he's going to have to show himself."

Get me out of here, Voice.

The iron door swung open, and Raven was pulled by the hair into a dark corridor. Her ears rang. Toady grinned, lifting her up by the neck. He slapped her face once. Twice. Thrice. He enjoyed listening to the smack of his open hand against her cheek. He laughed madly.

Voice, are you controlling him?

No . . . I . . . can't anymore.

Another smack and her face went numb. Toady's ugly mug smirked when she tried to kick him in the testicles. He squeezed her left breast. The pain surged immediately to her head and the ringing was louder, earsplitting.

"I'm taking you to the leader." His fetid breath made her gag. He slapped her again. "And don't think your Sorrow friend can help you this time." He laughed, pushing her head on the damp concrete floor. He dragged her by the hair. When she fidgeted, he kicked. "Or I might not take you to him at all. I might accidently lose you first, bitch."

Raven . . .

Voice? What should I do?

I'm sorry. I have to go now.

But you said you would help me find my son. Please. She begged. *Help me.*

They won't let me. He whispered as if others could hear him. *I don't think I'm supposed to remember you when I wake up.*

But you said—

I know. And he drifted away.

The pull was stronger than previous times, wider and permanent. The voice, her voice, the man who had guided her for an entire journey, the man she had learned to trust, care for, and believe in, had abandoned her for good.

She found no trace of his link, not hidden in any of the billions of neurons, not in her memories, her lobes. The voice was gone for good, and she knew it as much as she knew Toady would try to kill her.

But you never told me your name.

PROMISED LAND

Soldiers armed with a diverse amount of weapons guarded all corners of rebel territory. All soldiers rotated shifts, many settled miles away from the town. The working men were not allowed to drink while on duty, and only after their shifts ended could they do as pleased: sex and booze. The adventurous types often volunteered to go on missions, invading countless counties, broadening their range. The most accomplished soldiers quickly moved up rank. Once on top, there was no limiting the amount of slaves a rebel could own.

They were, however, cautious of ensnarement from within. According to Zemi, the incident happened once. A rebel had been drunk and his abused slaves loathed him. Jointly, they cut off his head and ran off to the river where guards eventually caught them and dragged them back to camp.

The militia enjoyed capital punishment, and as a casual warning they brought along their slaves to witness the tortures. All three females were publicly whipped and mutilated, repeatedly raped and then hanged with their hands behind their backs for days on end. They were eventually thrown in a dingy cell, left to die from their wounds. Escape was never tried again. In fact, most slaves tried hard to keep their masters happy. No one wanted to be bartered, starved, or beaten for disobedience.

"How long have you been a slave?" Camden asked Zemi, interrupting her story. "Which rebel do you belong to?"

The candles spurts danced in her eyes. She blinked, capturing the flames. "I don't have a slaver. I don't belong to anyone."

"You have to belong to someone." She smelled good, foreign, a rare scent he couldn't name. "Why do you smell the way you do?"

"My pheromones are probably different than yours. You've had to adapt to your environment and mine was less harsh, sad really." She sat gnawing one of her fingernails. "If county folks were smart, they'd attack the rebel regiment."

"Towns are not allowed guns," he told her. "Rebels check for them."

"Camden, I need to tell you something." She adjusted herself on the bed. The move shifted the quilt covering Camden's lap, revealing his tender penis.

"Bowie will be back soon." He cupped his sore member. "I don't want you to get caught or end up his slave."

"He won't be back yet," she said, with sureness. "There's a celebration at the mansion tonight."

Camden smirked. "Don't you have it all figured out."

"As a matter of fact, I do."

He knew little about his precious, random angel except for what she told him. Zemi had visited Camden every night for the past four days. She sneaked out of the mansion and ducked through the corn fields, slipping inside Bowie's house through the backyard garden. It was lucky for her the plantation crops were high that time of year. No one ever saw her.

"There's a slave woman, Camden." Her company was humbling and there was never any pretense of pride or superiority with her, not even when she had come to find him shackled, drugged, bruised and broken. "This house slave told me to reach out to you, give you hope." Zemi was his only hope, his only refuge. Yet at times, the need to own her overwhelmed him, a shameful example of rebel indoctrination.

Camden wanted to kiss her. One kiss from Zemi would linger long after she was gone. The memory of her lips would stay with him through the Bowie tribulations. Her caress would make the rebel's touch non-existent. "This slave girl sounds like a kind person," he answered.

"Camden—"

"Call me Cam." He leaned forward, inhaling her scent, indulging in her beauty. Her eyes were enormous, so dark and challenging. "Can I kiss you?"

"Do you want more *juice*? You're talking funny." She had been giving Camden a tonic to remove the effects of the opium in his system.

"Zemi, would you consider me for a husband if I somehow managed to get us out of this mess?"

"No, Camden," she said. "I need to talk about your sister."

He straightened up. "What do you know about my sister?"

"She's a slave here."

"No. Can't be. Lucy's married." Camden could scarcely control the urge to whine like a child. "She lives far away."

"Her husband was killed. She was brought here as a slave. Luckily, her kitchen talents won her a place inside Isaac's mansion. She's a sous-chef now."

The room door swung wide open, fanning a chilly breeze and the pungent smell of whiskey. "What's this?" Bowie stood at the threshold, weaponless, drunk, but sturdy.

Zemi leaped off the bed.

"What hole did this runty whore crawl out of?" He hurried toward her, giving Zemi no room to dodge him. "Come here, slut."

Camden, shackled, waited patiently for his chance. Bowie would try to punish his new victim with his closet toys, and just as Camden suspected, the rebel dragged Zemi by the hair to his wardrobe. He jerked it open and reached for the wooden paddle. His first swing missed. She wiggled away from the second strike. The third blow struck her in the face. Blood trickled down her nose. Bowie, still grabbing her by the hair, dragged her to the bed. Camden wasted no more time. He yanked on Bowie's long hair and brought the man down. Once down, he began kicking him. Zemi helped. Together they made a vicious pair.

Bowie picked himself back up by swinging his fists in the air. He aimed mostly at Zemi. Camden locked his arms over and around the rebels head and used his shackles as a lariat. Bowie crouched away as Zemi attacked his knees with the paddle. The man buckled. On the ground he was helpless, on the floor, *he* was the victim. Camden's weight fell on his slaver's chest and before the man struggled, Camden pounded mercilessly. He clouted Bowie until his knuckles bruised, until his joints stiffened, until the man's face was nothing but blood and broken bones, until the rebel barely breathed.

"We're leaving this godforsaken town tonight." Zemi removed a set of keys from Bowie's pocket. She released Camden's arms and legs. Frustrated, she ripped the dog collar off his neck. "You don't belong to anyone."

They shackled and gagged Bowie.

Her covert tactics led them out of the house through the garden, squatting all the way to the plantation mansion. Few men were out patrolling on the moonless night, and no one guarded the kitchen's back door. Zemi knocked five times. Someone returned four knocks. She knocked again, three knocks. The answer was another two knocks. Zemi pounded the iron door one last time. It opened.

Lucy illuminated the darkness with an oil lamp. "What took you so long?" Her tone of voice was higher-pitched than he remembered. "Bowie left hours ago."

"Yeah, but he didn't get home until a little bit ago. I couldn't come back later for Camden." Zemi's whispers veiled the night with its muffled cadence. She clutched Camden's hand and dragged him inside the mansion's dark kitchen. "Are the guards sedated?"

"Everyone who isn't joining us is asleep, except for the general and his daughter." Lucy led them to a snug pantry. Rack after rack of fresh foods filled the shelves. Camden's stomach rumbled. "Are you hungry, Brother? Do you want something to eat?"

What he wanted was to touch her, make sure she was real. "Lucy, look at you, my sister."

"Let's do the family reunion thing later." Battle mode Zemi was tall and authoritative. "How did everything go tonight, Lucy?"

The evening feast had been in celebration of Wafer's thirteenth birthday. Off duty soldiers had come from all around Lawrenceburg to partake in the young man's coming of age event. Several rebels brought offerings, young girls close to Wafer's age. "The offerings," Lucy said, "babies, little girls, all terrified and shaking. We perfumed and scrubbed them clean. These girls were then forced to keep their heads bowed, standing motionless in a straight line for the entire evening, while the men dined and enjoyed themselves."

"Did he choose?" Zemi asked.

The young lady most appealing to Wafer became his first slave, and the second choice, his first whore. Risk of attachment prevented the rebels from keeping their first virgin. Isaac was not a man who took chances with 'sympathy'.

"Wafer picked a twelve-year-old blonde as his first whore," said Lucy, "and a teensy brunette for his home slave."

"And?" Zemi's frame remained rigid, unaffected by the injustice of it all.

Lucy put her hands on her hips. She grinned. "The potion was supposed to take affect exactly four hours after consumption. This gave the men plenty of time to party some more before getting home and passing out for the rest of the night. Your plan was perfect."

"What do you need me to do?" Camden wiped his nose; he really wanted to wipe Zemi's. She still bled from the paddle to the face. "I don't have many skills, but I'll try anything that gets me out of this hell hole."

Zemi turned to him. "I need you to get the basement keys from Isaac's room. Give it to one of the girls. They'll get the weapons we need to defend ourselves. All the guards are sedated. We've been planning this for weeks. Don't fail us."

"What if he wakes up and—"

"We'll give you a gun," she said. "Lucy will tell you what to do afterwards. We may also need you to help load the wagons with food and water."

"Wagons?" He didn't know where to begin. "What are we doing, exactly?"

"The male slaves need the weapons from the basement to help us get to the stables. We're going to need a lot of horses in order to move everyone out."

"That sounds like a giant undertaking." Camden wasn't so sure he wanted to help anymore. "I thought only you and my sister were escaping. Are you trying to rescue all the slaves?"

"Let my people go," she said. "Didn't the Bible teach you anything?"

"Yes, not to believe everything I read."

"No one gets left behind, Camden. No one."

"Alright, I guess I have to believe you know what you're doing." He trusted her, foolishly or not. He had no choice but to trust her. "What about you? What will you do?"

She smiled. "I'm setting the distillery on fire."

Doors creaked and voices murmured in the silence of the night. Tiptoes scurried from one end of the dark hall to the other. The slave girls gathered their belongings and rushed down the stairs in eerie silences interrupted only by the occasional bumping of elbows and arms. The guards, resting in awkward positions on every corner of the mansion, snored loudly. One snort produced more noise than all the house slaves combined.

The general's door was locked. The two rebels guarding his room lay tangled on top of each other, one drugged and the other had a bruised forehead. How many more sober rebels roamed the streets, guarding the river and the stables? Camden was grateful to have been given the easiest task. Isaac Mullin was just a man, a fat one at that. Camden did not fear him. In fact, he loathed him for having knowledge and using it solely to lead men back into the dark ages. If the devil did exist, Isaac Mullin was his son. If Camden had to kill the devil's son in order to steal a pair of keys, he would do so without the slightest hesitation.

He heard the moaning sounds, the grunting of an old man trying too hard to climax. Camden shivered in disgust. He checked to make sure his gun was loaded before he kicked the door open. The shadowy room had a single candle, half-spent. It illuminated Ida's startled face. Her fat father lay on top of her. Isaac's sweat radiated rage, displeasure of having been interrupted in mid-thrust. Camden raised the gun as Isaac dived for cover. The man hid behind the bed and ordered his daughter to do the same.

Ida sat up, naked as he had always imagined her, but to his displeasure, he saw nothing but a whore with a whore's smile. He could never again desire such a creature. Her lure vanished. She was weak, thin and disturbingly white, too pale, manufactured that way through the lab. Natural redheads no longer existed. To make the DNA needed to create red hair, pills needed to be traded. Ida had to be the sperm of Isaac, and the egg of a woman of many decades ago.

He fired one shot, close to her head, grazing her right ear. She cupped it, looked appalled, and then confused. Ida turned around. Her dead father lay sprawled naked on the carpet, a red carpet, the color of her hair, her father's blood. His shriveled penis was still erect. Camden laughed. Maybe it was hysteria, or maybe release. He had never killed a man or used a gun for anything other than blasting rotten tomatoes. Red oozed out of Isaac's chest. Ida's red hair veiled her face as she cried over her father's body.

Camden gave the key to the girl patiently waiting by the door. She thanked him, kissed his hand, and ran off to join the others. Ida's sobbing followed him for many rooms, and he had no inclination to comfort her. Instead, he rushed down the stairs to find his sister.

Lucy worked inside the pantry, handing sacks of food to other girls. She ordered the ones standing around to get busy and gather the children. One girl asked if it was okay to wake Bran. Lucy told her no. Bran would come down whenever he was ready. The girl nodded and hurried up the stairs, other girls hurried down. They reminded Camden of mice, scurrying all over the place, squeaking and running, stumbling into each other, whispering apologies into the darkness. They treated their freedom like another chore to accomplish, quickly, efficiently and with minimal sound.

"Sister," Camden said, and many girls turned to him. "What do you need me to do next?"

"Get along, ladies. There's no time to waste." And to Camden, "Go help in the basement. Get as many rifles, handguns, and knives as you can carry. Women won't know what to choose from."

"Neither would I." He caught the whine in his tone, but was not embarrassed by it. "Pat and Gad, they knew guns."

Lucy approached him. She held him at arm's length. "Mother always said you would do great things someday. I still believe that. Now, you go down there and help those girls choose weapons. Without firepower we don't stand a chance against the rebels."

The pep talk hardly motivated him. "A lot of these girls aren't going to make it, Lucy."

"Are they alive?" Her gaze bore through him, and she was Camden's mirror image. "Why aren't they here with you?"

"They're both dead, Lucy. I'm sorry."

Her mourning was one prolonged blink.

The house slaves and the ladies-in-waiting had lived among rebel men long enough to know what constituted good firepower—to Lucy's assumption of the contrary. The girls chose better ammunition and blades. They gave him a look of disapproval whenever he grabbed a rifle that was too bulky, or when the bullets belonged to a different gun. He was useless in the weapons armory, and they knew it as much as he did.

Camden left the ladies to it and hurried back up the stairs. He exited the house through the front door. The wind wafted fresh air. The loud thunderous sounds of caving buildings brought him outside the mansion. A remarkable fire swept through the distillery, sending flames hundreds of feet into the air. Oceans of burning whiskey flowed into the street. Many rebels ran wild, but not enough to overpower the crowds of girls abandoning their houses with their master's firearms. Camden had no idea what Zemi had used to blow up the factories, or how she sneaked inside the distillery without coming across a single guard, but he was proud of her, proud of his sister as well for taking their lives back, for saying no to slavery.

Chaos erupted from all sides of Lawrenceburg. Camden knew the fire would draw the guards from outside of the town. They would come heavily armed and with liquor-free minds. The girls rushed outside the mansion with weapons stuffed in pillow cases, sheets, sacks, and buckets. Slave men came from all parts of the town to claim rifles and handguns. These men brought horses and wagons and everything else needed for the lengthy trip. No one spoke. They all worked in hurried silence, allowing the furious flames of a burning town to speak for them.

Zemi crashed into Camden, panting, wiping the black smudges off her face. She wore a rebel's uniform, yet her wild hair gave her away. He steadied her, saved her from falling. The rifle in her hands came up. Zemi's finger closed on the trigger. She looked up at him, and instant relief brightened her large brown eyes. "For a second I thought you were one of them."

"You're amazing!" Camden was sure he was in the presence of greatness, such a fierce leader. He envied the passion that exuded out of her every pore. "So, what happens now? Where do we go from here?"

She smiled. "We take everyone to the Promised Land."

"I want to go there." He knew she was referencing the Bible, the story of Moses. "You know, you're a real leader, Zemi. I think you're the fire Joshua wanted me to find."

And just like that, the fiery spirit vanished from Zemi's eyes. The confidence melted away. Her shoulders flopped, her gun dropped. She wasted her draining effort in a slow parting of lips, the inaudible whisper of an unasked question. She tried voicing the word again, exhaling as if someone had struck her in the stomach, as if a gut wrenching ache unable her to breathe.

Zemi said, "Joshua?"

I WILL WAIT

The man seemed no more threatening than the average rebel or bounty hunter. He looked nothing like the mindless drones, and his pale skin projected the same transparency as his cunning grin. The glass wall separating them from each other didn't comfort the man as much as it eased Saul, who remained abjectly beside his puppeteer. The man's blue eyes lacked fear, and his gaze gored the mind of Atabey. He kept her dull. He exuded a confidence much older than his apparent years. But it was the black tattoo on his shoulder of the squatting zemi goddess that truly baffled Nico.

"Who are you?" He asked as soon as the man's eyes centered on Ata. "Why are you trying to kill her?"

"If I'd had my way, she would have been dead long ago," the man answered. His dialect was neither southern, modern, nor of the current century. "Listen, Daniel, truth is, I thought I'd lose my freaking mind if I ever saw you again. But as you can see, I'm actually quite calm. I can't say the same for you, though. Do me a favor and don't get all Hulk-like, you'll blow us all up."

"My name is Nico Lowell, Sorrow." Nico tried to regulate his heartbeat. He generated an excessive amount of energy. "What is your name?"

"Joshua Sorrow." His laugh had a husky tone, a throaty rasp. "My son was egoistical. He gave his species our family surname."

"I don't understand. Why did you call me Daniel?"

Joshua frowned. His expression revealed a hint of Saul. "Time is not linear. You used to tell me this all the time. You used to tell me a lot of bullshit, Daniel. I knew I'd recognize you. Those eyes of yours are the same fucking color as your birthstone, and why are you always blond?"

Saul moved to the background and stooped to cradle Mary. He appeared less anxious than before his guiding voice had showed up in the flesh. Saul must have thought himself safe. Nico loathed the man. "Are you such a coward you need to hide in the heads of your puppets?"

"Look who's talking," Joshua said. "I learned most of my tricks from you."

"You're a spineless—" Nico reached for Ata too late. She ran into another wall, collapsing immediately after. "Damn you!"

"You should really watch what you say, big bro. My feelings are easily hurt." Joshua shook all over, loosening his tense limbs. "Reincarnation, you keep coming back, always to the wrong time. You've been looking for dunce over there," He pointed to Atabey, "For longer than you think. Millions of years. I don't fucking know. I'll tell you this, Dan. I hope you enjoyed your short time with Blue, because now I'll have to exit you out of this world, again. This is already getting old."

Nico had skipped through time regenerating over and over again, hoping to eventually land on the right century. It took him decades to conclude Ata had failed to do the same. Storing all of her energy in one vessel was impossible for one as young as she, and so she had stored at intervals, losing herself in the great vastness of humanity. She needed Nico to live; he needed her to survive.

He had dwelled in human vessels for years at a time as a shaman, a medicine man, a doctor, or a surgeon, whatever the century termed his abilities. The charade never lasted a full life's worth. Not without Ata's stabilizing touch. His expanding energy had destroyed his various hosts. He could never store enough information inside a single brain to stop the cycle, for him to realize he needed to help Atabey come into full, human existence.

Nico and Atabey equaled pure energy. They had long surpassed the need for a physical body. Were they the last of their kind, the first, or the only? He had ignored her unhappiness and loneliness for ages in the hopes she would eventually move past it. She never did. The sea was Atabey's oldest friend, and to the sea she swam for comfort, for company. Her essence had seeped into a human, into a specific bloodline, and there it remained for centuries.

"It was pointless, wasn't it? I kept coming back, trying to rescue her from the human species, but she didn't want my help." His pure form held the answers to everything. Nico Lowell did not.

Joshua was somewhat content with Nico's hazy memory. He grinned. "You helped, asshole."

"How? I hardly know how to do so now?"

"By storing more information in your vessel, that's how."

"But I can't," Nico said. "The human brain with its billions of neurons, its intricate pumps, and long battery life, is still insufficient. I tried it. I must have tried for centuries, or maybe I never did. But why would I let her risk losing herself for that long, for what purpose?"

"She left you. You were angry. It happens." Joshua's statements were not meant to be sympathetic, but honest. He knew Nico's past life, Daniel, more than Nico knew himself.

"Humans have been around for a long time," Nico said. "How long ago did Ata join them?"

Joshua smirked, a truly satisfied smile. "You used to know all this. Are you spanking new?"

"I have twenty years inside this vessel."

"Yeah, you're new."

"When did she leave me?"

"Fourteenth century, I think."

"For what country?"

"This is sad." Joshua headed toward Saul. "You see Saul here, he's a descendant of Alexander Sorrow, every Sorrow is. That makes me the grandfather to the entire race. You, Daniel, are the uncle."

"I don't understand?"

"Twenty-first century," Joshua answered. "You gave her seven centuries to figure it out on her own. And then you interfered. You tried twice and failed. Eventually, you realized you needed more than one vessel to store all of your energy."

The sensors in Nico's lungs sent signals to his diaphragm; his carbon dioxide levels had risen drastically. "You're the first Sorrow." He took a much needed breath.

"We're brothers, except, I'm also human. I'm not a freaking advance, mythological species. I'm half you, half human, half Sorrow, and with a tiny bit of schizophrenia. Time is not linear my, soon-to-be dead, brother. I see the past, the present, and well, the future. I don't experience the world like everyone else. So as you can imagine, I'm not always sure where I am, or what's going on. I see things. I've traveled to places that don't make sense to me. I understand truths a human never should, but then I'm stuck in a limbo. I can't die, or age, or breathe a day without knowing elephants exist, but I'll forever be an ant. You fucked me up real good, and then you died."

A strange pull drew Nico to Joshua to the point of physically wanting to collide with the man. "Why would I give a human being superior understanding, unmanageable knowledge? What sort of information did I store in you?"

"Wouldn't you like to know?" Joshua laughed again, haughty and husky. "You've reincarnated too many times, always looking for your precious Blue. I don't know how many times you've humanized, but I've been around once, and this once is eternal. Sorrows are freaks, freaks created by me. Oh yes, and my son has killed over seven billion people."

"Why didn't I kill your son in a previous life?" The coalescing magnetic field around Nico pulsed, distorting the air around his body. "Alexander wants Atabey dead. Why would I let him live?"

"The same reason your precious would never attempt to kill me. He's a part of her. I'm a part of you. Blue stored data inside a twin vessel. The birthed result was Alexander. But his mother wouldn't let me kill him."

"If Alexander's birth had been prevented," Nico said, "if his mother had been eliminated—"

"You fuck!" Joshua's bellow mimicked a thunderclap, rumbling and expanding across the room.

Ata sprang up again, and Nico caught her before she ran into another wall. She cried out in pain, screamed to the top of her lungs, and the walls trembled with the fury of her agony. Blood gushed from her nose, mouth, and ears. Coppery red fluid leaked down her thighs, soiling her dress. Every orifice flooded with blood. She was in pain, dying.

Nico grasped her arm and pushed repairing cells her way. None would take. Ata rejected the flow of energy by going taut, by allowing his touch to burn her skin. His energy caused more harm than good. Nico repaired. She tore. The cycle became endless in the seconds he struggled to keep her from bleeding to death.

"Ata, help me." He trembled with a need to merge deep within her. He needed to be light. "Open your mind to me, Atabey. Please."

Her tears tore at his heart. What could he do? *Patience, be energy. Slow and steady.* He dived inside his own body, and from within he led the army directly through her skin. Nico never anticipated the burn to be severe. Her skin melted. The cells died before doing her any good, committing suicide by the hundreds, and thousands. And Nico could not take the deaths as a part of the circle of life as he had always instructed his human patients to do.

His own body burned with rage. He could do nothing to save her. Joshua knew him better than he knew himself. He had known an older and wiser Nico. The man saw the future and the past. The outcome was unchanging. "Don't let her die. What do you want from me?" Nico grew desperate, sensing Ata's slow heartbeat.

"What's the password?" Joshua said, smoothly. "And don't tell me you don't know what I'm talking about."

The numbers were ingrained in Nico's memory since before he could speak, numbers his sick mother had insisted he memorize: "25-21-3-1-8-21," he recited.

Joshua's attention fell on Saul, whose dismay distorted all of his features. The man communicated with his puppeteer through thought. Saul rose to his feet and placed a limp Mary on the operating table. He mouthed an apology to Ata through the glass and marched out the room. Nico no longer hated him. Saul had acted out of love for the only person he perceived as family. He had led Ata into a trap, rightfully assuming distance wouldn't keep Joshua from destroying her. Saul had made a choice. He chose Atabey's pain over her death.

Nico took Atabey into his arms. He held her, squeezed her fragile body, yearning to be inside her. He wanted to hide in her sweet perfume, her satin skin. Her arm's third degree burns reached her bones. Nico swallowed the lump threatening to tear him to pieces.

"Joshua," he cried. "Get your tentacles out of her head. I need to make her better."

"I was waiting for you to say that." Joshua stretched his arms, popped his knuckles, fooled around with his neck, and smiled. He said, "I need you to do one more thing for me."

Nico knew the man expected a rejection. "What do you want?"

"Kill yourself."

"Impossible."

"It's not impossible." He insisted. "I've seen you do it before."

"Before," Nico hissed, "Atabey was not human."

"Yeah, but you can still burst."

"If I do, I'll be sentencing her to death. I will never do that."

Joshua stepped away from the glass, several feet away, then all the way to the other side of the operating room. He stood there, hands akimbo, feet apart. "I predicted you'd say that."

"You hate me," Nico said. "I know this much is true, but I can't undo the past. If you take your hatred out on Ata . . . if you let her die . . . if . . ." He stumbled, unable to finish his sentence, unable to control his multiplying cells, the molecules, the metals, the oxygen in the air, the space separating his energy from the visible world. "You're going to let her die. Aren't you?"

Joshua had nothing left to lose. The smile appeared slowly, a dignified satisfaction of a kind. He had waited a long time for the precise moment where he could utter practiced words. After many years of drinking from the cup of vengeance, he finally embraced his sweet victory. "If she dies, she dies."

The soles of Nico's feet vibrated. He placed his palm on the glass wall. It shattered. Thousands of tiny pieces of glass spread onto the floor. The computers went haywire, and the operating room's equipment hovered in the air, dangerous sharp objects gyrated to and fro. He hoped nothing stabbed Mary in her sleep. Nico's one and only objective was to murder the man who had cockily asked him to do the impossible—or possible. Nico's body fought itself the same way Atabey had once done after their first fusion. There would be no more fusions. He would die without touching her, feeling her one last time.

"I wouldn't come close to me, Danny boy. You might be strong, but I'm stronger." Joshua remained unafraid for good reason.

Nico, unable to merge with Atabey, would die. Nothing he could do would prevent it from happening. He had died many times in the past. If he staged his electric discharge and controlled his death, he could return again. He deliberately allowed the energy churning inside his core to envelope him. At times of passing, one sees everything clearly, and he finally understood Joshua's usefulness.

"If only you could see yourself." Joshua ducked the scalpel that flew over his head. The room spun a burning heat. "You're going to burst!"

Mary Carrier would be his new mother; Joshua's demented objective all along. He probably intended to go after his own son next. The man had a hit list, but his selfishness proved useful. Joshua wanted Alexander just as dead as Nico did. Joshua wanted his entire line of descendants gone. So did Nico. He finally understood why his brother, yes, brother, had destroyed an entire city.

Atabey, I promise to come back for you. Nico tried to communicate despite Joshua's mental block. *I won't leave you for long. Mary will be a healer while I grow inside her. Allow her to heal you. I know what I need to do now. Ata, I'll rectify everything on my final rebirth. Wait for me. Promise me you'll wait for me.* He regretted abandoning her in such a way, but someday, his new vessel would make right by her—by Earth.

Nico fell to his knees. He needed to enter Mary's small body without hurting her. If he maneuvered his entry just right, Mary would survive the nine month pregnancy, the labor, and the residual energy. He would spare her, unlike Rosette.

He reacted with the oxygen. He produced heat and light. His internal organs burst, and his blood boiled. He was slipping away, but could not let go, not yet.

Her internal kiss finally reached him, enveloped his expanding muscles. So beautiful was his last image of Atabey. Those eyes, those honey orbs of light. She held the image in her mind, shared her yearning for a last embrace.

I will wait for you, she whispered.

Nico exploded.

MOCKINGBIRD

The tunnel's dark corners were as ominous as any cave. Water trickled somewhere in the distance, rats squeaked, and decay crumbled cement chips. A lantern illuminated the dome around her. The sharp smell of rust stung her nostrils. She tasted the blood on her lips as her body was painfully dragged through damp crooks. Raven's eyes had not yet adapted to the light. She couldn't see anything beyond Pockmark's feet.

Toady slammed her head against a concrete wall. She slumped into a sitting position. He laughed when Raven moaned. He tried tearing at her clothes. She was too faint to stop him from clumsily groping her breasts. But how could she allow him to violate her? She couldn't, and she wouldn't. Raven slugged him in the dark. Toady smashed his fist into her eye. For an instant, bright light illuminated her surroundings, and then everything darkened. *Poof!* She shrunk, blending with the cold floor. Toady found her face. His wet mouth covered hers with slimy saliva, a probing tongue that tasted like putrid meat.

She struggled, scraping at his face with her fingernails. He smacked her over and over again with one hand and the other twisted her nipples. He shouted insults into her mouth. He pressed his knee hard against her thigh, held her down so he could tear off her jeans. Raven bit his tongue. She kicked him and scrambled on all fours. She attempted to distance herself from the yapping maniac. Toady came at her from behind, grabbed one leg, and dragged her toward him. He flipped her over. He struck her. His ugly face scowled at her with odium and conquest. Raven thrashed until her knuckles bled. His weight pressed her body down. He hammered her numb.

The tunnel exploded with light.

Toady hesitated for a moment, scanning his surroundings. No one appeared. He glanced back at Raven, ready to pound her some more when a yellow blast jerked him backwards. He landed several feet away, disoriented and fumbling.

She rose slowly, bending over. Every muscle in her body hurt like hell. One eye was swollen shut. Toady, back on his feet, charged her. Raven jabbed him in the throat. She kicked his kneecap as hard as she could and ran. She heard Toady's snarls and leaps, and then the thud of his fall. She turned around and found him on his stomach, writhing in pain. Her urgency to flee was almost greater than her need to end it once and for all.

The fading blast of light had come from the surgeon's room. She wondered if Nico and Ata were alright. *No time to think about them*, the voice would have told her. *Think about yourself.* Pockmark would keep coming for her until she was dead.

Raven lunged at Toady. She landed on top of the man. He sneered, mocking. She went for the thin skin in the hollow of his neck, accessing his windpipe. The jugular veins were easy enough to bite into. She bit down at his throat with her front incisors and then violently drew away. He emitted a gurgling sound from the hole in his throat, but Raven held on, only unclenching after his body stopped convulsing. She had the nerve and fury to taste his blood bubbling inside her mouth. She didn't gag.

Raven sat in the dimness of the damp cold tunnel for what seemed like hours. She hugged her legs and cried. Her body hurt. Her teeth ached. What was the point of it all? She had naively believed there was a chance of finding her son. Bran probably lived somewhere in rebel territory. Raven was worn, torn, and exhausted.

Did she have the courage to start a new search? Yes. She did. But why? How many more hoops did she need to jump through?

The tunnel's dark halls brightened again, close to where Raven lay huddled near a huge shut door. Saul, the bringer of light, pulled on a handle. He opened the metal box near the lever, and started reciting and pressing numbers: 25-21-3-1-8-21. He laughed as the screechy iron door—or at least it resembled watery iron—parted.

"The numbers can only be entered once a year," Saul mused. "Once a year, if you get it wrong the first time, you have to wait another twelve months before trying again. It's genius. Rosetta was a clever woman."

A boiling chemical odor mixed with corrosion wafted out the room. Saul strolled inside. Raven tried standing, only to collapse. She heaved and panted hard on her second try. She glanced over at Toady. Blood no longer seeped from the torn throat of his corpse. The filthy rebel deserved no sympathy. She shivered. Why had Toady hesitated to kill her? The shock blast must have minimized his strength. *But why didn't the blast hit me?*

"Thank Daniel for that, lucky you." The man sounded jovial, but his expression was cold. "Hello, Raven, pleasure to meet you in the flesh." He offered a hand.

She stared at him, confused, and with sudden need to puke.

"And Ata and Mary are fine, by the way, in case you were wondering." His scruffy and chaotic hair was darker than hers, his powder blue eyes resembled her mother's, and his stubborn facial features reminded her of her father. But it was the musical note, the voice of a man who could hum beautiful melodies for hours on end, that she recognized the most.

"Vo-ice." She choked on her words and tasted the bile in her mouth. "You're the voice."

"Was the voice," he corrected. "I was young then, probably in my late teens, eighteen or nineteen. I don't remember anymore, but as it turned out, mentally communicating with a girl from the future is a thing of crazies. Big brother had me put in a mental hospital, the prick."

"Huh? But . . ." Her throat ached.

"Don't try to wrap your head around it," he said. "Life is different now. I'm Joshua Sorrow, by the way." And as an afterthought, "Are you going to take my hand or not?"

Raven followed the voice—the man—inside the laboratory room, a test center. Destroyed computers cluttered the ground, and paper sheets soared from the pile Saul discarded. He rummaged through a table in front of a cracked, wall-sized screen. Joshua gazed up at the glass tube in a corner of the chamber, a device large enough to fit a grown person. It was filled to the brim with a clear milky substance, which reminded Raven of a giant placenta. Red cables floated inside, sparking electricity. Both Saul and Joshua frowned as if disappointed to find no one there.

"Do you think they killed her or—" Saul censored his words, tightened his lips. "Sorry."

"You're free, Saul," Joshua said. "When the war comes, you're not going to want to be anywhere near Kentucky. Go south, deep south."

Saul approached the tube and settled beside Joshua. "What about Atabey and Mary?"

"I'll condemn Daniel, again."

"It was your idea to—"

"He didn't deliver. He won't be delivered."

"I thought you couldn't hurt the fetus once it was formed."

"I'm not going to try to hurt the embryo. I'll kill the host."

Saul's frown lines deepened. "What does that mean?"

"You know what that means. Go."

"She's only a—"

Joshua grabbed Saul by the throat. He shoved him against the giant tube. "She's a fucking parasite." He released Saul, who gasped and coughed for air. "Go before I kill Blue, too."

Saul stumbled out of the lab, ignoring Raven's bent posture near the entrance. Her lethargy overwhelmed her. Her shaky legs moved as if stuck in sand, a body within an ocean. Had she ever visited the coast? Raven did not remember anything before the rebels, and the last thing she needed was to become someone else's slave. What if the passive-aggressive man attacked her? She lingered on the questions, on her choices. Still, she waited for his explanation, sensing Joshua Sorrow meant her no harm. He was the voice, after all. Wasn't he?

"You keep trying to figure me out." He turned to her, grinning. "It's only been an hour for you, but me, I haven't spoken to you in decades."

Joshua ambled about the room coolly, carefully inspecting every piece of paper, every cracked screen and unplugged wire. He was not the man who had helped her get to Arlington. Joshua's troubled face oozed grief, an old despondency. Misery lived trapped inside his skin. He carried himself like he had seen enough of the world to know nothing mattered. But he must live for something. His blue gaze carried determination, an angry conflict of wills. She wanted to ask him many questions. Would he answer them?

"I don't understand what you mean," she said. "None of this makes—"

"Toady banged you up pretty good." He surveyed her like a man looking through a box of childhood memories. "When I first met Toady a few years ago, I knew I was finally in your lifetime. I'd killed him then, but I remembered you said you wanted to do it yourself."

His strange scent overpowered the stench of the corroded laboratory. The black painting on his right shoulder . . . a raven. Did the bird relate to her?

Yes, he communicated. *It does.*

You hear me?

I always hear you.

247

She no longer detected the soothing strokes of his mental brush, his kindness. *What happened to you?*

Long story, won't bore you with it.

Make it short then.

Daniel or Nico. Joshua's gruff voice poorly suppressed his hatred. *Don't ask me what he is because I don't know. He's never been alive long enough to figure it all out himself. Ata took too long to form. He's dead now, by the way.*

But he can't die! Raven's eyes stung, blurring her vision. *Ata needs him to live.*

Daniel doesn't get a happily ever after, Raven. I won't allow it. Joshua despised more than just the world. He loathed the people in it. *Daniel should have never meddled with humans.*

Voice or Joshua, please tell me you didn't hurt Mary?

I haven't yet, but I will soon.

"No, you can't! She's a little girl. None of this is her fault."

"It's never anybody's fault, is it?"

"Not hers, for sure."

Joshua's crucial frown was similar to Saul's. "Blame Daniel. Pawn all of mankind's tragedies on him."

"Why do you hate him so much?"

"I have to kill Mary. Don't interfere, and perhaps, you'll get your son back."

Every heart beat hurt. Raven found it difficult to breathe.

"Isaac's rebel camp has Bran," he said. "What will it be? Do you want your son back, or do you prefer to save your cousin?"

On cue, Saul, Ata, and Mary entered the laboratory. Ata was no longer bruised or bleeding. Her face, her gait, all of it was pure, clean. Saul presented Joshua a glowing Mary. He begged the man to make it quick. Raven locked eyes with Ata and mentally—at least she hoped—told her to protect the child from a certain death. Raven didn't have the courage, or the strength, to do it herself.

Ata leaped for Mary and clutched her. Her act of bravery made her the target. Joshua grabbed Ata by the neck. Killing either female was good enough for him. Saul begged for her life and presented Mary, thrusting the little girl forward, telling Joshua to take the child instead. But Joshua wanted Ata. Joshua had always wanted Ata.

Raven pushed Saul out of her way and nabbed her cousin. She wrapped her arms around the girl, protectively. And stepped back, avoiding confrontation. She was too weak to fight—a lie. Flows of soft waves, an internal current, healed her legs, throat, and her arm muscles. Her headache vanished. *Mary?* Did the little girl possess Nico's healing abilities? Raven was touched that even after death Nico was still looking out for her. She owed him so much and would soon repay him—her.

Don't try, Raven. It's pointless. Blue will be dead before she hits the ground. A few feet away, Saul collapsed. *Don't make me do the same to you.* Ata's feet dangled. Joshua had her by the throat. *This will be easier if Saul doesn't object.* Ata wiggled and struggled as Joshua tightened his grip on her neck.

Raven breathed, slowly. *Look at her first.*

She's a blue-haired abomination. His humorless laughter was loud inside her head. *What's to look at?*

Mary's watching you. She's trembling. Raven gathered her cousin closer still. *I hear the kid's stomach rumbling.*

I don't care about all that. He squeezed and Ata gagged.

If you're going to kill her in front of a child, at least have the decency to look at her when you do it. Raven pushed the wild laughter out of her head through sheer will, veiling her mind with the image of a lactating newborn. Her son.

"Do you know what you are?" Joshua let go of Ata, and she started to run. He yanked her hair and pushed her back down. Ata stopped resisting. She stared up at him, tears in her eyes and confused. "Tell me, Blue. Do you know what you are?"

She shook her head.

"You're the reason the human species is almost extinct. Your brother's unbeatable virus wiped everyone out."

Ata cried. She tried to form words. "I'm sorry—"

"*Hush, little baby, don't say a word.*" Joshua sang the lullaby with a haunting intonation. Ata rocked forward and back, screaming in pain. "*Daddy's going to buy you a mockingbird.*"

Mary's arm's tightened around Raven's waist, and Raven felt Nico's plea through the nine-year-old girl. "Stop it, Joshua! What kind of a man are you?"

He turned to her, his eyes lost in rage. "Stay out of this."

"What do you want from her?" Raven was unsure anyone but Nico knew the answer, and Nico was gone, obliterated, fragmented into currents of energy, voltage so vast it was a wonder any of them survived the impact. Raven took the image of the bursting healer from Joshua's head. He offered the information freely. Some good remained in the voice—the man—layered on top of agony and hatred. He struggled with goodness, almost non-existent, but still there. "Look at your daughter, Joshua. She doesn't know what you want from her."

Joshua did look. He glared at the sobbing, shaking figure beneath him. His taut shoulder muscles visibly softened. Ata was no more a threat to him than a baby kitten. Her expressions, her sobs, he scrutinized them with disdain. Her huge amber eyes darken into a brown color. The effect emerged from his mind. Ata's eyes still shone amber but to him, they had changed to a brown, almost black color. Taken aback by the effect, Joshua clawed at his own face, angry at himself, disappointed, distressed. He shouted in high octaves of indecision. Nothing made sense to him.

"Where's your mother?" His voice returned to a natural soothing note. "I need to find her before your brother does. I need to help her. I need her." Ata had never met any of her relatives, yet her reluctance to reply only served to anger Joshua. "Answer me!"

"I don't know." Her nose and ears trickled thin lines of blood. "Is my mother Zemi?"

Ata's screams pierced through Raven's bones. Her cry echoed through the walls and it was agonizing, inhumane. She deteriorated, corroded from the pain her shrieks emanated. Ata would burst into a pile of human entrails because unlike Nico, she was mostly human, but no human deserve such cruelty.

Raven lamented never getting the chance to see her son again, and then she charged Joshua.

WHERE, OH WHERE

Weary slaves trudged along with their heavy belongings, noisy wagons, and neighing horses. Heads drooped low and vigor diminished from the steps and hearts of the free people. The men and women had rushed out of a burning town unsure of what to expect, or what horrors awaited them beyond the unknown.

They marched for two days, avoiding the skeletons of former cities. Why live in ruins when one could prosper in the countryside? Crops thrived in fertile land while cities crumbled.

A crooked and rusted sign just beyond the horizon announced the exit of one town to the comfort of the next. But the news encouraged no one and so silence lingered until the sun was high in the brilliant sky, smiling, but brazenly burning their exposed skin.

The green mountain tops lacked marked trails. Thirsty streams fondled by rocks never led to a river. Wild animals of every breed wandered over from every corner, unafraid of the free slaves. The sun beat at them day in and day out. Plagues of mosquitos, bloodsuckers of the worst kind, stung relentlessly. The road to the Promised Land was not as promising as he had expected, beautiful, but vast and endless.

Camden suggested everyone take a break, and the men and women halted, all tired. The people considered him a liberator, a leader. Zemi had marched in front of the pack, but so did Camden, a man. She never bothered to dispute the assumptions and instead focused on finding the quickest and best route to the Promised Land. They would settle and start a new home, a new village, somewhere where the rebels could never find them.

While the folks aided the injured and fed the sick, Camden approached his sister. "Have you seen Zemi?"

"She headed into the woods with Bran."

"When?"

"Not too long ago. But she did seem a bit anxious, afraid." Lucy remarked about the girl who had outsmarted, fought, shot, and outran a whole camp of rebels.

Zemi had remained silent and pensive for two whole days where she never addressed anyone's concerns; the rumors of another rebel invasion had spread among the people. Camden shivered. He would never go back to Lawrenceburg. Not alive.

The rumors reached a point of panic. Camden saw no other choice but to calm the men, women and children. The people had lost a great deal without the guarantee of permanent safety. They deserved some sort of solace. He stole his motivational speech on commitment and endurance, fighting for the freedoms wanted, for the dream of a better tomorrow, from presidents of various nations, and a few civil rights leaders. Camden gave the people hope. He fired up their spirits. The free slaves clapped in unison at the end of his sermon, and it was not until he finished that he understood why Joshua had insisted he read all those books.

Camden searched for Zemi further in the woods. He thought he found her emerging from a moving bush until a big coyote leapt out of cover and strutted toward him. He stared into the animal's eyes and leered, immobile. The coyote watched him but ceased its approach. Camden waited for a chance to run. He cursed himself for not having brought along a rifle. The pending challenge lasted a few seconds before Bran—out of nowhere—bypassed the still creature to get to Camden. He tugged at his pant leg.

Bran said nothing—as usual. He glanced up at Camden and squeezed his hand. Zemi appeared soon after, fatigued, but glad to see him. She petted the coyote. The animal first recoiled from her touch but then encouraged it, settling on the grass, momentarily harmless. Camden didn't know where to start with the questions. Many would have ended with *marry me*. A girl capable of taming a wild coyote deserved an immediate marriage proposal.

"You missed my speech," he told her.

"Are you on my side, Camden? I need to know that you'll always be on my side."

"Of course I am."

"Okay, I need . . . need you to do me a huge favor." Her tone of voice trapped an abrupt sadness deep in her throat. "This is important and if you say no, I don't know if I could confront him myself, not yet." Mountains of pain clogged her hoarse words. "I need you to go somewhere because I . . . can't."

"You freed me and my sister," he said. "I will go anywhere you want me to go."

"Thank you so much." Zemi embraced him, held him for longer than he expected her to. He used the opportunity as a chance to sneak a kiss on her cheek. She laughed, stepping back, and holding him at arm's length. "With your blessings first, I'll take your people the rest of the way home, Moses."

"You do know I don't believe in any of that Bible stuff, right?" He smiled. "Where am I going?"

A wasteland, his destination was a hideously decomposing city. The stench of death emanated from every rusted, old ruined thing. He hated himself for agreeing to the mission, and he was starting to doubt whether the coyote knew where it was taking him. Zemi had said to trust the animal, said it with a straight face. Bran had come along, too. The slow mute was to be taken to his mother, a promise, Zemi said, a mentally ill teenager had once made to a raven-haired girl.

The underground tunnels preserved an eerie darkness. Camden plowed through hazardous materials to get to a narrow hall of parallel entrances. He searched for a wide and thick door, a mysterious metal entrance. He recognized the structure right away. The gray door was a solid acting as a liquid. Camden took a breath and entered, bracing himself for more carnage. He had already bypassed a dead Dagan, Orion and Toady. He expected more deaths. Silence always meant more death.

The coyote rushed to the blue-haired girl, nudged her with its muzzle, and licked her battered body. Black, Blue and Mary all lay unconscious. The man slumped near the metal door also appeared inert, for a total of four.

"Joshua?"

The rebel leader was sitting on the floor, his back against a giant tube full of something milky. His limp legs shaped a V pattern, his arms dangled—the image of a starving survivalist.

He squinted up at Camden. "Do you know who they are?"

"You don't?" Camden approached the rebel and signaled Bran to stay outside. "You know the girls, all of them. You brought Mary here yourself. Do you know your men are all dead?"

"What men?" His blue, weary gaze wandered over to the unconscious figure by the door. "That one looks familiar."

"He looks like you, a little bit." So did Black. She too resembled the rebel leader: hair and skin tone. Mary's cheekbones and nose mirrored Black's. Blue, well, Blue . . . "Is that Blue, Joshua, the one with the coyote?" Camden couldn't believe how much the girl looked like Zemi.

Joshua rose. "Where is she?"

"Who? Where's who?"

"Where, oh where is my Zemi now?"

Camden hesitated, a bit struck by the word *my*. He truly had come to think of Zemi as his bride-to-be.

Joshua laughed, hatefully, cruelly. "Young Camden, of eighteen or nineteen, your naiveté has always amused me. Did you kill Bowie?"

"No, but I'm sure—"

"To think I nearly killed this one," he said, observing Blue. "If I do now, I won't have anything to leverage with later. It all just recently came to me in another one of my blackouts."

"You said the jackal would lead the way," Camden said. "It was actually a coyote, and by fire, you meant Zemi. Didn't you?"

"Camden." Joshua's eyes hinted at murder. "I want to know exactly where she is."

Camden would never tell the crazy rebel where Zemi and the others were headed to, not that he knew where in Eastern Kentucky—

"Thank you, that wasn't so difficult, was it?" Joshua smiled or smirked, Camden could never tell. "You see this here, Cam." He pointed at a shoulder tattoo of a squatting Indian woman. "This here is Atabey, a zemi goddess. I drew her up, got most of my tattoos as reminders of the things I'm not supposed to forget. The goddess is supposed to knock out two birds with one stone: Zemi and Atabey." He glanced at Blue, "One down."

"Is Zemi a goddess? Or is she like an angel of—"

"Don't be ridiculous, Cam. Gods don't exist. It's all myth. And didn't I warn you not to get attached. Humans depend on it." He barked his frustration like a parent who was sick and tired of repeating himself to a stubborn child. "You're supposed to be smart. You're supposed to create the army that will eventually bring down the Sorrows. Zemi knows that. Fuck, your sister knows that. Did you find her? Big sis will be useful."

Camden figured the rebel already knew the answer.

"I'm not a rebel, Cam," he said. "I'm simply paving the road for your safe passage. I won't always remember this moment or why Zemi thinks it's her job to help me sort it all out. I see she completed one of my tasks." He glanced at Bran. The mute boy walked into the room and ran to Mary, the only person he recognized. "It's not a crow, Cam. It's a raven, and that too I forgot to do."

"You forgot to do what?"

"Bring Bran to his mother." He sighed and started for the exit. "Take them all back to your remote countryside. You'll prosper there. I forgot why I came here."

"What about Zemi?" Camden would run and warn her if he had to. "If you hurt her—"

Joshua took a deep breath, inhaling the whole room. "You smell like her. Zemi touched you. Didn't she? She tortures me like that, always out of reach. But don't worry, Cam, I won't find her. She won't be in Eastern Kentucky or anywhere else. She'll continue to evade me for a while longer." At the door, he turned one last time toward the blue-haired girl, and then Mary, lastly, he studied Black. "This one attacked me knowing she didn't stand a chance, knowing I'd put her to sleep before she reached me. A Sorrow worth sparing, who knew."

The moment he left, all four of his victims awoke.

Blue sat up. Her yellow eyes brightened at the sight of the coyote. "Oak!" She hugged the animal like a child might cuddle a house pet.

The one man staggered toward her. He embraced her and helped to her feet. Blue then headed over to Mary. The two girls stared at each other, both cried, both hugged.

The man caught the sight of Bran and gasped. His surprise quickly turned into relief. He took the boy by the arm and directed him to Black, who was still having a hard time standing. "Raven, I think this is your son."

Black gazed up at the mute boy and reluctantly stroked his cheek. Satisfied, she pulled him to her lap. She squeezed him. Bran neither flinched nor scurried away. He wrapped his arms around her as if flooded with familiarity. He resembled his mother.

"I love you so much, Bran. I promise, I promise to . . . to never, ever let anyone take you away from me ever . . . ever again." Her tears came in spurts of out of breath anguish. She wiped her eyes as another mini waterfall flooded her face.

Bran smiled shyly.

Black asked the boy many questions and then nodded at his silence. "Did George tell you about me?" She bobbed her head, listening. Bran remained silent. The scene was bizarre. A delusional mother imagining her mute son answered her questions. It took Camden several minutes to realize the boy understood her, and was indeed replying—but not aloud. Sorrows, they both were. Incredible.

Mary and Blue joined the others in the reunion of embraces. The one man spotted Camden. He shielded the women with his frame and demanded to know who he was. Camden told him, told all of them his story. He finished with the promise to take them to a safe haven, Eastern Kentucky, away from rebels and Sorrows. He omitted Joshua's involvement and allowed them to believe the leader had disappeared before Camden arrived.

"Tell me about her," Blue said. The girl's eyes were as bright as a full moon on a mysterious night. Enchanting. She sauntered toward Camden with slow steps that made her appear as if she were gliding above the ground. Blue stopped inches from his face and tilted her head in odd directions as if studying an extinct creature. "Is my mother beautiful?"

"Uh-huh." Camden coughed into his fist. "Yes."

Blue's resemblance to Zemi drew him to her. Not the hair, eyes, height, or smell . . . something about the girl—maybe the large eyes. Both women shared an aura of being something altogether strange in the world, something not quite belonging among humans. Zemi, however, was more organic. Atabey almost cornered the edges of imitation, a replica of a sort, a clone? No. A descendent. All Sorrows descended from a new kind of Adam and Eve.

"Will I meet my mother in your new land?" Blue's whisper reached him in a warm gust.

He shivered. "Probably not."

Her shiny gaze brimmed with tears that sparkled like the jewels found in rivers. "Does she not want me like my father?"

"I don't know." He felt helpless in front of her sadness.

Mary stepped forward. She wrapped her arms around Blue's waist and smiled up at her. A teardrop landed on the little girl's forehead. Mary's right palm glowed; she examined all angles of her hand in astonishment. She clasped Blue's wrist. The bright spark and static from the touch created goosebumps on Blue's entire arm.

"Listen," Camden interrupted. "Think of Zemi as a guardian angel who's looking out for you from a distance. Maybe for your own safety she stays away. But Zemi did send me here to fetch you and your friends. I'm sure you'll meet her when the time comes."

Blue smiled at him. "You think?" She turned to the man two steps behind her. "Is it true, Saul?"

"Sure," said the man, "but don't get your hopes—"

"I believe." Atabey's delight was almost magical. She considered Mary with a fascinated and elated smile and cried. "I'm going to take good care of you during and after the pregnancy."

"You'll have plenty of help." Black gripped her son's hand and headed to the exit; Bran tagged along like a little duckling, stumbling and trying to catch up. "Let's get out of this dump."

Sunrise crept over the hills and veiled the highway's overgrowth, a sweet mandarin shade meant to ease morning strollers. They ran into another coyote, two horses and a foal just outside the rotting city. Black laughed as she petted and then mounted the mare. Her son examined the colt in delight before his mother lifted him up on the saddle. She promised he could befriend and ride the foal once the horse was old enough and Sable approved; the mare neighed as if understanding the discourse. Blue and Mary climbed the chestnut stallion. The journey to Eastern Kentucky would take them a few days.

"Saul, aren't you coming?" Blue's smile diminished as she considered the cross-armed man a few yards away.

"No, Ata, I plan to spend my life far away from the war." His straight as arrow stance and deadpan expression left little room for a debate.

"But you're like a father to me," she said. "What shall I do without your companionship?"

His lips curved slightly in an attempt at a smile. He gestured at the little girl beside Blue; Mary gazed up at the winking sun in wonder. Saul said, "I think you have all you need and want."

"Will I see you again?"

"If you ever need me," he said, tapping his forehead. "You know how to reach me."

Blue stroked Mary's long hair. She kissed the top of the girl's head before regarding the man again. "Goodbye, Saul." She waved. The chestnut horse started in a trot.

"Yeah, bye," Black said. Her mare followed the stallion. The foal cantered behind its parents with young and stuttering eagerness.

Saul grabbed Camden, stopped him from joining the group on foot. He waited patiently for the women and children to move out of hearing distance before he let go of Camden's arm. "What's your number one priority, kid?"

Camden blinked.

"Well, what is it?"

"Can't you just read my mind? Don't all Sorrows do that?"

"Not all Sorrows can read minds without hurting a regular brain." Saul snickered as if disgusted with the ability. His entire face contorted into hostile nausea. "I'm not that talented."

A crow cawed in the distance and then a flock of them invaded the muggy and desert-like atmosphere. Perspiration trickled down Camden's back, and he worried whether he could safely escort the group of travelers to Eastern Kentucky without coming across danger.

"Don't play their little games, or you'll find yourself a pawn in their chess set. Ata was one to her brother before she learned to block him. But Alexander will keep trying to find ways to lure his sister to Sorrow territory. You can't let that happen. If Atabey collides with her brother, humans won't stand a chance."

"O-kay," Camden said. "See, I'm more concerned with protecting Zemi from Joshua."

Saul frowned. "That's a centuries old marital dispute you should really stay out of, kid."

"Marital?" He took skeptical step back. "Is Zemi married to Joshua?"

"Unfortunately, yes, they birthed the first Sorrows. Also, you should probably know they're no longer on the same team. Joshua's fighting for humans. Zemi fights for her children. The latter does not benefit you."

"But Zemi has been good to—"

"It doesn't matter, does it?" Saul exhaled a slow and almost painful breath He hung his head and groaned at the broken concrete. "Joshua has already set you on a course. Go live your life. Spend time with your sister while you still can. Please, try to forget Zemi. Don't allow Sorrows to control or influence your thoughts. Let them inside your head and this war will be over before it begins. Good bye. I'm done."

And he was done. Saul marched back into the cracked streets of Crystal City, heading in the opposite direction of the horses and coyotes, vowing never to return again, presumably, to live far away from the coming war. Maybe the man was right and Camden was a pawn. *No.* He shook his head in denial. He rejected the idea of a set destiny. He believed in choice. Camden would lead people into a new era where sane logic reigned supreme.

Promised Lands did not exist. He would travel to the farthest corner of Eastern Kentucky, the uncharted wilderness. There, his people would survive because humans had done so for millions of years and would continue to endure if educated properly. He believed in knowledge. In his new country no one would be allowed to act on weak will. Ignorance was not bliss. It was the reason why countless of civilizations had crumbled many times before. Camden vowed to focus on what really mattered . . .

Where, oh where is my Zemi now.

Acknowledgements

Hard work and many, many drafts later, we come to the final product. I hope everyone enjoys reading the story as much as I enjoyed writing it. This novel came into existence and publication because of the helpful guidance of a few lovely people.

First, I would like to thank my agent T.L. Gray. She is a rock, solid. Always ready to guide me in the right direction and pull me back when I stray—I tend to stray a lot. Thank you for believing in my world, in my potential.

A special thanks to the early readers who helped dust and shape Hear Me Scream: Douglas O., Libby L., Robert T., Justin N., Jeff S., just to name a few. Thank you for the advice given, the tips suggested, and for the errors ejected. You folks keep me humble.

To my family: Papi, my brother, my sisters, thanks for loving me. To my brother and sister-in-law, you guys are kind and helpful people. To my mother in heaven, I miss you. For my husband Jason, you have always believed in my dream. Your love and support means the world to me.

Another special thanks goes to my writer and Insomniac friends. You guys need to stay in the asylum. You crazy folks, love you all. Thanks for pushing me Jenna. To the publisher: Vabella, John, thank you for the opportunity.

Last but not least, my in-laws: Jeff and Jamie James. Their home in Taylorsville, the acres, the property, their environment served as my inspiration. Thanks Jamie for listening to me blab on and on about the plot, and thank you Jeff for discussing survival methods, guns, ammo, hunting, and gardening with me.

Okay, I think I've exhausted the thank yous. If I forgot anyone, wait for the sequel.

ABOUT THE AUTHOR

R.M. James wrote plays as a child and forced her sisters to read them. As she got older, her stories evolved into short movies. Her film and literature studies edged her into one of her truest callings: fiction writing. The majority of her time goes into caring for her family, taking nature shots, reading, and imagining new scenes for another novel. She lives in Kentucky.